"The prize is immortality," Henry said.

"It's not something we give out lightly, and we need to make sure it is something you can handle."

I felt a cold block of ice form in the pit of my stomach. So my choices now were to live forever or die trying. Somehow it didn't seem fair.

"You will do well," Henry said. "I can feel it. And afterward, you will help me do something that no one else is capable of doing. You will have power beyond imagining, and you will never fear death again. You will never grow old and you will always be beautiful. You will have eternal life to spend as you wish."

But would I have my mother?

* * *

Advance Praise for
THE GODDESS TEST
by
Aimée Carter

"A fresh take on the Greek myths
adds sparkle to this romantic fable."
—Cassandra Clare, *New York Times* bestselling author of
the Mortal Instruments series

"Enchanting and compulsively readable,
The Goddess Test twists classic myth and modern storytelling
into a fun, whimsical shape. A great story for teen girls."
—Melissa Anelli, *New York Times* bestselling author of
Harry, A History

THE GODDESS TEST

AIMÉE CARTER

HARLEQUIN®
TEEN

HARLEQUIN®
TEEN

ISBN-13: 978-0-373-21026-8

THE GODDESS TEST

Copyright © 2011 by Aimée Carter

Recycling programs for this product may not exist in your area.

For Dad, who has read every word.
You were right.

And in memory of my mother.

PROLOGUE

"How did it happen this time?"

Henry tensed at the sound of her voice, and he tore his eyes away from the lifeless body on the bed long enough to look at her. Diana stood in the doorway, his best friend, his confidante, his family in every way except by blood, but even her presence didn't help rein in his temper.

"Drowned," said Henry, turning back to the body. "I found her floating in the river early this morning."

He didn't hear Diana move toward him, but he felt her hand on his shoulder. "And we still don't know...?"

"No." His voice was sharper than he'd intended, and he forced himself to soften it. "No witnesses, no footprints, no traces of anything to indicate she didn't jump in the river because she wanted to."

"Maybe she did," said Diana. "Maybe she panicked. Or maybe it was an accident."

"Or maybe somebody did this to her." He broke away, pacing the room in an attempt to get as far from the body as possible. "Eleven girls in eighty years. Don't tell me this was an accident."

She sighed and brushed her fingertips across the girl's white cheek. "We were so close with this one, weren't we?"

"Bethany," snapped Henry. "Her name was Bethany, and she was twenty-three years old. Now because of me, she'll never see twenty-four."

"She never would have if she'd been the one."

Fury rose up inside of him and threatened to bubble over, but when he looked at her and saw compassion in her eyes, his anger drained away.

"She should have passed," he said tightly. "She should have *lived*. I thought—"

"We all did."

Henry sank into a chair, and she was by his side in an instant, rubbing his back in the sort of motherly gesture he expected from her. He tangled his fingers in his dark hair, his shoulders hunched with the familiar weight of grief. How much more of this was he supposed to endure before they finally released him?

"There's still time." The hope in Diana's voice stabbed at him, more painful than anything else that had happened that morning. "We still have decades—"

"I'm done."

His words rang through the room as she stood still next to him, her breathing suddenly ragged and uneven. In the several seconds it took for her to respond, he considered taking it back, promising he would try again, but he couldn't. Too many had already died.

"Henry, please," she whispered. "There's twenty years left. You can't be done."

"It won't make a difference."

She knelt in front of him and pulled his hands from his face, forcing him to look at her and see her fear. "You promised me a century, and you will *give* me a century, do you understand?"

"I won't let another one die because of me."

"And I won't let you fade, not like this. Not if I have anything to say about it."

He scowled. "And what will you do? Find another girl who's willing? Bring another candidate to the manor every year until one passes? Until one makes it past *Christmas?*"

"If I have to." She narrowed her eyes, determination radiating from her. "There is another option."

He looked away. "I've already said no. We aren't talking about it again."

"And I'm not letting you go without a fight," she said. "No one else could ever replace you no matter what the council says, and I love you too much to let you give up. You're not leaving me any other choice."

"You wouldn't."

She was silent.

Pushing the chair aside, Henry stood, wrenching his hand away from her. "You would do that to a child? Bring her into this world just to force her into *this?*" He pointed at the body on the bed. "You would do that?"

"If it means saving you, then yes."

"She could die. Do you understand that?"

Her eyes flashed, and she stood to face him. "I understand that if she doesn't do this, I *will* lose you."

Henry turned away from her, struggling to hold himself together. "That is no great sacrifice."

Diana spun him around to face her. "Don't," she snapped. "Don't you dare give up."

He blinked, startled by the intensity in her voice. When he opened his mouth to counter, she stopped him before he could speak.

"She will have a choice, you know that as well as I do, but no matter what happens, she will not become *that,* I promise you." Diana gestured toward the body. "She will be young, but she will not be foolish."

It took Henry a moment to think of something to counter her, and when he did, he knew he clung to false hope. "The council would never allow it."

"I've already asked. As it falls within the time limit, they have given me permission."

He clenched his jaw. "You asked without consulting me first?"

"Because I knew what you would say," she said. "I can't lose you. *We* can't lose you. We're all we have, and without you— please, Henry. Let me try."

Henry closed his eyes. He had no choice now, not if the council agreed. He tried to picture what the girl might look like, but each time he tried to form an image, the memory of another face got in the way.

"I couldn't love her."

"You wouldn't have to." Diana pressed a kiss to his cheek. "But I think you will."

"And why is that?"

"Because I know you, and I know the mistakes I made before. I won't repeat them again."

He sighed, his resolve crumbling as she stared at him, silently pleading. It was only twenty years; he could make it until then if it meant not hurting her more than he already had. And this time, he thought, glancing at the body on the bed once more, he wouldn't repeat the same mistakes either.

"I'll miss you while you're gone," he said, and her shoulders slumped with relief. "But this will be the last one. If she fails, I'm done."

"Okay," she said, squeezing his hand. "Thank you, Henry."

He nodded, and she let go. As she walked to the door, she, too, looked at the bed, and Henry swore to himself that this would never happen again. No matter what it took, pass or fail, this one would live.

"This isn't your fault," he said, the words tumbling out before he could stop himself. "What happened—I allowed it. You aren't to blame."

She paused, framed in the doorway, and gave him a sad smile.

"Yes, I am."

Before he could say another word, she was gone.

CHAPTER 1
EDEN

I spent my eighteenth birthday driving from New York City to Eden, Michigan, so my mother could die in the town where she was born. Nine hundred and fifty-four miles of asphalt, knowing every sign we passed brought me closer to what would undoubtedly be the worst day of my life.

As far as birthdays go, I wouldn't recommend it.

I drove the whole way. My mother was too sick to stay awake for very long, let alone drive, but I didn't mind. It took two days, and an hour after we'd crossed the bridge to the upper peninsula of Michigan, she looked exhausted and stiff from being in the car for so long, and if I never saw a stretch of open road again, it'd be too soon.

"Kate, turn off here."

I gave my mother a funny look, but turned my blinker on anyhow. "We're not supposed to exit the freeway for another three miles."

"I know. I want you to see something."

Sighing inwardly, I did as she said. She was already on borrowed time, and the chances of her having an extra day to see it later were slim.

There were pine trees everywhere, tall and looming. I saw no signs, no mile markers, nothing but trees and dirt road. Five miles in, I began to worry. "You're sure this is right?"

"Of course I'm sure." She pressed her forehead to the window, and her voice was so soft and broken that I could barely understand her. "It's just another mile or so."

"What is?"

"You'll see."

After a mile, the hedge started. It stretched down the side of the road, so high and thick that seeing what was on the other side was impossible, and it must've been another two miles before it veered off at a right angle, forming some kind of boundary line. The entire time we drove by, Mom stared out the window, enraptured.

"This is it?" I didn't mean to sound bitter, but Mom didn't seem to notice.

"Of course it isn't—turn left up here, sweetie."

I did as I was told, guiding the car around the corner. "It's nice and all," I said carefully, not wanting to upset her, "but it's just a hedge. Shouldn't we go find the house and—"

"Here!" The eagerness in her weak voice startled me. "Right up there!"

Craning my neck, I saw what she was talking about. Set in the middle of the hedge was a black wrought-iron gate, and the closer we got to it, the bigger it seemed to grow. It wasn't just me—the gate was monstrous. It wasn't there to look pretty. It was there to scare the living daylights out of anyone who thought about opening it.

I slowed to a stop in front of it, trying to look between the bars, but all I could see were more trees. The land seemed to dip in the distance, but no matter how I craned my neck, I couldn't see what lay beyond it.

"Isn't it beautiful?" Her voice was airy, almost light, and for a moment, she sounded like her old self. I felt her hand slip into mine, and I squeezed hers as much as I dared. "It's the entrance to Eden Manor."

"It looks…big," I said, mustering up as much enthusiasm as I could. I wasn't very successful. "Have you ever been inside?"

It was an innocent question, but the look she gave me made me feel like the answer was so obvious that even though I'd never heard of this place, I should have known.

A moment later, she blinked, and the look was gone. "Not in a very long time," she said hollowly, and I bit my lip, regretting whatever it was I'd done to break the magic for her. "I'm sorry, Kate, I just wanted to see it. We should keep going."

She let go of my hand, and I was suddenly keenly aware of how cool the air was against my palm. As I pressed the accelerator, I slipped my hand back into hers, not wanting to let go yet. She said nothing, and when I glanced at her, she was resting her head against the glass once more.

Half a mile down the road, it happened. One moment the road was clear, and the next a cow was in the road not fifteen feet in front of us, blocking the way.

I slammed on the brakes and twisted the wheel. The car spun a full circle, throwing my body sideways. My head hit the window as I fought for control of the car, but it was useless. I might as well have been trying to get it to fly for all the good I was doing.

We skidded to a stop, miraculously missing the tree line. My pulse raced, and I took great gulps of air, trying to calm myself down. "Mom?" I said frantically.

Beside me, she shook her head. "I'm fine. What happened?"

"There's a—" I stopped, focusing on the road again. The cow was gone.

Confused, I glanced in the rearview mirror and saw a figure standing in the middle of the road, a dark-haired boy around my age wearing a black coat that fluttered in the breeze. I frowned, twisting around to try to get a proper look out the back window, but he was gone.

Had I imagined it then? I winced and rubbed my sore head. Hadn't imagined that part.

"Nothing," I said shakily. "I've just been driving too long, that's all. I'm sorry."

As I cautiously urged the car forward, I looked in the rearview mirror one last time. Hedge and empty road. I gripped the wheel tightly with one hand and reached out to take hers again with my other, futilely trying to forget the image of the boy now burned into my brain.

The ceiling in my bedroom leaked. The real estate agent who'd sold us the house, sight unseen, had sworn up and down there was nothing wrong with it, but apparently the jerk had been lying.

All I did after we arrived was unpack the essentials we'd need for the night, including a pot to catch the dripping water. We hadn't brought much, just whatever could fit into the car, and I'd already had a set of secondhand furniture delivered to the house.

Even if my mother hadn't been dying, I was sure I'd be

miserable here. The nearest neighbors were a mile down the road, the whole place smelled like nature, and no one delivered pizza in the small town of Eden.

No, calling it small was being generous. Eden wasn't even marked on the map I'd used to get here. Main Street was half a mile long, and every shop seemed to either sell antiques or groceries. There were no clothing boutiques, or at least no place that would ever carry anything worth wearing. There wasn't even a McDonald's, Pizza Hut, Taco Bell—nothing. Just an outdated diner and some Mom and Pop store that sold candy by the pound.

"Do you like it?"

Mom sat curled up in the rocking chair near her bed, her head supported by her favorite pillow. It was so worn and faded that I couldn't tell what color it had originally been, but it had survived four years of hospital stays and chemotherapy. Against all odds, so had she.

"The house? Yeah," I lied, tucking in the corners of the sheet as I made her bed. "It's…cute."

She smiled, and I could feel her eyes on me. "You'll get used to it. Maybe even like it enough to stay here after I'm gone."

I pressed my lips together, refusing to say anything. It was an unspoken rule that we never talked about what would happen after she died.

"Kate," she said gently, and the rocking chair creaked as she stood. I looked up automatically, ready to spring into action if she fell. "We need to talk about it sometime."

Still watching her out of the corner of my eye, I tugged the sheet down and grabbed a thick quilt, arranging it on the bed. Pillows soon followed.

"Not now." I pulled the covers back and stepped aside so

she could crawl in. Her movements were slow and agonizing, and I averted my eyes, not wanting to see her in so much pain. "Not yet."

Once she was settled, she looked up at me, her eyes red and tired. "Soon," she said softly. "Please."

I swallowed, but said nothing. Life without her was unfathomable, and the less I tried to imagine it, the better.

"The day nurse is going to come by in the morning." I pressed my lips to her forehead. "I'll make sure she's all set up and knows what to do before I head to school."

"Why don't you stay in here tonight?" she said, patting the empty space next to her. "Keep me company."

I hesitated. "You need your rest."

She brushed her cold fingertips against my cheek. "I'll get more with you here."

The temptation of curling up against her like I'd done when I was a child was too much to resist, not when every time I left her, I wondered if it would be the last time I'd see her alive. Tonight I would let myself avoid that pain. "Okay."

I crawled into bed next to her, making sure she had enough blanket before I used the rest to cover my legs. Once I was sure she'd stay warm, I wrapped my arms around her, inhaling her familiar scent. Even after spending years in and out of a hospital, she still smelled of apples and freesia. She nuzzled the top of my head, and I closed my eyes before they started to water.

"Love you," I murmured, wanting to hug her tightly but knowing her body couldn't take it.

"I love you too, Kate," she said softly. "I'll be here in the morning, promise."

As much as I wished it could be, I knew that was no longer a promise she would always be able to keep.

★ ★ ★

That night, my nightmares were relentless and full of cows with red eyes, rivers of blood, and water that rose around me until I woke up gasping. I pushed the blanket off me and wiped my clammy forehead, afraid I'd woken my mother, but she was still asleep.

Even though I didn't sleep well, I couldn't take the next day off. It was my first day at Eden High, which was a brick building that looked more like a large barn than a school. There were hardly enough students to bother building one in the first place, let alone keep it running. Enrolling had been my mother's idea; after I'd missed my senior year to take care of her, she was determined to make sure I graduated.

I drove my car into the parking lot two minutes after the first bell rang. Mom had gotten sick that morning, and I didn't trust the nurse, a round, matronly woman named Sofia, to take care of her properly. Not that there was anything particularly menacing about her, but I'd spent most of the past four years caring for my mother, and as far as I was concerned, no one else could do it right. I'd nearly skipped to stay home with her, but my mother had insisted I go. As difficult as the day had been so far, I was certain it was about to get worse.

At least I wasn't alone in the walk of shame through the parking lot. Halfway to the building, I noticed a boy following me. He couldn't have been old enough to drive, and his white-blond hair stuck out almost as much as his overgrown ears did. Judging from his cheery expression, he couldn't have cared less that he was late.

He dashed forward to reach the front door before I did, and much to my surprise, he held it open for me. I couldn't think of a single guy at my old school who would've done that.

"After you, *mademoiselle*."

Mademoiselle? I stared at the ground to avoid giving him an odd look. No use in being rude the first day.

"Thanks," I mumbled, stepping inside and walking faster. He was taller than me though, and he caught up in no time. Much to my horror, instead of passing me, he slowed so we were walking together.

"Do I know you?"

Oh, God. Did he expect me to answer? Luckily, he didn't seem to, as he didn't give me a chance to respond.

"I don't know you."

Brilliant observation, Einstein.

"I should know you."

Right outside the office, he swung around, placing himself between me and the entrance. Sticking out a hand, he looked at me expectantly.

"I'm James," he said, and I finally got a good look at his face. Still boyish, but maybe he was older than I thought. His features were hardened, more mature than I'd expected. "James MacDuffy. Laugh, and I'll be forced to hate you."

Seeing no other choice, I forced a small smile and took his hand. "Kate Winters."

He stared at me for longer than was strictly necessary, a goofy grin on his face. As the seconds ticked by, I stood there, shifting uncomfortably from one foot to the other, and finally I cleared my throat.

"Er—could you maybe…?"

"What? Oh." James dropped my hand and opened the door, once again holding it open for me. "After you, Kate Winters."

I stepped inside, drawing my messenger bag closer. Inside

the office was a woman dressed head to toe in blue, with sleek auburn hair I'd have given my right foot to have.

"Hi, I'm—"

"—Kate Winters," interrupted James, falling into place next to me. "I don't know her."

The receptionist managed to simultaneously sigh and laugh. "What is it this time, James?"

"Flat tire." He grinned. "Changed it myself."

She scribbled on a pink pad of paper, then tore off the sheet and handed it to him. "You walk."

"Do I?" His grin widened. "Y'know, Irene, if you keep doubting me like this, I'm going to start thinking you don't like me anymore. Same time tomorrow?"

She chuckled, and finally James disappeared. I refused to watch him go, instead staring down at an announcement taped to the counter. Apparently Picture Day was in three weeks.

"Katherine Winters," said the woman—Irene—once the office door closed. "We've been expecting you."

She busied herself looking through a file, and I stood there awkwardly, wishing there was something to say. I wasn't much of a talker, but I could at least carry on a conversation. Sometimes. "You have a pretty name."

She raised her perfectly plucked eyebrows. "Do I? I'm glad you think so. I rather like it myself. Ah, here we go." She pulled out a piece of paper and handed it to me. "Your schedule, as well as a map of the school. Shouldn't be too hard to find—the hallways are color-coded, and if you get lost, just ask. We're all nice enough around here."

I nodded, taking note of my first class. Calculus. Joy. "Thanks."

"Anytime, dear."

I turned to leave, but as my hand touched the doorknob, she cleared her throat.

"Miss Winters? I just—I wanted to say I'm sorry. About your mother, I mean. I knew her a very long time ago, and—well. I'm very sorry."

I closed my eyes. Everyone knew. I didn't know how, but they knew. My mother said her family had lived in Eden for generations, and I'd been stupid to think that I could get away with coming here unnoticed.

Blinking back tears, I turned the knob and hurried out of the office, keeping my head down in hopes that James wouldn't try to talk to me again.

Just as I turned the corner, I ran directly into what felt like a wall. I stumbled to the ground, the contents of my bag spilling out everywhere. My cheeks burned, and I tried to collect my things as I mumbled an apology.

"Are you okay?"

I looked up. The human wall stared down at me, and I found myself face-to-face with a varsity football jacket. Apparently James and I weren't the only ones running late that morning.

"I'm Dylan." He knelt next to me, offering me a hand. I only took it long enough to sit up.

"Kate," I said. He handed me my notebooks, and I snatched them from him, shoving them back into my bag. Two textbooks and five folders later, I stood and brushed off my jeans. That was when I noticed that he was cute. Not just in Eden, but cute by New York standards, too. Even so, there was something about the way he looked at me that made me want to pull away.

Before I could do just that, a pretty blonde girl attached herself to his side and gave me a once-over. She might've been smiling, but with the way she was leaning against him and clutching his arm, she might as well have peed on him. He was clearly marked territory.

"Who's your friend, Dylan?" she said, tightening her grip.

Dylan looked at her blankly, and it took him a moment before he wrapped his arm around her. "Uh, Kate. She's new."

Her fake smile grew, and she stuck out her hand. "Kate! I'm Ava. I've heard *so* much about you. My father, he's a real estate agent, told me all about you and your mom."

At least now I had someone to blame for the leak in my room. "Hi, Ava," I said, biting the bullet and taking her hand. "It's nice to meet you."

Everything about the way she looked at me screamed she wanted nothing more than to take me out into the woods and bury me alive. "It's a pleasure to meet you, too."

"What's your first class?" said Dylan, craning his neck to look at my schedule. "Calculus. I—we can show you where that is, if you'd like."

I opened my mouth to object, figuring there was no reason to tempt fate more than I already was by continuing the conversation now that Ava was here, but before I could say a word, he took me by the elbow and paraded me down the hall. I looked at Ava, about to apologize for hijacking her boyfriend, but when I saw the flush of red on her cheeks and the clench of her delicate jaw, the words died on the tip of my tongue.

Maybe my mother would outlive me after all.

CHAPTER 2
AVA

I wasn't spectacularly pretty. I wished I was, but I was just me. I'd never modeled, never had guys drooling over me, and never looked like much of anything next to the genetically blessed socialites that attended my preparatory school back home.

Which was why I couldn't for the life of me figure out why Dylan was still staring at me.

He stared at me all through History, all through Chemistry, and all through lunch. I ate alone at the empty end of a table, my nose buried in a book, not wanting to bother with making friends. I wasn't going to be here for very long anyhow, so there wasn't much of a point. Once this was over, I had every intention of going back to New York City and picking up what few pieces of my former life I'd be able to find.

Besides, I was used to eating lunch alone. I hadn't had many friends back home either, since my mother had gotten sick at the beginning of my freshman year, and I'd spent all my time outside of school camped out next to her hospital bed as she went through round after round of chemo and radiation. It hadn't left much time for sleepovers and dating and hanging out with people who couldn't possibly understand what we were going through.

"Is this seat taken?"

Startled, I looked up, half expecting to see Dylan standing there. Instead, carrying a cafeteria tray full of french fries and wearing a huge pair of headphones that hid his elephant ears, James stared back at me, a jaunty grin on his face. I didn't know whether to be horrified or relieved.

Silently I shook my head, but it didn't matter anyway. He was already sitting. I stared at my book, trying my best to avoid looking at him in hopes he would go away. But the words blurred in front of me, and I read the same sentence four times, too aware of James to concentrate.

"Technically, you're in my seat," he said conversationally. Reaching into his backpack, he pulled out a full-size bottle of ketchup, and my eyes nearly popped out of my head as I abandoned all pretense of reading. Who carried around a bottle of *ketchup?*

He must've seen my look, because as he squirted it all over the massive pile of fries, he nudged the tray closer to me. "Want some?"

I shook my head. I had an apple and a sandwich, but the arrival of James made me a little queasy. It wasn't that I didn't think he might be a sweet kid—I just wanted to be left alone. As an excuse to avoid talking to him, I took a bite of my apple, taking my time as I chewed. James started to dive into his fries, and for a few brief seconds, I hoped the conversation was over.

"Dylan's staring at you," he said, and before I could swallow and make it clear I wanted nothing to do with Dylan, James nodded to something behind me. "Incoming."

I frowned and twisted around, but Dylan was still sitting across the cafeteria. It didn't take long for me to see what he was talking about though. Ava was heading straight toward us.

"Great," I muttered, dropping my apple onto a napkin. Was it really too much to ask that I get through my senior year unscathed? And if that really was so impossible, couldn't I at least have a day to settle before all of the drama started?

"Kate?" Ava's high-pitched voice was unmistakable. I sighed inwardly and forced myself to turn around, plastering an innocent smile on my face.

"Oh, hi—Ava, right?"

The corner of her lips twitched. I bet no one had ever asked for her name twice before.

"Right!" she said, her voice dripping with fake enthusiasm. "I'm so glad you remembered. Listen, I wanted to ask—do you have plans for tomorrow night?"

Other than scrub bedpans, change my mother's sheets, and measure out her medication for the following week? "I've got a few things going on. Why?"

She sniffed haughtily, but then seemed to remember that she was trying to play nice. "We're all having a bonfire in the woods—it's a pep rally, sort of, except it's not…well, you know. School-sponsored." She giggled and tucked a lock of blond hair behind her ear. "Anyway, I was wondering if you wanted to come. I thought it might be a nice way for you to meet everyone." Glancing over her shoulder at a long table full of jocks, she grinned. "I know a few of them are really eager to meet you."

Was that what this was about? She wanted to find me a boyfriend so Dylan would leave me alone? "I don't date."

Ava's mouth dropped open. "Really?"

"Really."

"Why not?"

I shrugged and glanced at James, who seemed to be determined not to look at Ava as he built an elaborate teepee made of fries. He wasn't going to be any help.

"Listen," said Ava, dropping her fake act. "It's just a party. Once everyone meets you, they'll stop staring at you. It's no big deal. Just an hour or whatever, and then you won't have to do it again. I'll even help you with hair and makeup and stuff—you can borrow one of my dresses, if they're not too small."

Did she even realize she'd just insulted me? I tried to refuse, but she kept going.

"Please," she said, her voice cracking with sincerity. "Don't make me beg. I know it's probably not what you're used to in New York, but it'll be fun, I promise."

I eyed her as she gave me a helpless, pleading look. She wasn't going to take no for an answer. "Fine," I said. "I'll stay for an hour. But I don't need your makeup or your dresses, and after this, you leave me alone, all right?"

Her smile was back, and this time it wasn't fake. "Deal. I'll be at your place at seven."

After I scribbled down my address on a napkin, Ava sauntered back to her table, her hips swaying outrageously as virtually every male eye turned her way. I glared at James, who was still focused on building that ridiculous hut. "Some help you are."

"You seemed like you were handling it."

"Yeah, well, thanks for throwing me to the wolves." I reached over and took a fry from the plate, making sure it was the one that was holding up the structure. It came toppling down, but

James didn't seem to mind. Instead he popped another fry into his mouth and chewed thoughtfully.

"Well," he said once he'd swallowed. "Seems you've officially made a date with the devil."

I groaned.

As I walked to my car after the last bell had rung, James caught up with me, music blasting from the headphones that hung off his neck, but at least he was silent. I was still annoyed he hadn't stepped in and helped me with Ava, so I waited until I'd reached my car to acknowledge him.

"Did I drop something?" I said, unable to think of any other way to make myself clearer. I didn't want to talk to him.

"What? No, of course not. If you did, I'd give it back." His bewilderment confused me. Did he really not understand?

I lingered with my key in the lock, wondering how long this was going to last. Was it just for today, or did I have to wait for my status as a new curiosity to wear off? I'd been stared at all day long, but no one but James, Dylan and Ava had approached me. I wasn't surprised. They'd all known each other since diapers, and they'd carved out their groups since kindergarten, more than likely. I had no place here. I knew it, they knew it, and that was perfectly fine with me.

"I don't date."

The words came out before I could stop myself, but now that I'd said them, I had to keep going.

"Even back home, I didn't date. I just—I don't. It's nothing personal. I'm not making excuses. I really mean it—I don't date."

Instead of looking disappointed or crestfallen, James stared at me with wide blue eyes and a blank expression. As the seconds ticked by, I felt my cheeks grow warm. Apparently dating me had been the last thing on his mind.

"I think you're pretty."

I blinked. Or maybe not.

"But you're at least an eight, and I'm a four. We're not allowed to date. Society says so."

Eyeing him, I tried to figure out if he was being serious. He didn't look like he was kidding, and he was staring at me again, like he expected some sort of answer other than a snort.

"An eight?" I blurted. It was the only thing I could come up with.

"Maybe a nine, if you put on some makeup. But I like eights. Eights don't let it go to their heads. Nines do. And tens don't know how to be anything other than tens—like Ava."

He was serious. I turned the key in the lock, wishing I had a cell phone so I could pretend someone was calling me. "Well... thanks, I guess."

"You're welcome." He paused. "Kate? Can I ask you something?"

I bit my lip to stop myself from pointing out that he already had. "Sure, shoot."

"What's wrong with your mother?"

I froze, and my stomach churned. I didn't say anything for several moments, but he still waited for an answer.

My mother. Her illness was the last thing I wanted to talk about. It seemed wrong to spread it around, like I was somehow spreading her around as well. And selfishly I wanted to keep her to myself for these last few days, weeks, months—however much time I had left with her, I wanted it to be just her and me. She wasn't a freak show they could stare at or some piece of gossip they could whisper back and forth, and I wouldn't let them do that to her. I wouldn't let them taint her memory like that.

James leaned against my car, and I saw a flicker of sympathy in his eyes. I hated being pitied. "How long does she have?"

I swallowed. For someone with zero social skills, he could read me like a damn book. Or maybe I really was that obvious. "The doctors gave her six months to live when I was a freshman." I clutched my car keys so hard that the metal cut into my skin. The pain was a welcome distraction, but it wasn't enough to make the lump in my throat disappear. "She's been hanging on for a really long time."

"And now she's ready."

I nodded numbly. My hands were shaking.

"Are you?"

The air around us seemed unnaturally heavy for September. When I focused on James again, racking my brain for something to say that would make him leave before I started crying, I realized that nearly all of the other cars had left.

James reached around me and opened the door. "Are you all right to drive home?"

Was I? "Yeah."

He waited as I climbed into the car, and he gently closed the door behind me. I rolled my window down as soon as I started the engine.

"Do you want a ride?"

He smiled, tilting his head as if I'd said something remarkable. "I've walked home every single day of high school so far, in the rain, snow, sleet, hail, doesn't matter. You're the first person to ever offer to drive me home."

I blushed. "It's not a big deal. Offer stands, if you want."

James stared at me for a moment, as if he were making some

sort of decision about me. "No, it's all right, I'll walk. Thanks though."

I wasn't sure whether to be relieved or to feel guilty for wanting to feel relieved. "See you tomorrow then."

He nodded, and I put the car into reverse. Right before I took my foot off the brake, James was next to the window again.

"Hey, Kate? Maybe she'll hang on a little longer."

I said nothing, not trusting myself to keep my composure. He watched as I backed out of the space, and when I turned onto the main road, I caught a glimpse of him walking through the parking lot. He'd put his massive headphones on again.

Halfway home, I had to pull over and give myself time to cry.

Mom spent most of that night hunched over a basin retching, and I spent most of it holding her hair back. By the time morning came and Sofia, the day nurse, showed up, my mother barely had enough energy to call in, excusing me from my classes, and we both slept the day away.

After another round of chilling nightmares, I woke up shortly after four, my heart pounding and my blood cold in my veins. I could still feel the water fill my lungs as I struggled to take a breath, could still see the dark swirls of blood that surrounded me as the current pulled me under, and the more I struggled, the deeper I sank. It took me several minutes to calm myself down, and once I could breathe steadily again, I dabbed a bit of concealer underneath my eyes to hide the dark circles. The last thing I wanted was my mother to worry about me as well.

When I went to check on her, Sofia sat in a chair outside her door, humming softly to herself as she knit what looked like half a puce sweater. She looked so cheerful that you would've never known my mother was dying on the other side of the door.

"Is she awake?" I said, and Sofia shook her head. "Did you attach her medication to her IV?"

"Of course, dear," she said kindly, and I slumped my shoulders. "Are you going to the party tonight?"

"How do you know about that?"

"Your mother mentioned it," she said. "Is that what you're wearing?"

I looked down at my pajamas. "I'm not going." It was an hour with my mother that I would never get back, and we didn't have many of those left together. Sofia clucked disapprovingly, and I gave her a dirty look. "Wouldn't you do the same if she was your mother? I'd rather spend tonight with her."

"Is that what she would want you to do?" said Sofia as she set down her knitting. "For you to put your life on hold while you wait for her to die? Do you think that's what would make her happy?"

I looked away. "She's sick."

"She was sick yesterday, and she'll still be sick tomorrow," said Sofia gently. I felt her warm hand in mine, and I pulled away, crossing my arms tightly over my chest. "She'd want you to have a night to yourself."

"You don't know that," I snapped, my voice quavering with emotion that refused to stay buried. "You don't know her, so stop acting like you do."

Sofia stood and carefully arranged her knitting on the chair. "I do know that all she talks about is you." She gave me a sad smile I couldn't bear to see, so I looked at the carpet instead. "She wants nothing more than to know that you'll be happy and okay without her. Don't you think an hour or two of your time might be worth giving her a little peace and reassurance?"

I gritted my teeth. "Of course, but—"

"But nothing." She squared her shoulders, and even though she was my height, she suddenly looked much taller. "She wants you to be happy, and you can give her that much by going out tonight and making friends. I'll stay and make sure she's taken care of, and I won't take no for an answer."

I said nothing, glaring at Sofia as my face burned with anger and frustration. She stared back, not giving an inch, and finally I had to look away. She didn't know how precious each minute was to me, and there was no way to make her understand, but she was right about my mother. If it would make her happy, I would do it.

"Fine." I wiped my eyes with my sleeve. "But if something happens to her while I'm gone—"

"It won't," said Sofia, the warmth back in her voice. "I promise it won't. She may not even notice you're gone, and when you get back, you'll have a story to tell, won't you?"

If Ava had her way, I was sure I would.

CHAPTER 3

THE RIVER

My last hope was Ava forgetting to pick me up, but when I reluctantly dragged myself to the porch five minutes after seven, I saw a massive Range Rover parked in the driveway, making my car look like a toy in comparison. My mother had still been sleeping when I'd gone to check on her, and instead of letting me wake her up to say goodbye, Sofia shooed me away. By the time I left, I wasn't a happy camper.

"Kate!" squealed Ava as I opened the passenger door, oblivious to my bad mood. "I'm so glad you're coming. You're not contagious, are you?"

With effort, I climbed in and fastened my seat belt. "I'm not sick."

"Whew," said Ava. "You're so lucky your mother lets you skip."

My hands tightened into fists, and I said nothing. *Lucky* wasn't exactly the word for it.

"You're going to love it tonight," said Ava, not bothering to glance in the mirror as she backed out of the driveway. "Everyone's coming, so you'll have a ton of people to meet."

"Is James coming?" I braced myself as Ava slammed on the gas, and the Range Rover lurched forward, taking my stomach with it.

For a split second, Ava looked so disgusted by the thought of James showing up that I almost took my question back, but the look was gone as soon as it'd come. "James isn't invited."

"Oh." I let it drop. I hadn't been expecting James to come anyhow—he and Ava didn't exactly run in the same circles, after all. "Is Dylan?"

"Of course." Her cheery voice sounded as fake as her nails, and when I looked at her through the dim light of the car, I saw a flash of something in her eyes. Anger, maybe, or jealousy.

"I'm not after him," I said, in case she hadn't gotten the message yet. "I meant it when I said I don't date."

"I know." But the way she refused to look at me spoke volumes, and I sighed. I shouldn't have cared, but in New York I'd seen plenty of boys taking advantage of their girlfriends while eyeing someone else in the background. It never ended well. No matter how much Ava might've hated me, she didn't deserve that.

"Why are you with him anyway?"

For a moment, she looked startled. "Because he's Dylan," she said, as if it were obvious. "He's cute, he's smart and he's captain of the football team. Why wouldn't I want to be with him?"

"Oh, I don't know," I said. "Because he's a pig who probably only dates you because you're gorgeous and almost certainly a cheerleader?"

She sniffed. "I'm captain of the squad *and* captain of the swim team."

"Exactly."

Ava spun the wheel, and the tires squealed against the pavement as the car turned sharply. The image of a cow in the middle of the road flashed through my mind, and I squeezed my eyes shut and silently prayed.

"We've been together for ages," said Ava. "I'm not going to dump him because some girl who thinks she's better than us comes along and tells me I'm being stupid."

"I don't think I'm better than you," I said tightly. "I just didn't move here to make friends."

She was silent as we drove through the darkness. At first I thought she wasn't going to say anything, but when she did a minute later, her voice was so small I had to strain to hear her. "Daddy said your mom's really sick."

"Yeah, well, Daddy's right."

"I'm sorry," she said. "I don't know what I'd do without my mom."

"Yeah," I mumbled. "Me neither."

This time when she turned the corner, I didn't feel as if we were suddenly flying through the air. "Kate?"

"Mm?"

"I really love Dylan. Even if he's only with me because I'm a cheerleader."

"Maybe he's not," I said, leaning my head against the window. "Maybe he's different."

She sighed. "Maybe."

Ava parked her gas-guzzling monster on the side of a dark road. Trees rose above us, and the moon cast shadows on the ground, but for the life of me I couldn't figure out where we were. There wasn't another car or house in sight.

"Where are we?" I said as she led me into the forest.

"The bonfire's in the woods," said Ava as she nimbly avoided the low-hanging branches. I wasn't as lucky. "It's not that far."

Muttering a string of profanities under my breath, I followed her. This effectively destroyed my intentions of leaving early, and I'd be stuck here until Ava left, unless I caught a ride with one of my many suitors.

I made a face at the thought. I would have rather walked.

"It's right on the other side of the hedge," said Ava, and I stopped. The hedge?

"You mean the hedge around that huge property?"

"You know about it?" Ava turned to look at me.

"My mom told me."

"Oh—well, it's where we have our parties. Daddy knows the owner, and he's totally cool with it."

Something about the way she said it made my stomach twist into knots as I remembered the figure I thought I'd seen in the rearview mirror, but there wasn't much I could do. Maybe she was telling the truth. She had no reason to lie to me, did she? Besides, as far as I knew, the only way past those hedges was the front gate, but we weren't anywhere near the road anymore.

"How are we supposed to get in?"

She continued walking, and left with no choice, I followed. "There's a stream up ahead. There's an opening in the hedge we can climb through, and the party's just on the other side."

I paled, my nightmares of drowning coming back to me. "I don't have to swim, do I?"

"No, why?" She must've caught something in my voice, because she stopped again to look at me.

"I can't swim. I never learned how." It was the truth, but I also didn't want to tell her about my nightmares. It was bad enough I had to relive them at night; if I told Ava, I was sure she would only use them as ammunition against me.

She laughed lightly, and I could've sworn her tone grew more cheerful. "Oh, don't worry, no swimming required. There are rocks you can step on and stuff that makes it easy to get in."

I could see the hedge now. My hands were sweaty and my breath was coming in short gasps, and I didn't think it had anything to do with our brisk pace.

"It's right up there." Ava pointed to a spot about twenty feet ahead of us. The sound of rushing water floated in the night air toward us, and it took every bit of willpower I had to keep following her.

When we reached the stream, my mouth dropped open. It wasn't a stream—it was a damn river. The current didn't look very powerful, but it was strong enough to carry me away if I fell. And without much light to work with, it was almost impossible to see the stones Ava referred to. She'd been telling the truth about the opening in the hedge though: it was small, as if the river narrowed just enough for the hedge to form over it. We'd have to walk on rocks and duck to get underneath, but it was doable without actually going swimming.

"Follow me," said Ava in a hushed voice. Holding her hands out for balance, she stepped into the river, searching until she found a wide stone. "Path's here—are you okay?"

"I'm fine," I muttered through gritted teeth. I was careful to place my feet exactly where she'd walked and hold my arms out like she did, but every step made me feel as if I were going to fall into the dark water below.

She ducked underneath the hedge, and I could no longer see where she was going. My stomach tightened as panic set in, and I placed a shaking hand against the hedge and bent down, taking each step one at a time.

Miraculously, I arrived on the other side dry. The stones ended immediately, and I had to jump to reach solid land, but I'd done it—I was safe. I let out a sigh of relief. If Ava thought she was getting me through that hole again, she was out of her mind.

Looking up, the first thing I saw was Ava unzipping her skirt, her top already discarded. Underneath she wore a bikini, the colors muted in the dark.

"What're you doing?"

She ignored me. Instead of pressing the issue, I took a moment to look around. We were in a wooded area, and had I not known any better, I'd have thought we were still on the other side of the hedge. It looked exactly the same.

"Sorry, Kate," said Ava. She pulled a trash bag out of her pocket and placed her folded clothes inside.

"Sorry? Why are you sorry?"

"For leaving." She tossed the bag over her shoulder and flashed me a wide smile. "Don't take it personally. If Dylan didn't like you so much, we might even be friends. But I'm sure you can understand why this has to happen."

"Why what has to happen?"

"This." She stepped into the water and shivered. Apparently it was as cold as it looked. "Consider this a warning, Kate. Don't touch my boyfriend. Next time it'll be much, much worse."

And with that she dove headfirst into the river.

Two things happened at once: first, I realized what was going on. She was leaving me here, knowing full well I was afraid of the water. There was no bonfire—she'd done this on purpose.

The second thing happened when Ava hit the river. Instead of watching her swim away, I heard a sickening crack as she hit her head on a rock, and the next thing I knew, Ava floated limply as she was carried away by the current.

I winced. The water carried her nearly twenty feet as I watched, but Ava didn't move. The blow must have knocked her senseless.

Good.

No, not good, the moral part of my brain insisted. Not good at all. If she was really unconscious and not just dazed, then she would drown if the current didn't push her onto the bank of the river.

I mentally groaned. Let her suffer—it wasn't a very wide river. She'd come to her senses and find the edge eventually.

But that do-gooder voice in my head pointed out that if something happened to her, I'd be responsible. And even if she had tried to pull a cruel prank on me, I couldn't bear the thought of something awful happening to another person in my life. I'd had enough tragedy for one lifetime.

My body moved before my mind was made up. I might not have been very good at swimming, but I could run. Kicking off my heels, I closed half the distance between us before I'd even realized what I was doing. The current was strong, but it wasn't as fast as I'd first thought. I caught up to Ava quickly, skidding to a stop on the muddy bank, but then I had a whole different problem to deal with—the water.

Images from my nightmares flashed through my mind, but I pushed them aside. Ava was in the center of the river and facedown, which meant I didn't have time to wait for her to come closer. There were only two options: let her drown or jump into the river after her. Not much of a choice.

Cringing, I entered the ice-cold water and splashed toward her, leaping sluggishly to keep up. My foot caught a rock and I fell in, drenching myself, and before I knew it, the current had me, too.

Panic rose up inside of me as soon as my head was submerged. But I was conscious, and even though I couldn't swim, the water wasn't deep. Unlike my nightmare, I managed to find my footing and push myself toward the surface. I struggled to reach Ava, and once I did, I grabbed her arm and yanked her toward me. My heart beat painfully fast, but I kept breathing as steadily as I could. I was going to kill Ava once she was awake, and if there was any justice in the world, she'd need stitches and permanently scar that pretty little face of hers.

I pulled Ava toward the shore and out of the freezing water, relieved to be on dry land. Even though she'd only been in for half a minute, her skin was beginning to turn blue, and I turned her on her side, hoping that would help if she'd swallowed any water.

"Ava?" I said, kneeling down next to her. My teeth chattered. "Ava—wake up."

She was still. I leaned in closer, waiting for her to take a breath, but she didn't. I swallowed the lump of dread in my throat. CPR. I could do that.

Roll her onto her back, palms against her diaphragm, one, two, three, four, five, six…

I looked at her and waited. Nothing.

"If this is some kind of joke…" I tried again. I wasn't giving her mouth-to-mouth unless I absolutely had to.

It was then that I noticed the gash on her head. I don't know how I'd missed it before—blood stained her hair scarlet, and I momentarily abandoned CPR to see how bad it was.

It wasn't just a cut. My stomach twisted violently when I pulled her hair back to see the wound. Her skull wasn't round on the top of her head—it was flat.

I shrieked and covered my mouth, seconds away from vomiting. Even in the dark, I could tell I wasn't just looking at hair and blood. Her scalp was exposed and part of it flapped open, revealing a crushed skull and bits of—oh, God, I didn't even want to think about it.

Quickly my fingers went to the side of her neck, searching in vain for a pulse. My breath was coming in rapid gasps now, and the world spun as I automatically resumed CPR. She couldn't be. It wasn't possible. It was a joke, just some sick joke where I was supposed to drag my sorry ass to the front gate and walk home. She wasn't supposed to be—

"Help!" I yelled as loudly as I could as hot tears streamed down my face. "Somebody *help!*"

CHAPTER 4

THE STRANGER

Sobbing, I thrust my hands against Ava's abdomen. She couldn't be dead. Two minutes ago, she'd been telling me off for…for what? It didn't matter. I wiped my eyes with the back of my hand, taking a deep, shuddering breath. No. Not possible. This wasn't happening.

"Help!" I cried, looking around wildly, hoping for some sign of life. But all I saw on either side of us were trees, and the only sound I heard was the flowing river. If anyone lived on the property, they could've been miles away.

I looked back at Ava, her face swimming as my eyes filled with tears again. What was I supposed to do?

My shoulders shook, and my body was useless. I stumbled backward, falling into a sitting position as I stared at Ava. Her eyes were wide open, unblinking and lifeless, and she was still as blood trickled from her head. It was useless.

I drew my knees to my chest, unable to tear my eyes away. What would happen now? Who would find us? I couldn't leave her. I had to stay here until someone found us. Oh, God, my poor mother—what would everyone say? Would they think I killed Ava? Hadn't I, in a way? If I hadn't agreed to go with her, then she would've never jumped headfirst into a river.

"May I help you?"

My heart skipped a beat. Standing beside me was a man—a boy? I couldn't tell, as his face was partially obscured by the darkness. But what I could see of him made my breath hitch in my throat. His hair was dark, and the jacket he wore was long and black, flapping in the cold breeze.

I hadn't imagined him after all.

"She's—" I couldn't finish.

He knelt next to Ava and examined her. He had to see the same things I saw—the bloody head, the too-still body, the angle of her neck. But instead of panicking, he looked up at me, and a jolt ran down my spine. His eyes were the color of moonlight.

I heard rustling a few feet away. Startled, I twisted around, only to see a black Great Dane approach us, tail wagging. The dog sat next to him, and he scratched the dog behind his ears.

"What's your name?" he said evenly.

With trembling hands, I tucked my wet hair behind my ears. "K-Kate."

"Hello, Kate." There was a calming quality to his voice, almost melodic. "I'm Henry, and this is Cerberus."

I could see his face clearly now that he was closer, and something about it looked off. He couldn't have been more than a few years older than me, twenty-two at the most, but even that was pushing it. And he was too beautiful to be out in the middle of the woods like this. He should've been on magazine covers, not spending his time hidden away in the Upper Peninsula of Michigan.

But his eyes drew my attention. Even in the darkness, they shone brightly, and I had a hard time tearing myself away from his gaze.

"M-my friend," I said, my voice trembling. "She's—"

"She's dead."

He spoke with such a matter-of-fact tone that my stomach turned inside out. I threw up what little dinner I'd eaten, the horror of the evening hitting me so hard I felt as if the wind had been knocked out of me.

Finally, once I'd finished, I turned back into a sitting position and wiped my mouth. Henry had arranged Ava so she looked as if she were sleeping, and now he was staring at me like I was some strange animal he didn't want to scare off. I looked away.

"So she is your friend?"

I coughed weakly, struggling to keep the sob bubbling up inside of me from bursting. Was she? Of course not. "Y-yes," I managed to say. "Why?"

I heard the rustle of fabric and opened my eyes to see Henry placing his jacket over Ava, the way people covered dead bodies. "I didn't realize friends treated each other the way she treated you."

"She—it was a joke."

"You didn't think it was very funny."

No, I hadn't. But it didn't matter anymore.

"You're afraid of the water, yet you jumped in after her, even though she was going to leave you behind."

I stared at him. How did he know that?

"Why?" he said, and I shrugged pathetically. What did he expect me to say?

"Because," I said. "She—she didn't deserve to…" She didn't deserve to die.

Henry was quiet for a long moment, and he looked at Ava's covered body. "What would you do to have her back?"

I struggled to understand what he was saying. "Back?"

"Back in the condition she was in before she jumped in the water. Alive."

In my panic, I already knew my answer. What would I do to have Ava back? What would I do to stop death from tightening its chokehold over the remaining shreds of my life that it hadn't already stolen? It had marked my mother and was waiting in the wings to take her from me, inching closer every day. She might've been ready to give up, but I would never stop fighting for her. And like hell I was going to let it claim another victim right in front of me, especially when it was my fault Ava was here in the first place. "Anything."

"Anything?"

"Yes. Can you help her?" An irrational hope flared up inside of me. Maybe he was a doctor. Maybe he knew how to fix her.

"Kate…have you ever heard the story of Persephone?"

My mother loved Greek mythology, and she used to read the stories to me as a child. But what did that have to do with anything? "What? I—yes, a long time ago," I said, bewildered. "Can you fix her? Is she—can you? Please?"

Henry stood. "Yes, if you promise me one thing."

"Whatever you want." I stood, too, daring to hope.

"Read the myth of Persephone again, and you will figure it out." He took a step toward me and brushed his fingertips against my cheek. I jerked away, but my skin felt as if it were on fire where he'd touched me. He placed his hands in his pockets, untroubled by my rejection. "The autumn equinox is in two weeks. Read it, and you'll understand."

He stepped back, and I stood there, confused. Turning to look at Ava, I said, "But what about—"

I glanced up, and he was gone. Stumbling forward, my feet numb, I looked around wildly. "Henry? What about—"

"Kate?"

My heart leaped into my throat. Ava. I fell to my knees next to her, too afraid to touch her, but her eyes were open and she wasn't bleeding anymore and she was *alive*.

"Ava?" I gasped.

"What happened?" she said, struggling to sit up and wipe the blood from her eyes.

"You—you hit your head and…" I trailed off. And what?

Ava stumbled to her feet and swayed, but I reached out to steady her with trembling hands. "All right?" I said, dazed, and Ava nodded. I wrapped my arm around her bare waist to help keep her upright. Henry's jacket was gone. "Let's get you home."

By the time I crawled into bed that night after scrubbing the blood out from underneath my fingernails, I'd almost convinced myself he wasn't real. That seeing him today and from the car earlier that week—it'd all been my imagination. It was the only logical explanation. I'd hit my head when I jumped into the river, and in the car I'd been exhausted. Ava had been fine all along, and Henry…

Henry was just a dream.

That weekend the phone rang on the hour, nearly every hour before I unplugged it. My mother needed her rest, and after what had happened, all I wanted to do was cut myself off from the world and keep her company. I didn't know who it was, and I didn't care.

The freezing river hadn't done me any favors, and I slept most of the weekend away in the rocking chair beside my mother's bed. It was a restless sleep, littered with the same nightmares I'd been having nearly every night since coming to Eden, but now there was a new one. It went exactly as the night had gone, with Ava diving into the river and hitting her head, and me jumping into the water to save her. But when I pulled her body out of the river, it wasn't her face I saw, pale and lifeless as blood pooled on the ground. It was mine.

I had to wear a surgical mask around my mother. I felt feverish and achy, and there was a deep cough in my chest that I couldn't shake, but someone had to take care of her. I poured medicine down my throat hoping it'd make me feel better, and by the time Monday rolled around, I felt well enough to brave school once more.

The moment I entered the cafeteria at lunchtime, James attached himself to my side, already holding his tray full of french fries. He babbled on happily about a new CD he'd picked up over the weekend and even offered to let me listen, but I shook my head. I wasn't in the mood for music.

"Kate?" We'd taken our seats, and he had already drenched his fries in ketchup. "You're really quiet today. Is your mom okay?"

I glanced up from my uneaten sandwich. "She's hanging in there."

"Then what's wrong?" The look on his face made it clear he wasn't going to let it go.

"Nothing. I was just sick all weekend, that's all."

"Oh, right." He popped a fry into his mouth. "You missed Friday. I got your homework for you."

"Thanks." At least he wasn't pressing the issue.

"Did you go to that party with Ava?"

I froze. Was it that obvious? Was there something in my expression that told him? No, it was only idle conversation.

"Kate?"

Terrific. Now he knew something was wrong. "I'm sorry," I mumbled, slouching.

"Did something happen at the party?"

"There wasn't any party." No point in lying to him about that. He'd be able to ask around and find out anyhow, if he ever bothered to talk to other people. "It was just Ava and a stupid prank."

"What sort of stupid prank?" The way his voice dropped and his eyes hardened should have set off alarm bells in my mind, but I was too busy trying to come up with some sort of feasible reply. How was I supposed to describe the impossibility that had happened beside the river? There was no way he'd believe me. I didn't even believe me. And Ava—

I mentally smacked myself. The whole thing had been a prank, hadn't it? Not only leaving me there, but her smashing her head against a rock, and Henry showing up and pretending to do…to do whatever it was that he'd done. He was probably someone's older brother. Maybe even Ava's.

But what about her skull? The way she'd stopped breathing? The angle of her neck? Could that really be faked?

"Speak of the devil," said James, eyebrows raised as he looked over my shoulder. I didn't need to turn around to know who it was.

"Kate!" squealed Ava, and she sat down beside me without

waiting for an invitation. I tensed, gripping my apple so hard I could feel the fruit bruise beneath the skin.

"Er, hi." What was I supposed to say to her? "How—how was your weekend?"

She swung her legs underneath the table and set down her tray of food. Unlike James, she had a chicken sandwich and a pile of Tater Tots. There was no possible way she ate that every day for lunch and managed to stay so skinny.

"It was good. You know, rested and swam and stuff." She took a bite of her sandwich and didn't bother swallowing before continuing. "I tried calling you, but you never picked up. Did my dad give me the wrong number?"

I nearly choked. That had been Ava? "N-no, that was my house." I looked at James, silently willing him to say something, but he seemed to be making a very real effort not to look at us. "I was sick, so I didn't pick up."

"You're feeling better now though, right?"

I hesitated. "Yeah, I feel better."

"Oh, that's perfect then! I was hoping you'd come over this week sometime. We've got a swimming pool, and I was think-ing maybe I could teach you how to swim."

I gaped at her. After everything that had happened, she wanted me to go swimming with her? "I don't—I don't swim." And after what had happened on Friday, I didn't want to go anywhere near a body of water ever again. It seemed unusually cruel to keep dragging a stupid prank out like this, and I silently wished she would drop it already.

Ava pursed her lips, and it was clear that something in my voice or expression must've clued her in. "No hard feelings about what happened, right?" Maybe I was imagining it, but she seemed almost nervous. "I mean…that's sort of what I wanted to talk to you ab—"

"Ava," I interrupted. "Why are you sitting with me?"

Her face fell, and she put down her sandwich. "I broke up with Dylan."

"What? Why?" I glanced at James again, but he was now engrossed in making a fry fort. "I thought you said you loved him."

"I do! I did."

"Then why?"

"Because." She glanced over her shoulder at the jock table. At least half a dozen pairs of eyes were watching us, and she lowered her voice to a whisper. "You saw me, right? I dove into the river and hit my head, and the next thing I know I'm on the ground with a throbbing headache."

I forced a nonchalant shrug. "So you hit your head and I dragged you out before you drowned. No big deal."

"Yes, it is." Her voice dropped. "There was blood everywhere. My mother saw me when I got home, and she had a fit. I had to tell her it was yours."

"But it wasn't mine."

Our eyes locked. Hers were red and shining with tears. "I know," she whispered. "Kate, what happened to me?"

Across the table, James stilled, and I noticed he was no longer wearing his headphones. On top of telling Ava what had happened, now I'd have to explain it to him once she was gone. He wouldn't believe me—no one in their right mind would. *I* wasn't even sure I believed me, and I still wasn't convinced it wasn't all some elaborate hoax.

Ava watched me closely, waiting for me to speak, and I knew there was no way I could lie my way out of this. Even if they did think I was crazy, the need to tell someone, to understand what had happened was overwhelming. I took a deep breath, kissed my sanity goodbye, and I told them everything.

Once I was done, Ava stared at me, her eyes shining. "Oh, Kate—you really jumped into the river to save me?"

I shrugged, and before I knew it, she wrapped her arms around me and buried her face in my neck. The hug lasted for nearly half a minute, things growing more awkward with each second that passed. Finally she let me go, although her hands were still on my shoulders.

"That's the nicest thing anyone's ever done for me. When I tried to tell Dylan…" She bit her lip. "He laughed at me and told me to stop making stuff up."

At the jock table, Dylan sat surrounded by his friends, laughing loudly. Next to me, Ava looked crushed. "So you broke up with him?" I said.

"It doesn't matter," she said, picking at her sandwich. "He'll be begging to get back together with me in a week. What about Henry? You really promised him anything? What did he want?"

Out of the corner of my eye, I saw James look up.

"I'm not really sure," I said. "He asked if I knew about the myth of Persephone, and he told me the autumn equinox was in two weeks. He said once I read about her, I'd know what he wanted me to do. I've heard it before, but I don't get what that has to do with anything—"

Across the table, James dug through his backpack, tossing heavy books and binders onto the table. They landed with a thud, and half the cafeteria looked at us. I ducked my head, amazed as I tried to figure out how all of it fit into his bag, but finally he yanked out a thick book I recognized as our English text. He flipped it open seemingly at random, but when I craned my neck to see what he'd turned to, I saw it wasn't random at all.

"This is the story of Persephone," he said, pointing to a picture of a girl emerging from a cave. A woman stood on the grass, her arms open wide in greeting. "Queen of the Underworld."

"The Underworld?" said Ava, leaning over to get a better look. "Which one?"

James gave her a look that could've withered a plant. "The one where the dead go. Tartarus? The Elysian Fields?"

"Greek mythology," I said, turning the page. "See this guy?" I pointed to a dark-haired man half covered in shadow. "He's Hades, God of the Underworld. Ruler of the dead."

"Like Satan," said James.

"No, not like Satan," said Ava. There was a hint of anger in her voice, but James either didn't notice or didn't care. "Satan's Christian, and the Underworld isn't hell. Hades isn't a demon. He's just…some guy who was put in charge of dealing with the souls of the dead. He sorts them out and stuff."

I stared at her. "I thought you didn't know anything about this?"

She shrugged and looked down at the book. "Might've heard a few things before."

"He kidnapped her," said James in a voice so low it sent a shiver down my spine. "She was playing in a field, and he dragged her down to the Underworld with him to be his wife. She refused to eat, and while her mother, Demeter, appealed to Zeus—king of the gods—the world grew cold. Eventually Zeus made Hades give Persephone back, but by then she'd eaten a few seeds, and he insisted that it meant she had to spend part of the year with him. So whenever she's with him as his wife, winter comes. It's the myth that explained the seasons to the Greeks."

The temperature felt as if it'd dropped twenty degrees. A horrible thought crossed my mind, and I stared at James, trying to figure out if the implications of the deal I'd made with Henry were even remotely possible.

Ava, on the other hand, snorted. Loudly. "So he was lonely. It doesn't make him a bad guy—you don't know if she wanted to go down there with him. She might have, y'know."

I ignored her and looked at James. "Do you think Henry's going to try the same thing on me?"

"That's ridiculous," said Ava, rolling her eyes. "If he was going to kidnap you, he'd have already done it, right? It's not like he didn't have the chance when we were in the woods."

"I don't know," said James. "It's possible. Maybe he's waiting for the autumn equinox to do it. It's just a few weeks away, at the end of September." He stared at me, blue eyes so wide I wondered if they were going to fall out of his head. "What if he wants you to stay with him during the winter?"

"He can't really expect me to drop everything and move in for a while," I said uncertainly. "Or permanently."

"He might not ask," said James. "What happens then?"

Silence settled between the three of us, with only the buzz of the cafeteria around us. Finally I straightened my shoulders and said with as much conviction as I could, "Then I'll kick his ass and the police will arrest him. End of story."

But it wasn't the end, because none of us were mentioning what had happened on the bank of the river. He'd somehow brought Ava back from the dead, and I didn't know how to explain it.

James slammed the book shut, and I jumped.

"Maybe so," said James, "but it doesn't change the fact that you agreed to marry a complete stranger."

CHAPTER 5
THE EQUINOX

Over the next two weeks, I had one option: forget about the deal I'd made, write it off as ridiculous, and move on with my life. Even if I'd had any other choice, my mother's health made sure that all of my attention was focused on her.

But James and Ava wouldn't let me forget it. With each day that passed, they argued in hushed whispers across the lunch table, sometimes seeming to forget I was even there. James seemed determined to talk me out of it, pointing out how little I knew about Henry and how he had to be a few colors short of a rainbow to even think about inviting me to stay with him for half of the rest of my life. But for every flaw in the deal that James brought up, Ava countered. She defended Henry relentlessly, even though none of us knew anything about him, but it was easy enough to figure out why. Without Henry, she'd be dead; of course she felt some amount of loyalty toward him.

They dissected the myth, both borrowing heavily from it to give weight to their argument, and asked me repeatedly to tell them exactly what Henry had said, but there was only so much information I could give them. Part of me worried and counted the days with them, but most of me was too focused on my mother to care. The nightmares also continued, leaving me with only a few hours of sleep a night, but no one commented on the dark circles under my eyes. Eden was a small town, and they all knew about my mother.

A few days before the beginning of autumn, I came home to find her sitting in the middle of the weed-choked garden, and a knot of panic formed in my throat. Scrambling out of my car, I hurried to her side, kneeling next to her so I could get a good look at her face.

"Mom?" I said, my voice choked with worry. "You should be inside resting." How did she even have the energy to do this? I glared at Sofia, who sat on the porch knitting.

Sofia shrugged. "She insisted."

"I'm fine, slept all day," said Mom, waving me away, but not before I could get a good look at her. Her skin was pale and paper-thin, but there was a spark in her eyes that hadn't been there the past few weeks.

"Come on," I said, taking her elbow gently and trying to guide her upward. She stubbornly remained sitting, and I was too afraid of hurting her to put much force behind it.

"Just another few minutes," she said, looking up at me pleadingly. "I haven't spent time outside in ages. The sun feels wonderful."

I dropped back down to my knees. There was no point in arguing with her anymore. "Do you need any help?" I made a face at the tangled bed of weeds. How long had it been since anyone had tended to it?

Her expression brightened considerably at my offer. "I don't need any, but I'd like some. Just start tugging."

It was dirty work, but together we continued to weed out

the small clearing she'd already managed to create. I didn't want to think about how long she'd been out here. She didn't have the energy to waste on this sort of thing, but when my mother set her mind to something, there was no talking her out of it.

"I'll be back in a few minutes," said Sofia from the porch, and she ambled inside, closing the door behind her and leaving us alone. I watched my mother out of the corner of my eye as I yanked out a weed that was nearly half as tall as I was. At the first sign of trouble, I was taking her inside.

But she hadn't been this energized and lucid in days. I hadn't told her about what had happened at the party, not wanting to worry her, but with the autumn equinox approaching and James and Ava at odds with each other, I found I wanted to tell her—if not the whole story, then at least something. I'd never kept anything like this from her before, and I wouldn't have many more chances to talk to her about it.

"Mom?" I said hesitantly. "You know Eden Manor?"

"Of course." The crease in the middle of her forehead deepened as she tugged at a particularly stubborn weed. "What about it?"

I gripped the base of the stem below her fist and helped. After we tugged together, it came loose with a shower of dirt.

"Does someone named Henry live there?"

She straightened, not bothering to try to hide her surprise. "Why do you ask?"

"Because." I shifted uneasily on the grass, my knees already starting to ache. I knew I should have told her and that she'd want to know, but what if she tried to do something about it? What if I scared her, and it hurt her?

So I lied.

"Some kids at school were talking," I said, unable to look at her as guilt gnawed at me. I never lied to her unless I had to. "I just wondered if you knew anything about him."

Her shoulders slumped, and she reached forward to tuck a loose lock of long hair behind my ear. "If you insist on bringing up difficult subjects, can we at least talk about what's going to happen when I die?"

I was on my feet in an instant, all thoughts of Henry flying out of my head. "It's time to go inside."

Her eyes narrowed. "I'll go inside when you agree to talk to me."

"I *am* talking to you," I said. "Please, Mom. You're going to make yourself worse."

She smiled humorlessly. "I don't see how. Are you going to talk to me about it or not?"

I closed my eyes, ignoring the sting of tears. This wasn't fair. We still had to have some time left, right? She'd made it this far—surely she could make it a few more months. Christmas, I thought. Just one more Christmas together, and then I could accept saying goodbye. I'd made the same deal for the past four years, and so far, it'd worked.

"I don't want you to miss me," she said. "You should live your own life, sweetie, and not be weighed down by me anymore, especially once I'm gone."

My throat felt rough, but I didn't say anything. I didn't know how to live my own life. Even back in New York, she'd been my best friend—my only friend for the past four years. What did she expect me to do, pack up and move on?

"And I want you to fall in love and start your own family, one that'll stick around a lot longer than I did." She reached out to take my hand, squeezing it gently. "Find someone who'll be good to you and never let him go, all right?"

I felt like I was drowning. "Mom," I choked, "I don't know how to do any of that."

She smiled up at me sadly. "No one does, Kate, not at first. But you're ready for this, I promise you. I did everything I could." For a moment she trailed off and looked at our joined hands. "You *are* ready, and you will be great, sweetheart. You're going to do the impossible, I can feel it, and even if you don't think I'm there with you, I always will be. I'm never going to leave you—remember that, okay? Sometimes it might feel like I'm gone, but I'll always be there when you need me the most."

I wiped my eyes with my free hand, my grip on her tightening. Something inside of me was crumbling faster than I could glue it back together, and I didn't know what to do anymore. I couldn't imagine life without her in it, and I didn't want to, either. But it was a reality I'd be facing far sooner than I was prepared for. I wanted her, my mother—not a memory.

"Promise me you'll be yourself and do what makes you happy, no matter what," she said, taking my hand in both of hers. "You're meant for great things, sweetie, but the more you struggle against who you are, the harder it will be. Whatever obstacles you face, remember you can get through anything if you want to badly enough. And you will." She smiled, and whatever was left standing inside of me broke. "You're so much stronger than you think you are. Do you promise me you'll try to be happy?"

I wanted to tell her that I didn't know how to be happy without her, that I didn't know who I was when she wasn't there, and I wasn't strong enough to do this, but her pleading look was too much for me to take. So I lied a second time.

"Okay," I mumbled. "I promise."

Her smile only made me feel guiltier. "Thank you," she said. "It'll be easier to go when I know you'll be okay."

I helped her to her feet, not trusting myself to speak. Leaving the uprooted weeds abandoned in the middle of the lawn, I brushed the dirt off her knees and half carried her into the house, wishing with all my might that she never had to go in the first place.

The next day, as the teacher droned on about conjugating irregular French verbs, the door to the classroom opened, and Irene from the front office stepped inside. Every head, including mine, turned to stare at her, but the only person she looked at was me.

Feeling as if my insides had turned to liquid, I stood, able to sense James and Ava's stares burning into the back of my head. I stumbled across the length of the classroom, ignoring the whispers that followed.

"Kate," said Irene in a gentle voice once we were in the hallway and the door to the classroom was closed firmly behind me. "Your mother's nurse called."

The walls spun around me, and for a moment I forgot how to breathe. "Is she dead?"

"No," said Irene, and relief flooded through me. "She's in the hospital."

Without another word, I turned around and ran down the hallway, class forgotten. The only thing I wanted was to get to the hospital before it really was goodbye.

"Kate?"

It was late in the afternoon, and I sat in the waiting room of the hospital, exhausted. I'd spent the past three hours alone and flipping through a stack of magazines without reading a word, waiting for the doctors to come tell me how she was.

"James!" I stood on wobbly legs and hugged him as if my life depended on it. It lasted longer than was strictly necessary, but I needed to feel his warm arms wrapped around me. It'd been a long time since I'd hugged someone who wasn't frail. "My mother's sick and they're not telling me—"

"I know," he said. "Irene told me."

"What if this is it?" I said, burying my face in his chest. "I didn't even get to say goodbye. I didn't get to tell her I love her."

"She knows," he murmured, running his fingers through my hair. "I promise she knows."

He spent the next few hours with me, only disappearing to get us something to eat, and he was next to me when the doctor finally came and told me what I'd feared: my mother had slipped into a coma, and it wouldn't be long now.

James stayed by my side when I went in to see my mother, who looked so small and fragile lying in the middle of the hospital bed, her body connected to more machines and monitors than I could count. Her skin was ashen, and even if the doctor hadn't told me, I knew she wasn't going to last much longer. Mentally I went over everything that had happened the day before, hating myself more each time I thought about how I'd let her stay out and garden. Maybe if she hadn't exerted herself like that, she'd still be hanging on.

Now, lying there inside that dying body, there was no sign of her. This wasn't how I wanted to remember my mother, as a lifeless shell of who she'd once been, but I couldn't let go.

Shortly before ten, a nurse came in and told me that visiting hours were over. Several minutes later, when I still couldn't make myself leave, James stepped beside me.

"Kate." I felt his hand on my back, and I tensed. "The sooner you get some sleep, the sooner you can come back and see her in the morning. Come on, I'll drive you home."

"It's not home anymore," I said hollowly, but I allowed him to lead me away.

I stared out the window as he drove my car back to Eden, grateful he didn't try to start a conversation. Even if he had, I wasn't so sure I'd have been able to answer. It wasn't until we sat in my driveway, the engine of the car still running, that James spoke. In the background, a song played so softly on the radio that I had to strain to make it out. I was stalling. I didn't want to go back inside that house. I'd prepared myself for what was coming for years, but now that it was happening, I couldn't stand the thought of being alone.

"Are you sure you're okay?"

"I'm fine," I lied. James smiled sadly.

"I'll come by and pick you up tomorrow morning, first thing."

"I'm not going to school."

"I know." He didn't take his eyes off of me. "I'll take you to the hospital."

"James…you don't have to do that."

"Isn't that what friends do?" It hurt to hear the uncertainty in his voice. "You're my friend, Kate, and you're miserable. What could possibly be more important than taking care of you?"

My chin trembled, and it was only a matter of time before the waterworks started. Not knowing what else to do, I leaned over the driver's seat and wrapped my arms around him. I'd never had a friend like him, someone who would've given up their day to keep me company at my dying mother's bedside. I'd come to Eden expecting to be alone when this was over, and instead I found James. If there was ever a reason to stay in Eden, it was him.

"At least take the car," I said into his shoulder. "You shouldn't walk home in the dark like this."

He started to protest, but I pulled back and gave him a look, and he nodded. "Thanks."

By the time I managed to pry myself away from him and exit the car, I was a tearful, snotty mess, but I didn't care. Next to the sidewalk, I could see the bare patch of dirt in the garden and the pile of weeds still sitting on the lawn.

"I'll see you tomorrow," he said, his voice carrying from the driveway. I nodded, unable to speak, and waved goodbye to him, using the last of what little strength I had left to force a smile.

I stepped inside, my hands trembling, but I knew there was no point being afraid of an empty house, no matter how strongly my mother's scent lingered. I would be living alone for a very long time.

Wandering listlessly through the halls, I ran my hand across each surface I passed, staring blankly ahead into the darkness. Tonight marked the end of the only chapter in my life I'd ever known, and I didn't know how to live in the emptiness ahead.

When midnight came and the doorbell rang, I was curled up in my mother's bed, still wearing my clothes from that day. It took me two rings to decide to answer it, and even then, I took my time rolling out of bed and making my way down the

stairs. Clutching my mother's pillow to my chest, I opened the
door, expecting it to be James.

It was Henry.

My stomach dropped to my knees, and the fog that clouded
my head evaporated.

"Hello, Kate." His voice was like honey, and I was suddenly acutely aware of how awful I looked. "Do you remember
me?"

How could I possibly forget? "Yeah," I said hoarsely. "You're
Henry."

"I am." There was something sad behind his smile, something
I related to all too well. "This is my valet, Walter."

I eyed the second man, my hand still gripping the doorknob.
He was older, his hair gray and skin wrinkled, and his pale face
was drawn. "Hi," I said uncertainly.

"Hello, Miss Winters." He smiled warmly. "May we come
in?"

There was no point in worrying about whether or not they
were here to kidnap me. Ava was right; if that was Henry's plan,
I would have been in the back of a van with my hands duct
taped together by now. Besides, it didn't matter anymore. With
a nod, I opened the door wide enough for them to enter.

I nervously led them into the living room. After flipping
on the lights, I sat down in the armchair, giving them both no
choice but to sit on the couch. Henry took a seat as if he'd been
here a thousand times before, and in the light, it was easier to
see his face. He looked as young and gorgeous as before. "Do
you know what day it is?"

I wasn't even sure what month it was anymore, but there was
only one reason Henry would show up on my front porch. "It's
the—the autumn equinox, right?"

"Very good," said Henry. "Did you read up on Persephone?"
My mouth went dry, and I nodded.

"And are you prepared to uphold your end of our bargain?"

I looked back and forth between them uncertainly. Maybe they were here to kidnap me after all. "I'm not really sure what our bargain is."

Walter was the one who spoke. "In exchange for the life of your friend, you have agreed to spend the autumn and winter at Eden Manor. Every autumn and winter, if things go as planned."

I stared at him. "Excuse me?"

"As our honored guest, of course," he added. "You will be treated with the utmost care and respect, and you will have everything you could ever ask for."

"Wait." I stood too quickly, and the blood rushed to my head. I fought off the dizziness, refusing to stumble in front of them. "You mean for the rest of my *life,* I have to spend six months with you? That was our deal?"

"Yes," said Henry. He raised a hand to silence Walter, and he, too, stood. "I am aware it will not be easy, and you will face certain—challenges. But I assure you that I will do everything I can to ensure you are safe and happy. For the other six months a year, you may do whatever you wish. You may have an entirely separate life, if you would like—you will have complete freedom. And while you are with me, you will be treated like a queen. I will do everything in my power to make you happy."

He was dead serious, I realized. Latching onto one word in particular, I remembered the myth and my blood ran cold.

"Queen," I said, spitting the word out bitterly. "You mean you want me to be your *wife?*"

Henry frowned. "I am not proposing marriage to you, Kate. With your mother's death, you will soon have nothing holding you here, and I am offering you a chance at a life you cannot possibly imagine."

I bristled. How did he know about my mother? "What do you get in return? I'm not going to sleep with you if that's where you're going with this. I'm not that kind of person."

He and Walter exchanged amused glances. "I assure you that all I want is the pleasure of your company. The platonic sort."

Somehow I didn't think that was all he was getting, but there was no point in even pretending it was an option. I wasn't about to spend six months of the rest of my life with a stranger no matter what he offered me.

"No," I said. "Thank you for your offer, but you're crazy, and no. Now if you don't mind, I have to sleep."

They didn't argue. Walter stood to join Henry and me, and I led them both to the front door, holding it open so they had no excuse to linger. As Henry exited, he stopped, his body less than a foot away from mine. He really was beautiful, and with him so close, it was hard to remember exactly why spending six months with him would be such a bad thing.

"Do you understand what will happen if you do not uphold your end of our deal?"

Ah, right. Because no matter how gorgeous he was, he was still crazy. "I don't know, and I don't care," I said firmly. "Now please leave."

"I will give you until midnight," he said, joining Walter on the front path. "But I am afraid I cannot wait any longer. Don't be so quick to dismiss my offer, Kate. This is the only time I will make it."

Instead of answering, I slammed the door shut, trying to ignore how violently my hands were shaking.

James came by the next morning, and he was nice enough to bring me a bagel. I picked at it as we drove to the hospital, my appetite nonexistent. Luckily he didn't make me talk.

As I sat by my mother's bedside, holding her hand, a traitorous thought crept into my mind. If Henry had saved Ava—if it really hadn't been my imagination or some horrible prank—could he save my mother, too?

I pushed the idea away. I couldn't afford to think like that, not when I had to prepare myself for the end that was coming. Besides, what Henry had done was impossible. A fluke, or a trick of the light, or some horrible joke that Ava still hadn't confessed to—whatever it was, my mother was on death's door, and no magic trick was going to save her. She'd held on years longer than she should have, and I knew I should've been grateful for the time I'd had with her, but watching her slip away as the hours passed made it impossible.

It wasn't until that evening as we walked slowly through the hospital parking lot that I finally told James what had happened that morning. He was silent as I finished the story, his hands stuffed in the pockets of his black jacket.

"You mean they just showed up like that, no warning or anything?"

I nodded, too empty to think much about it anymore. "They weren't rude about it, I guess, but it was just—weird."

He opened the car door for me, and I lowered myself into

the passenger seat. It wasn't until he sat down in the driver's seat that he spoke. "You can't go, Kate."

"I wasn't planning on it. She'd never leave me if I were like this."

"Good," he said.

We drove through the parking lot, and in front of us, the sun was setting. I blocked my eyes as I tried to find the courage to voice what I'd wanted to say all day. "What if he can save my mother?"

He scowled. "What else would he demand from you in order to do it?"

"Whatever it was, it'd be worth it," I said quietly. "If it meant she'd be alive."

James reached across the seat to set his hand over mine. "I know it would be, but sometimes all we can do is say goodbye."

My face grew hot and my vision blurry, and I turned away from him to stare blankly out the window. "What do you think will happen when I don't show up? Do you think he'll hurt Ava? That was our deal—I did what he wanted, and he'd save her."

"He won't hurt her," said James, though out of the corner of my eye I saw his grip on the steering wheel tighten. "Not if he's any kind of human being."

I wiped my eyes with the sleeve of my sweater. "I'm not so sure he is."

When I got home, there were six messages on my machine. The first was from the school, calling to find out where I was, and the next five were all from Ava, her tone growing more and more worried with each message.

Even though I was exhausted, I called Ava back. It was good to hear her voice, despite her being as annoyingly cheerful and talkative as ever. She blabbered on enough for the both of us, and she didn't seem to mind that I barely said a word. Even though James seemed sure nothing would happen to her, I couldn't shake the worry that something might. Even though I'd only known her for a few weeks, after the incident by the river, I felt responsible for her. I couldn't do anything to help my mother, but if something happened to Ava because of me—I couldn't bear it.

"Ava?" I said as we were about to hang up.

"Yeah?" She sounded distracted.

"Do me a favor and take care of yourself tonight, okay? Don't do anything stupid like climb a ladder or pet a lion."

She laughed. "Yeah, whatever. I'll call you in the morning. Say hi to your mom for me."

After hanging up, I couldn't sleep. Instead I watched my clock tick over from 11:59 to 12:00, and a sick sense of dread filled me. What if something happened to Ava? What was I supposed to do then? It'd be my fault. Against all odds, she had become my friend, and I was supposed to protect her from that sort of stuff, not deliberately antagonize the man who apparently thought she owed him her life. Or thought I owed him mine.

I didn't want to think about Henry. I didn't want to think about how he'd brought her back that night at the river, and I didn't want to think about his offer. I tried to picture my mother's face, but the only image I could come up with was the one of her lying in the hospital bed and dying.

I rolled over and buried my face in my pillow. There wasn't anything I could do now, and feeling this helpless was gut-wrenching. But I'd already made my decision, and I was going to stick to it. If I had it my way, I would never see Henry again.

Half past seven I awoke to loud banging on the door. I groaned, having only fallen asleep shortly after four, but I couldn't ignore it. Throwing open the door, the string of curses on the tip of my tongue disappeared. It was James, looking like he hadn't slept since the day before. I opened the door, running my fingers through my mess of mousy brown hair.

"James? What's going on?"

"It's Ava."

I froze.

"She's dead."

CHAPTER 6

EDEN MANOR

The rumor around town was that she'd had a brain aneurysm, but I knew better. As James drove past the school on our way to the hospital, I saw the entire student body huddled together in the parking lot, hugging each other and sobbing. I couldn't look away. "Turn around."

"What?"

"I said turn around, James. Please."

"And go where?"

I stared out the window, unable to tear my eyes from their faces. Even the kids who'd hated Ava were crying. I breathed in shallowly, struggling not to do the same.

It was my fault. Ava was seventeen years old. She'd had her whole life ahead of her, and now she was dead because of me. If he was going to take somebody, why hadn't he taken me? I was the one who'd stupidly brushed his warning aside, not her.

I squeezed my eyes shut once we passed the school, the image of the crowd mourning together burned into the back of my eyelids. Was this how it was going to be my whole life?

Everyone I knew dying? Would James be next, or would it mercifully be me?

Anger swelled up inside of me, engulfing my guilt until I was clutching the armrest so tightly that my nails created permanent half-moon indents in the worn leather. Ava didn't deserve this, and no matter how much Henry had disliked her for the prank she'd pulled, that didn't give him any right to do this to her, to her family, or to this town. And for what? Because I didn't believe him? Because I didn't want to waste half of the rest of my life catering to the desires of a lunatic? Is that what he did when he didn't get his way—throw a tantrum and kill someone?

I ignored the little voice in the back of my mind that reminded me Henry was the only reason she'd survived that night by the river in the first place.

I couldn't do anything to help my mother, but I could help Ava. And I would fix this.

"Kate," said James softly, reaching across the seat to set his hand over mine. "It's not your fault."

"The hell it isn't," I snapped, yanking my hand away. "She wouldn't be dead right now if it wasn't for me."

"She would've died weeks ago if it hadn't been for you."

"No, she wouldn't have," I said. "She'd have never tried to pull that stupid prank if I hadn't agreed to go with her. She wouldn't have hit her head if I hadn't moved to Eden. None of this would've happened if I hadn't come here."

"So because you moved here, it's all your fault." His grip on the wheel tightened in irritation. "Ava was the one who dove headfirst into that river. You were the one who agreed to give up half of the rest of your life to keep her alive. You gave her more time, Kate, don't you get that?"

"What good are a few more weeks?" I spat, wiping my cheeks angrily. "It's pointless. None of this should've ever happened."

"Kate..." James started, but I turned away again. We were past the school now.

"Just drive, James. Please."

"Where are we going?"

"If he brought her back to life once, he can do it again."

James sighed and said in a voice so soft I wasn't positive I'd heard him right, "I'm not sure it works that way."

I swallowed thickly. "If you ever want to see Ava again, you'd better hope it does."

We arrived at the gate ten minutes later. By that time I was shaking, caught between despair and fury. How dare Henry do this? He had to have known that I hadn't understood or believed in the sorts of things he was talking about, and he'd done it anyway.

He had to bring her back. No matter what it took, I would make him do that much.

Instead of the gates being locked, as they had been when my mother and I had driven past, they were cracked open wide enough for me to slip through on foot. I glanced at James, not knowing what to say.

"You shouldn't do this," he said. "There's no guarantee he can bring Ava back, and once you go in there, you might not come back out."

"I don't care. I'll make him fix her."

"Kate, you know that's impossible."

I gritted my teeth. "I have to try. I can't let her die, James. I can't."

"She isn't your mother," said James gently. "No matter how hard you fight for Ava's life, it won't change what's already happened. It won't save her, and it won't save your mother, either."

"I know that," I choked, though a small part of me wondered if I really did. But I'd already seen Henry perform the impossible once. He could do it again, I was sure of it—and maybe if I did what he wanted, he could save more than Ava this time. "This is my choice, and if there's even a chance this can be changed, I'm going to figure out how. Please," I said, my voice faltering. "Please let me do this."

James was quiet for a moment, but at last he nodded, no longer looking at me. "Do whatever you have to do."

My hands shook as I tried to unfasten my seat belt. James reached over and did it for me. "But what if he's serious?" he said. "What if he wants you to stay for six months?"

"Then I'll do it," I said, staring up at the giant gates as a sense of foreboding filled me. I would stay all year if it meant he would save her. Save them. "Six months isn't the end of the world. I'll do what I have to do."

He nodded once, a distant look in his eyes. "I'll be here waiting then. But Kate…" He hesitated. "Do you really think he's what he says he is?"

My heart pounded. "I don't think he's said what he is."

James sighed. I was hurting him by doing this, but I had no choice. "What do you think he is?"

I frowned, remembering Ava's words. "A very lonely guy." Chances were if Henry was going to kill me, he'd have already done it. I knew a way out if he really did try to keep me hostage, but if he was going to force me into it, he'd have done that the day before. He really had given me a choice, and so far all

I'd done was make the wrong one. I could either accept Ava's death or do something about it—and frankly, I'd had enough of people dying. I wasn't going to let it happen again.

Remembering all of the promises I'd made to my mother, I sucked in a deep breath, wishing I could talk to her. She'd know what to do. "You'll take care of my mom, won't you?"

He apparently knew better than to insist she'd still be there when I returned, whenever that might've been. "I promise. I'll let school know you won't be coming back, too."

"Thanks," I said. One less thing to worry about.

The steps from the car to the gate were the hardest ones I'd ever taken, but if it meant bringing Ava back, I would surrender my freedom to Henry. He'd been right; I had nothing else in my life except my mother. Once she was gone, I would be empty. But now I had a chance to trade what was left of my shell of a life for someone who would make the most of it. Ava's life had barely begun. All the best parts of mine were already behind me. My mother wanted me to go out and find happiness, but I couldn't, not without her. At least this way what was left of me wouldn't go to waste.

I walked through the gate and on to the grounds, and immediately the atmosphere changed. It was warmer here, and there was a sort of electricity in the air that I couldn't identify. As I took another few steps, I heard the gate clang shut behind me, and I jumped. Turning around, I saw James standing next to the car, his eyes on me. I waved, and he flashed a pained smile.

The road was lined with trees that were evenly spaced, and it sloped upward. It took me a few minutes to walk over the hill, but when I did, I stopped, my mouth agape. Whatever I'd expected, it wasn't this.

A huge manor sat sprawled across the grounds, so large that I couldn't see what lay behind it even from the top of the hill. The road I was on became paved, and it circled around to the front of the manor, forming a perfect oval.

I'd only seen buildings like these in pictures of European palaces, and I was sure that nowhere else in the Upper Peninsula—maybe even the entire state—did a place like this exist. It gleamed white and gold, and everything about it looked majestic.

As I stood there, it took me a moment to notice that I wasn't alone. A dozen gardeners and workers stared at me, and I suddenly grew self-conscious. I was inside the gate; now what?

In the distance I saw a woman bustling toward me, holding up the hem of her skirt as she climbed the hill. Rather than taking a step back, I stood my ground, caught between awe, fear and determination. No matter how beautiful his home was, I still needed to see Henry—and soon.

"Welcome, Kate!" said the woman, and upon hearing her voice, I did a double take.

"Sofia?"

Sure enough, as she drew closer, I recognized her as the day nurse who'd helped me take care of my mother for the past few weeks. I stared at her, shocked, but Sofia acted as if none of this was a big deal. When she reached me, her cheeks were pink and she smiled ear to ear. She took my arm. "We were wondering if you'd ever show, dear. How's your mother?"

It took me a second to find my voice. "Dying," I said. "What are you doing here?"

"I live here." She started to lead me toward the house, and I let her, trying hard not to stare.

"You know Henry?"

"Of course I do," she said. "Everyone knows Henry."

"Can you raise the dead, too?" I muttered, and Sofia clucked her tongue.

"Can you?"

I clenched my fists. "I need to see him."

"I know, dear. That's where we're headed."

I glanced at her, uncertain if she was being patronizing or evasive or both. She ignored my look and led me down the oval drive until we reached the large French double doors, which opened without any prompting from Sofia. Instead of following her inside, I stopped and stared.

The outside was nothing compared to the magnificent entrance hall. It was simple and tasteful, not at all gaudy, but it was far from ordinary.

The floor was mostly white marble, and I could see a hint of plush carpet on the other end of the hall. The walls and ceiling were made of mirrors, and they made the massive hall look larger than it already was.

But it was the floor in the center of the room that caught my attention. There was a perfect circle made of crystal, and it was by far the most incredible thing about the hall. It shimmered, colors seeming to swim together, blending and dividing as I stared. My mouth hung open, but I didn't care—everything about it was surreal, and I could hardly believe that I was still standing in Michigan.

"Kate?"

I tore myself away and finally paid attention to Sofia. She stood a few feet ahead of me and gave me a hesitant smile.

"Sorry," I said. I walked toward her, stepping around the crystal circle as if it were really water. For all I knew, it was. "It's just—"

"Beautiful," she said cheerfully, taking my arm once more and steering me past a grand spiraling staircase that led up to a part of the manor I couldn't see. I didn't dare try to look, not wanting to waste another minute.

"Yeah." It was the best I could come up with, but I was otherwise speechless. Whatever I'd been expecting, it hadn't been this.

She led me through a series of rooms, each uniquely decorated and exquisite. One room was red and gold; another was sky-blue, with murals painted on the walls. There were sitting rooms, game rooms, studies and even two libraries. It seemed impossible that these were all in the same house—and apparently only belonged to one boy who wasn't much older than me, unless his parents lived here, too—but it never seemed to end.

Finally we turned down another hall and entered a room that had dark green walls and gold trim. The furniture seemed more worn and comfortable here than in the other rooms, and Sofia directed me toward a black leather couch.

"Sit, dear, and I'll have someone bring you refreshments. Henry should be with you shortly."

I sat, not wanting her to leave me alone, but I could do this. I had to. Ava's life was at stake, and this was the only chance I'd have to make this argument. If Henry wanted to keep me here, then fine. As long as he brought Ava back, I would do anything he wanted me to do, even if it meant spending the rest of my life behind the hedges. I pushed away what James had said in the car about Ava not being my mother. That wasn't why I was here.

But even as I thought it, I knew I was lying to myself. Wasn't the mere possibility of Henry being able to save my mother—or somehow save me from the pain of losing her—exactly why I was here? I would do everything I could to save Ava, but she'd been dead for hours, and the entire town knew. Henry would undoubtedly want a steeper price for bringing her back a second time, and no matter what brave face I put on, the thought of staying behind these hedges for the rest of my life terrified me. I'd meant what I'd said about doing everything I could to try to bring her back, but even if that was impossible like James had said, my mother wasn't dead yet. There was still a chance Henry could do something to save her.

I don't know how long I sat there in silence, staring blankly at a bookcase full of leather-bound books. I went over my speech in my head, making sure everything I wanted to say was there. He had to listen to me, didn't he? Even if he didn't want to do it, if I talked long enough, he had to at least hear me. I had to try.

Out of the corner of my eye, I noticed Henry standing in the doorway, holding a tray laden with food. My fingers dug into the sofa, and all of the words I'd practiced flew out of my head.

"Kate," he said in a low, pleasant voice. Stepping inside, he set the tray on the coffee table in front of me and sat on the sofa across from me.

"H-Henry," I said, hating myself for stuttering. "We need to talk."

He inclined his head, as if silently giving me permission to speak. I opened and shut my mouth, not knowing what to say. While he waited, he poured us both a cup of tea. I'd never had tea in a china cup before.

"I'm sorry," I said. My throat was dry. "For not listening to you yesterday, I mean. I wasn't thinking, and I didn't think you were serious. My mom's really sick, and I just—please. I'm here. I'll stay. I'll do whatever you want. Just bring Ava back."

He sipped his tea and motioned for me to take mine. I did so with shaking hands.

"She's seventeen," I said, my voice growing more desperate by the word. "She shouldn't have to miss out on her whole life just because of my stupid mistake."

"It wasn't your mistake." He set his cup down and focused on me. His eyes were still the same bizarre shade of moonlight, and I squirmed under the intensity of his stare. "Your friend made her choice when she decided to jump into the river and abandon you. I do not hold you accountable for your friend's death. You shouldn't either."

"You don't understand. I didn't know that you were serious. I didn't get it. I didn't know she'd really die—I thought you were kidding, or…I don't know. Not kidding, but something. I didn't know you could do that, and now that I do—please. She doesn't deserve to die for making a few mistakes."

"And you do not deserve to give up half of the rest of your life for her."

I sighed, so frustrated that I was close to tears. What did he want from me? "You're right, I don't want to stay here. This place terrifies me. *You* terrify me. I don't know what you are or what this place is, and the last thing I want to do is spend the rest of my life here. Maybe Ava wasn't the greatest to me at first, but she's my friend now. She didn't deserve to die, and her death—it's my fault. It should have been me, not her, and I can't live with that. I can't look at myself in the mirror every day knowing it's my fault that her family has to go through the pain of losing her just like—" I stopped. Just like I was going through the pain of losing my mother. "I can't. So if it means

Ava comes back, then I'll stay here for as long as you want, I promise. Please."

It wasn't exactly the speech I'd planned, but it was close enough. By the time I was through, there were tears in my eyes, and I gripped the teacup so tightly that it was a minor miracle it didn't break.

In front of me Henry was silent, staring into his own cup of tea. I didn't have the faintest idea what he was thinking, and I wasn't sure I wanted to know. All that mattered was that he agreed.

"You would willingly give up six months a year for the rest of your life in order to save your friend, even after what she did to you?" There was a note of incredulity in his tone.

"What she did doesn't deserve a death sentence," I said. "There are a lot of people out there who loved her, and they shouldn't have to hurt like that because of me." And maybe knowing I'd saved her would help me hurt a little less, too.

He drummed his fingers against the armrest of the sofa, his eyes on me once again. "Kate, I do not invite just anyone into my home. Do you understand why I offered this to you?"

Because he was crazy? I shook my head.

"Because even though she had abandoned you, instead of feeling spiteful or allowing her to die, you did everything within your power—including face one of your greatest fears—to save her."

I didn't know what to say to that. "Wouldn't anyone?"

"No." His smile was weary. "Very few would even consider it. You are rare, and you intrigue me. When you declined my offer yesterday, I thought perhaps I was wrong, but by coming here today, you have only proved yourself even more worthy and capable than I could have imagined."

I blinked, alarmed. "Worthy and capable of what?"

He ignored my question. "I will make my offer only once more. In return, I cannot give you your friend's life back. She is gone, and I am afraid that if I returned her to her body now, she would be something unnatural, and she would never find happiness. But I promise you that as she is now, she is content."

My chest felt hollow. "So it's all for nothing then?"

"No." He tilted his head, his eyes narrowing slightly. "I cannot undo what has already been done, but I can *prevent*."

"Prevent what?"

He stared at me, and with a rush of hope, I understood. I thought I would be the one to bring it up, but he'd done it for me.

He could stop my mother from dying.

"You—you can really do that?"

He hesitated. "Yes, I can. I cannot heal your mother, but I can keep her alive until you are ready to say goodbye. I can give you the chance to spend more time with her, and when you are ready, I will make sure it is peaceful."

His words settled over me, enveloping me in a strange warmth. "How?" I whispered.

He shook his head. "Don't worry yourself about that. If you agree, you have my word that I will uphold my end of our deal."

I'd always thought I'd get to say goodbye to my mother. None of the scenarios I'd played out in my head involved her falling into a coma and slipping away without me getting to tell her I loved her one last time, and now...

"Okay," I said softly. "You—you keep her alive. She has a really aggressive kind of cancer, so it might—it might be difficult." Suddenly it was hard to see with the way my eyes were swimming in tears. "But she won't be in any pain, right? I just—I want to be able to say goodbye."

"She won't be in any pain, I will make sure of it." He smiled sadly. "Is there anything else you would like? You are giving up much more than I am, and I want you to be certain."

I swallowed. "You can't keep her alive? You can't—you can't heal her?"

"I am sorry," he said. "But goodbyes aren't forever. The love you have for your mother isn't the sort that death can breach."

I ducked my head and stared into my tea, not wanting him to see me fall apart. "I don't know who I am without her."

"Then you will have a chance to find out before she goes." Henry set down his cup. "And when you say your goodbyes, she will have peace of mind knowing you will be all right."

I nodded, my throat too tight for me to speak. For her then, too. She wanted me to be all right, and that wasn't something I could promise her yet. But the chance to have one more conversation, to tell her I loved her one last time, and the glimmer of hope that I would be able to look her in the eye and promise her I would be okay so she could let go without worry or guilt—it was worth it.

"Then it is done," said Henry gently. "You will be my guest for the winter. Sofia will escort you to your room, and nothing will be asked of you until tomorrow."

Again I nodded. This was it then—I was trapped. This would be my home for the next six months. Suddenly the room seemed much smaller than it had before. "Henry?" I said with a squeak.

"Yes?"

"Did Sofia know this was going to happen?"

Henry eyed me for several seconds, as if trying to decide whether or not I would believe him. "We've been watching you, yes."

I didn't dare ask who *we* were. "What is this place?"

He looked amused. "Have you not figured it out already?"

I felt my cheeks color. At least there was some blood left in my head, which meant I had a chance at standing without passing out. "I've been a little busy thinking about other stuff."

Getting to his feet, Henry offered me his hand. I didn't take it, but it didn't seem to bother him. "It goes by many names. Elysium, Annwn, Paradise—some even call it the Garden of Eden."

He smiled as if he'd told a clever little joke. I didn't get it, and my confusion must have shown, because he continued without me asking.

"This is the gate between the living and the dead," he said. "You are still living. The others on the grounds died a very long time ago."

A chill ran through me. "And you?"

"Me?" The corner of his mouth twitched. "I rule the dead. I am not one of them."

CHAPTER 7

THE IMPOSSIBLE

My rooms were surprisingly comfortable. Unlike the rest of the house, they didn't seem to be too preoccupied with making sure everyone walking through them knew they were part of a very rich and powerful household. Instead my suite was relatively modest, the only real luxury being the bed, which was huge and canopied and exactly the sort I'd always dreamed of having. Part of me wondered if Henry had known that, too.

Everyone seemed to know I was there, as if I were someone famous. I heard whispers and giggles every now and then from the other side of my door, and whenever I looked out the huge bay window, I could see some of the grounds workers staring up at me, like they knew I was watching them. I didn't like being a topic of gossip, but there wasn't a whole lot I could do about it except close the curtains and bury my head in a pile of pillows.

The day passed quickly, and it wasn't long before Sofia brought me dinner. I was still annoyed that she hadn't warned me she was part of this earlier, so I muttered my thanks without looking at her and refused to answer any of her questions. How I was doing wasn't exactly a secret anyway.

After she left, I picked at the food, too worried about what was going to happen in the morning to eat. While I wasn't confined to my room, there wasn't much else for me to do, at least not now, not when I knew how easy it would be for me to get lost.

But no matter how nice the room was or how kind the staff was or how good the food tasted, the fact remained that I was essentially a prisoner. I thought of James and wondered how long he'd waited at the gate and whether or not he'd gone to see my mother afterward. Six months seemed to stretch on forever in front of me, the end nowhere in sight—would he keep his promise? Would he be there when this was over, or would he have moved on? Deep inside, I knew he would be there. I didn't deserve a friend like him.

But would my mother still be there at the end, too? Would Henry keep his promise? Was he even capable of it? I wanted to believe him, to believe that that sort of thing was possible— because if he really could keep her alive, then maybe I'd never have to say goodbye, not until it was my time to die, too. Or maybe he'd be able to keep her alive long enough for them to find a cure.

I couldn't save Ava, but there was still hope for my mother, and no matter what it cost me, it would be worth it.

I didn't remember falling asleep, but when I opened my eyes, I wasn't in Eden Manor anymore. Instead I was lying on a blanket in the middle of Central Park and staring up at a cloudless summer sky, the heat of the sun on my face.

I sat up, confused, and looked around. There was a picnic basket next to me, and other people were scattered around the grass enjoying themselves. Sheep Meadow. It was my favorite spot in the entire park, within view of the lake, but far enough away from the worst of the tourist traps that it didn't feel gimmicky. My mother and I hadn't been able to come here in years. I started to stand, determined to figure out what was going on, when my mouth dropped open.

My mother, looking as healthy as she had ten years ago, long before the cancer set in, walked up the gentle slope, wearing a long flowing skirt and peasant blouse I hadn't seen her in since she grew too thin to wear it.

"Mom?"

She smiled—a real smile, not a sickly smile or the smile she put on when she was trying to hide how much pain she was in. "Hello, sweetheart." She sat next to me and kissed my cheek.

I was still for a moment, too stunned to move, but when it finally sank in that she was here, healthy and glowing and my mother again, I threw my arms around her, hugging her tightly and inhaling her familiar scent. Apples and freesia. She was no longer frail, and she wrapped her arms around me with equal strength.

"What's going on?" I said, struggling to keep my eyes dry.

"We're having a picnic." She released me and began to unpack the basket. It was full of my favorite foods from when I'd been a child—peanut butter-and-jelly sandwiches, sliced tangerines, macaroni and cheese packed in plastic containers, and enough chocolate pudding to serve a small army. Best of all, she pulled out a box of baklava, just the way she always made it. I watched in amazement, wondering what I'd done to deserve such an amazing dream, even though it felt too real to be one. I could sense each blade of grass underneath my hands, and the warm breeze brushed the ends of my hair against my bare arms. It was like we were actually here.

And then a thought wormed its way through my mind, and I looked at her suspiciously. "Did Henry bring you here?"

Her smile widened. "He's lovely, isn't he?"

I gulped a lungful of air, and all the bad thoughts I'd ever had about Henry flew out of my head. He kept his promise. More than that, he could really do it. "Is this a dream then? Or is it—is it real?"

She gave me a container of macaroni, along with a look that only my mother could pull off. "Is there some rule I don't know about that means it can't be both?"

A sense of irrational hope filled me. "Is he really what he says he is?"

"And what would that be?" she said, unwrapping a sandwich.

I blurted out everything that had happened since we arrived in Eden. Seeing Henry after nearly crashing into an imaginary cow—the night by the river and how he'd seemingly resurrected Ava—the deal I'd made, and the way James had tried to stop me from taking it—the visit from Henry, and Ava dying the next day—my decision to go to Eden Manor to try to save her, and finally the deal I'd made with Henry that had gotten me this. Suddenly staying with him for six months didn't seem nearly as bad, not if I got to see my mother every night.

"Curious," she said, though her eyes were sparkling with amusement. I didn't see anything funny about the situation. "I wish you'd told me all of this earlier, Kate."

"I'm sorry," I said, my cheeks flushing as I stared down at my hands. "I thought I was going crazy or something."

"Hardly." She reached out and cupped my chin, guiding it

upward until I was looking at her. "Promise me you'll tell me everything that happens from now on, will you? I don't want to miss anything."

I nodded. More time with her—it was all I could possibly ask for. "Mom?" I said in a small voice. "I love you."

She smiled. "I know, sweetheart."

When I woke up early the next morning, at first I didn't know where I was. The heat of the sun from my dream still lingered on my skin, and I opened my eyes, half expecting to see my mother standing over me, but it was only the canopy of my bed.

Groaning, I sat up and blinked the sleep out of my eyes. Something wasn't right, and I couldn't put my finger on it. Then, after a long moment, the day before came flooding back to me, along with the deal I'd made with Henry, and my heart skipped a beat. So it hadn't been just a dream after all.

"D'you think she's awake now? She ought to be, yeah?"

"If she wasn't, she certainly is now."

I froze. The whispers were coming from the other side of the curtains hanging from my bed, and they weren't voices I recognized. The first was bright and bubbly; the second made it sound like whoever it belonged to wanted to be anywhere but here. I couldn't blame her.

"What d'you think she's like? Better than the last one, yeah?"

"Anyone's better than the last one. Now shut up before you really do wake her up."

I sat there for a long moment, trying to absorb what I was hearing. I'd locked the door the night before, I was sure of it, so how had they gotten in there? And what did they mean by "the last one"?

Before I could speak, my stomach growled. Loudly. The sort of epic loud that makes everyone in class turn around and giggle while you duck in your seat and try not to turn red. Whatever chance I had at eavesdropping was gone, thanks to my traitorous belly.

"She's awake!" The curtains snapped open, and I shielded my eyes from the morning light. "Oh! She's pretty!"

"And brunette. Haven't had one of those in decades."

"Thanks, I guess," I mumbled, but with the sun shining in my eyes, I couldn't see who I was talking to. "Who're you?"

"Calliope!" This was the one who spoke in exclamation points, the one who'd called me pretty. I pried my eyelids open just enough to get a decent look at her. Smaller than me, with blond hair that hung past her waist and a round face that flushed pink with happiness. She looked so excited that I was afraid she'd topple over.

"Ella," said the second girl dully. Still squinting, I got a good look at her and felt a stab of jealousy. Dark hair, tall, impossibly beautiful, and she looked bored to tears.

"And you're Katherine," said Calliope. "Sofia told us all about you, how you came here to help your friend and how you're staying with us for six months and—"

"Calliope, stop it, you're scaring her."

I didn't know if scaring was technically the right word, but it worked for now. As Calliope bounced up and down, getting closer to me with each move she made, I started to lean back. Her exuberance was intimidating.

"Oh." Calliope took a step back, blushing again. "Sorry. Are you hungry?"

Deep breath, I thought. In and out, in and out, and maybe things would start to make sense.

"She needs to get dressed first," said Ella, moving toward an armoire. "Katherine, what's your favorite color?"

"*Kate*. Call me Kate," I said through gritted teeth. It was too early in the morning for this. "And I don't have one."

"You don't have a favorite color?" said Calliope disbelievingly as she moved to help Ella. I stood and stretched, unable to see what exactly they were doing. Both of them stood in front of the armoire, which looked as if it were chock-full of clothing.

"Not today," I said, irritated. "I can dress myself, you know."

Ella and Calliope wrestled something long and blue and soft from the crush of clothing. They both turned toward me, holding—

Oh, no.

"Unless you've some sort of inhuman ability to lace yourself up into a corset, dressing yourself isn't an option," said Ella, her eyes glinting. I didn't know if it was out of amusement or malevolence. Quite possibly both.

They held up a blue dress that was so low-cut, not even Ava would've touched it. The sleeves were long and narrow, fanning out just toward the end, and there was lace. *Lace*.

My eyes widened. "You can't be serious."

"You don't like it?" Calliope frowned and ran a hand over the soft fabric. "What about something yellow? You'd look nice in yellow."

"I don't wear dresses," I said through a clenched jaw. "Ever."

Ella snorted. "I don't care, because you do now. I'm in charge of wardrobe, and unless you want to wear what you have on now until you stink so badly that no one comes near you, you're wearing this."

I stared at the blue monstrosity. "I'm not your doll. You can't make me play dress-up."

"Yes, I can," said Ella. "And I will. I've got thousands of years of fashion to choose from, and I can make your life a nightmare if you try to fight it. Ever try to sit down in a hoop skirt?" She gave me a pointed look. "Behave, and I might consider giving you a day off every once in a while. But this is my choice, not yours. You gave yours up the moment you agreed to stay here."

"Besides, everyone wears dresses here," said Calliope brightly. "You can't say you don't like it until you give it a chance."

Ella offered me the dress. "Your choice. Expensive, comfortable dresses you won't notice in a day or two, or jeans that'll stand up on their own in a week."

Letting out a low growl in the back of my throat, I snatched it from her and stormed into the bathroom. She could make me wear it, but that didn't mean I had to like it.

Lacing me up took nearly twenty minutes, and that was without a corset. That's where I drew the line, and Ella wasn't stupid enough to try to force me into that, too. The dress fit me well without me suffocating myself, and that was good enough. I didn't need to have my chest forced up to my chin in the meantime.

Once they'd finished dressing me, Calliope sat me down and fussed with my mousy hair for a few minutes. She hummed as she worked, and any questions I tried to ask were either ignored or cut off by random bursts of song. Just as I started to wonder if it would ever end, she announced that I was done and breakfast was ready.

Breakfast. I was so ravenous that I didn't even object as they forced my feet into a pair of heeled shoes. We would talk about those later, especially if I was expected to do stairs, but for now, as long as there was a promise of food, I'd put up with it.

Still feeling lost, I followed them out of the room, wishing I understood more about what was going on. Was this how every morning was going to go, or would I eventually be allowed to dress myself? Were they supposed to be my friends, like Calliope seemed to want to be, or were they supposed to keep an eye on me to make sure I didn't escape?

They weren't my most pressing questions, but those answers, I suspected, were ones only Henry could give me. In the meantime, there was still one response Calliope and Ella owed me.

"Calliope?" I said as she and Ella led me through the maze of rooms and corridors. Supposedly there was a breakfast room in the massive manor, but I wasn't so sure I believed them. It felt like we'd been wandering for hours. "What did you mean when you asked if I were better than the last one?"

She gave me a blank look. "The last one?"

"When you guys thought I was sleeping—you mentioned me being better than the last one. What last one?"

Calliope thought for a moment before realization dawned on her. "Oh! The last one. The last girl, I mean. The last one Henry had here."

There was another girl? "How long ago was that?"

Calliope exchanged a look with Ella, who remained silent. "Twenty years, maybe?"

So apparently Henry had been a toddler last time. Unless he was telling the truth about ruling the dead, but I wasn't quite ready to accept that. "Why do I need to be here then? Why isn't she here anymore?"

"Because she d—"

Ella slapped her hand over Calliope's mouth so hard that the sound reverberated through the room. "Because she isn't," said Ella sharply. "It isn't our job to explain this to you, Katherine. If you want to know why you're here, ask Henry. And you…" She glared at Calliope.

"Oh," I said softly as another thought occurred to me. "He—he said everyone here was dead. Is that true? Are you two…?"

Neither Ella nor Calliope seemed surprised by my question. Instead Ella pulled her hand away, letting Calliope answer.

"Everyone's dead here, yes," she said, rubbing her cheek and giving Ella a dirty look. "Or like Henry, never alive in the first place."

"When were you…uh, born?"

Calliope sniffed. "A lady doesn't reveal her age."

Ella snorted, and Calliope glared at her.

"Ella is so old, she doesn't even know what year she was born," said Calliope, as if that was something to be ashamed of. I shook my head, speechless, not knowing if I was really supposed to believe all of this or not.

Ella said nothing. Instead she pushed open another door, finally revealing a long room with a table so large it could've easily seated thirty. My head was spinning from Calliope's story, and it took me a moment to realize the room was already filled with people.

"Your court," said Ella drily. "Servants, tutors, anyone you'll ever have contact with. They all wanted to meet you."

I stopped dead in the doorway, feeling the blood drain from

my face. There were dozens of pairs of eyes staring at me, and suddenly I was painfully self-conscious.

"Are they going to stay here while I eat?" I whispered. I couldn't think of a better way of making sure I didn't eat a thing.

"I can send them away, if you'd like," said Calliope, and I nodded. She skipped forward and, with two claps of her hands, most of them began to file out. A few who handled the food remained, along with two men standing off to the side, each accessorized with formidable weapons. The tall blond was so still he might as well have been a statue, and the brunette fidgeted, as if standing still and being silent was something he wasn't very good at. He couldn't have been older than twenty.

"You will always be guarded," said Ella, and I looked at her, startled. She must have seen me staring. She moved forward with the grace of a deer and gestured to a place at the foot of the table. "Your seat."

I followed her, trying hard not to trip on the hem of my long dress, and sat down. Now there were only about a dozen people in the room, but they were still all looking at me.

"Your breakfast, Your Highness," said a man, stepping forward to set a covered plate in front of me. Ella lifted the cover, not giving me the chance to do so myself. She looked as bored as she had in my room.

"Um, thanks," I said, bewildered. *Your Highness?* I picked up a fork, prepared to spear a piece of fruit and eat it, but a pale hand snatched my wrist before I could do it.

I looked up, surprised to see Calliope standing over me, her blue eyes wide. "I taste first," she insisted. "It's what I'm supposed to do."

Shocked, I blurted, "You test my *food?*"

"When you decide to eat, yes," she said timidly. "I tested your dinner last night, too. But you don't have to eat while you're here, you know. Eventually you'll forget what it feels like. If you want to though, I have to—"

"No," I said, pushing my chair back so loudly it squealed against the marble floor. The stress of the day before and the confusion of that morning came crashing down on me, shattering every last bit of self-control I had. "No, this isn't going to happen. It's ridiculous—food tasters? Armed guards? Your *Highness?* Why? What am I supposed to be doing here?"

Everyone seemed stunned by my outburst, and it was several moments before anyone spoke. When they did, it was Ella. "You agreed to stay here for six months out of the year, yes?"

"Yes," I said, frustrated. They didn't understand. "But I didn't agree to food tasters or—or any of this."

"You did," she said calmly. "It's part of the deal."

"Why?"

No one answered me. I clenched my skirt so tightly that I thought it would rip. "Let me see Henry," I said. "I want to talk to him."

The silence was deafening, and something inside of me snapped.

"Let me talk to him!"

"I'm here."

The sound of his voice, low and smooth, startled me. Whirling around, I managed to lose my balance, barely catching myself on the chair. Henry stood in front of me, much closer than I'd expected. His young and flawless face was blank, and my heart skipped a beat. When I managed to regain my voice, it came out as more of a squeak, but I didn't care. I wanted answers.

"Why?" I said. "Why am I here? I'm not your princess, and I didn't sign up for any of this, so why is it happening?"

Henry offered me his hand, and I hesitated, but finally took it. His skin felt surprisingly warm against mine. I don't know what I'd been expecting—ice, maybe. Not heat. Not any evidence of life.

"Close your eyes," he murmured, and I did. A moment later, I felt a cool breeze against my cheek, and my eyes flew open. We were outside, in the middle of an elaborate and well-tended garden, with quiet fountains scattered throughout the flowers and hedges. A stone path led up from where we stood to the back of the manor, which loomed in the distance, an easy half a mile away. Cerberus, the large dog from the forest, trotted up to greet Henry, and he gave him a good scratch behind the ears.

My stomach dropped to my knees, and any color that was left drained from my cheeks. "How did you—"

"In time," he said. Numbly I sat down on the edge of the fountain. "You said yesterday that you did not want to do this, and I do not blame you. Now that the deal has been made, however, it cannot be undone. You showed courage the night you saved your friend's life, and I ask that you find it within yourself once more."

I took a deep breath, trying to find an ounce of that so-called courage he was convinced I had. All I could find was fear. "Back in Eden, you said—you said if I read the myth of Persephone, I'd understand what you wanted," I said in a shaking voice. "My friend James told me she was the Queen of the Underworld, and I read it in a book when I was—" I shook my head. It wasn't important. "Is that true?"

He nodded. "She was my wife."

"Was? She existed?"

"Yes," he said, his voice softer. "She died many years ago."

"How?"

Henry's expression was blank. "She fell in love with a mortal, and after he died, she chose to join him. I did not stop her."

There were so many parts of that statement that I didn't understand that I wasn't sure where to begin. "But she's a myth. It isn't possible she really existed."

"Maybe," he said, his gaze distant. "But if it is happening, who's to say what's possible and what isn't?"

"Logic," I said. "The laws of nature. Rationality. Some things just aren't possible."

"Then tell me, Kate—how did we get outside?"

I looked around again, half expecting it to fade away like some elaborate illusion. "You knocked me out and brought me out here?" I offered weakly.

"Or perhaps there was a trap door that you did not see." He reached out to take my hand, and I stiffened. Sighing, he brushed his fingers against mine and then pulled away. "There is always a rational explanation, but sometimes things may seem irrational or impossible if you don't know all the rules."

"So what?" I said. "You're telling me that a Greek god just happened to build a manor in the middle of the woods in a country halfway across the world?"

"When you have eons to live, the world becomes a much smaller place," he said. "I have homes in many countries, including Greece, but I favor the solitude here. It is peaceful, and I enjoy the seasons and the long winter."

I sat very still, not knowing what to say to that.

"Could you try to believe me?" said Henry. "Just for now. Even if it means pushing aside everything you've learned, would you please do me the favor of trying to accept what I am telling you, no matter how improbable it might seem?"

Pressing my lips together, I looked down at my hands. "Is that what you do? Play make-believe?"

"No." I could hear the smile in his voice. "But you may, if you'd like. If it will make it easier on you."

This wasn't going to go away. Even if it was all one big trick, if everything was planned out from the beginning to make me look like a fool or whatever his endgame was, then all I could do was wait for the punch line.

But the image of Ava lying in a pool of her own blood with her skull bashed in floated into my mind, as did the feeling of the cool breeze across my cheek when only moments before, we'd been in the heart of the manor. And my mother, alive and well in Central Park—whatever was going on, sooner or later I'd have to face the fact that it wasn't anything I'd ever experienced before.

"All right," I said. "Let's pretend this is really Paradise and everyone's dead, and Ella and Calliope are a million years old, and you're really who you say you are—"

"I do not claim to be anyone except for me," he said, the corner of his mouth twitching upward.

I made a face. "Fine, then let's pretend this is all real, that magic is possible and the tooth fairy exists. And somewhere down the line I didn't hit my head and you aren't certifiably insane. What does your wife dying have to do with me?"

Henry was silent for a long moment. "As I said, she chose to die rather than to stay with me. I was her husband, but she simply loved him more."

Judging by his pained expression, there was nothing simple about it, but I didn't press him. "You know you look way too young to have been married, right?" I said in a sorry attempt to lighten the mood. "How old are you anyway?"

The corners of his lips twitched again. "Older than I look." After a moment he added, "She may have loved me, but it was never her choice. It was my last gift to her, letting her go."

There was a note of sadness in his voice that I understood all too well. "I'm sorry," I said. "I am. I just—I still don't understand why I'm here."

"I have been ruling on my own for nearly a thousand years, but a century ago, I agreed to only a hundred more before my brothers and sisters take my realm from me. I cannot handle it on my own, not anymore. There are simply too many for me to do it alone. I have been searching for a partner ever since, and you are the last one, Kate. This spring, the final decision will be made. If you are accepted, you will rule with me as my queen for six months of the year. If you do not, you will return to your old life with no memory of this time."

"Is that what happened to the others?" I said, forcing the question past my dry lips.

"The others…" He focused on something in the distance. "I do not mean to scare you, Kate, but I will never lie to you. I need you to trust me, and I need you to understand that you are special. I had given up before you came along."

I clasped my hands together to keep them from shaking. "What happened to them?"

"Some of them went mad. Others were sabotaged. None of them reached the end, let alone passed the tests."

"Tests?" I stared at him. "Sabotaged?"

"If I knew more, I would tell you, but it is why we have taken such extreme precautions to protect you." He hesitated. "As for the tests, there will be seven of them, and they will be the basis on which it will be decided if you are worthy of ruling."

"I didn't agree to any tests." I paused. "What happens if I pass?"

He stared at his hands. "You will become one of us."

"Us? Dead, you mean?"

"No, that is not what I mean. Think—you know the myth, do you not? Who was Persephone? What was she?"

Fear stabbed at me, cutting me from the inside. If what he claimed was true, then he'd kidnapped Persephone and forced her to marry him, and no matter what he said, I couldn't help but wonder if he would try to do the same to me. But the rational part of me couldn't look past the obvious. "You really think you're a god? You know that sounds crazy, right?"

"I am aware of how it must sound to you," said Henry. "I have done this before, after all. But yes, I am a god—an immortal, if you will. A physical representation of an aspect of this world, and as long as it exists, so will I. If you pass, that is what you will become as well."

Feeling dizzy, I stood as quickly as I could while still in those damned heels. "Listen, Henry, this all sounds great and everything, but what you're telling me is from a myth that people made up thousands of years ago. Persephone never existed, and even if she did, she wasn't a god, because there's no such thing—"

"How do you wish for me to prove it?" He stood with me.

"I don't know," I said, faltering. "Do something godlike?"

"I thought I already had." The fire in his eyes didn't fade. "There may be things I will not—cannot—tell you, but I am not a liar, and I will never mislead you."

I shrank back from the intensity of his voice. He really did believe what he was saying. "It's impossible," I said softly. "Isn't it?"

"But it is happening, so maybe it is time for you to reevaluate what is possible and what is not."

I thought about kicking off my heels, heading down the path to the front gate, and leaving, but the thought of my dream with my mother stopped me. As the part of me that wanted to stay for her overruled my skepticism, the temperature dipped twenty degrees, and I shivered.

"Kate?"

I froze, my feet glued to the ground. I knew that voice, and after yesterday, I'd never expected to hear it again.

"Anything is possible if you give it a chance," said Henry, focusing on something over my shoulder. I whirled around.

Not ten feet away from us stood Ava.

CHAPTER 8

AVA'S RETURN

I don't know how long I stood there, hugging Ava so tightly that she couldn't have possibly been able to breathe. Time moved slowly, and all I could think about was the way her arms felt around my shoulders as I struggled not to cry.

"Ava," I said in a strangled voice. "I thought—James said—everyone thought you were dead."

"I am," she said, her voice soft, but still hers. "Or at least that's what they tell me."

I didn't ask how. Henry had done it once, and even though he'd said he couldn't do it again, maybe he'd tried. Maybe he'd discovered it wasn't so impossible after all.

But if she were dead—really, truly dead—did that mean he'd been telling the truth after all? Was this how he was trying to prove it? The ground felt uneven underneath me. Even though every rational part of my mind screamed that this couldn't be happening, Ava felt warm and real in my arms, and there was no way anyone would go to such lengths to pull off a prank. The whole school thought she was dead. *James* thought she was dead, and I trusted him not to lie to me like that.

"Kate," she said, prying me off of her. "Calm down. I'm not going anywhere."

I pulled away, tears stinging my eyes and blurring my vision. "You better not be. You get to stay?"

"For as long as you want."

Over her shoulder I saw Henry standing to the side, his eyes averted.

"Henry? She can stay?"

He nodded. "She can stay on the grounds, but she may not leave."

I looked at Ava again, wiping my eyes with the back of my hand. "This isn't fair."

"What isn't fair?" she said.

"That I get to leave and you don't."

Ava laughed, the lighthearted sound of it jolting. "Kate, don't be ridiculous. I've got about forty years before my parents get here and tell me what I can and can't do, and I bet there are tons of cute guys here. I'll have plenty of things to do."

"Not too much, I hope," said Henry. "Ava, would you mind giving us a few more minutes alone?"

Beside me, Ava grinned. "Yeah—can I get something to wear?" It was then that I noticed she was wearing nothing more than a long white robe.

"I've got a whole closet upstairs," I said. "Ask for Ella. She'll show you where everything is."

"Thanks." Ava gave me one last hug, whispering, "He's *cute*," in my ear, then bounded off toward the manor. I watched her go.

"I didn't think I'd ever see her again."

"Understandable," said Henry. He stood so close to me that

I could feel the warmth of his body. "Sometimes we misjudge what is possible and what is not."

I looked up at him, a strange and unpleasant tension spreading through me. A dozen questions ran through my mind, but there was only one that was surrounded by a delicate bubble of hope. If I waited much longer before asking him about it, that bubble might burst. "Was it real then? My dream with my mother?"

Henry looked decidedly pleased with himself. "Did you enjoy it?"

"Yes." I hesitated. "Was it—was it just once?"

"No." He watched me closely, as if he was afraid I would pass out. I wasn't so sure I wouldn't. "For the duration of your stay, you will get to see her every night."

I studied the pattern in the marble fountain, my eyes tracing the jagged lines and swirls. "Thank you. So much."

"There is no need to thank me." He sounded confused. "I told you I would honor our agreement, and I will."

"I know." But I'd never thought it meant I would get to spend more time with her. Not by her bedside holding her hand and hoping she would wake up, but talking to her like she wasn't sick, like the past four years had never happened. It was beyond everything I'd hoped for.

But him honoring his side of our agreement meant I had to honor mine as well, and it crept up on me, terror slowly penetrating my mind and body as I realized I was trying to do something no one had been able to do before. In a way, it felt like I'd signed my own death warrant. "What now? What am I supposed to do?"

"Just be yourself." He set his hand on my shoulder, like he'd done for Ava. Unlike Ava, however, he seemed afraid to touch me, and the contact lasted for only a few seconds. "The tests will most likely come when you least expect them. I am not in charge of administering them, nor am I the final judge."

"I'm not really good at pop quizzes," I said.

He chuckled, and it washed over me, helping to dissolve some of my anxiety. "These are not the sort of tests any teacher would grade you on. They test who you are, not what you have stored in your brain. It is possible you will recognize them as they are happening, and it is possible you will not. But just be yourself. That is all anyone can ask of you."

His fingers brushed against my cheek, lingering. This time I didn't pull away.

"Why the tests?" I said. "Why are they necessary?"

"Because," he said. "The prize is not something we give out lightly, and we need to make sure it is something you can handle."

"What's that?"

"Immortality."

I felt a cold block of ice form in the pit of my stomach. So my choices now were live forever or die trying—or forget the last conversations I would ever have with my mother. Somehow it didn't seem fair.

"You will do well," he said. "I can feel it. And afterward, you will help me do something that no one else is capable of doing. You will have power beyond imagining, and you will never fear death again. You will never grow old, and you will always be beautiful. You will have eternal life to spend as you wish."

A shiver ran through me, and I didn't know if it was because of the way he spoke, what he said, or the way he looked at me.

Eternal life without my mother wasn't something I wanted to contemplate. But if he could bring Ava back...

"Perhaps," he whispered, "you may even learn how to swim."

That broke the spell. I snorted loudly, unable to help myself. "Good luck with that."

He smiled. "Or perhaps some things are impossible after all."

Once Henry returned me to the breakfast room, I ate so quickly that I could barely taste the food, despite how mouth-watering it all looked. Stacks of buttered toast, piles of bacon, even a side of pancakes with maple syrup, but Ava was some-where in the manor, and I wanted to see her again. I needed to confirm that she was really here. It wasn't until after I'd finished my eggs, cooked exactly like my mother used to make, that I realized for the first night in weeks, I hadn't had a nightmare. I made a mental note to ask Henry about that, wondering if it was because of my dreams with my mother. It had to be. If anything, I'd expected Eden Manor to make my nightmares worse rather than chase them away.

Before I could see Ava, however, Calliope informed me that I had to meet my tutor. Once I'd finished my meal, she was the only one there to show me the way, with Ella conspicuously absent. I hoped it meant she was busy helping Ava, but given how much she already seemed to hate me, I expected her to stick around as little as possible.

On our way, we passed a bowl of fruit, and I remembered the question I hadn't been able to ask Henry. "Why do you taste my food?"

Calliope held a door open for me. "To make sure no one's trying to kill you."

"Why would they try to do that?"

She gave me a look that made me feel like an idiot for not already knowing the answer. "Because if Henry relinquishes his control over the Underworld, someone else will take his place. Not everyone's rooting for you, you know."

"Wait, what?" I'd been so concerned about what would happen to me if I passed that I hadn't stopped to think what might happen to Henry if I failed. "Who?"

"I can't tell you that. Watch out!"

I stopped abruptly, narrowly missing a vase set on a pedestal. It looked expensive. And ancient. And handmade. I sucked in a breath and moved gingerly around it.

"In here," said Calliope, gesturing toward another door. She pushed it open, and I stepped inside, focusing on the only thing worth looking at: a small wooden table with a matching chair on either end. Everything else was a dull white, and it smelled as if it had recently been painted.

"I'll see you afterward," said Calliope as she pulled the door shut behind me. I spun around and hobbled toward her, managing to trip over the thick carpet.

"Wait!" I called, but it was too late. The door was already closed, and to my horror, I noticed there was no handle. It would be impossible to open without someone on the other side.

I stood there like an idiot for the better part of a minute, trying to figure out how to get out. There was a large window on the far wall, but we were three stories up. Jumping wouldn't likely be suicidal, but it'd hurt. Other than the door, there were no other exits, so the only thing I could do was wait.

Kicking my shoes off my aching feet, I took a seat at the table and crossed my arms over my chest. The chair was uncomfortable, and the room was hot, but at least I didn't have to walk in those heels anymore.

The thick smell of incense filled the air, making me sneeze. Looking over my shoulder, I caught sight of a familiar face, and my eyes widened. Behind me stood Irene, the receptionist from the high school office, dressed in a white robe similar to Ava's. It flowed behind her and was stunning, but it was nothing compared to her hair. While it'd been red before, now it was vivid ruby, so bright in the sunlight that it almost glittered. It couldn't possibly be natural.

"Hello, Kate," she said with a friendly smile. "It's good to see you again."

I hesitated. "Nice to see you again, too?"

She sat down across from me with the sort of grace that a dancer would've given their right arm for, and I couldn't help but feel a stab of bitterness. What was she supposed to teach me, how to be beautiful?

"Is there anyone else from Eden here that I should know about?" I said. First Sofia, and now Irene—was Dylan due to mysteriously appear as well?

The corners of her lips twisted into an amused smile. "I suppose you'll have to wait and see, won't you? Sorry about the subterfuge, darling. I promise it was only for the best."

"Yeah, I figured," I grumbled. I didn't like knowing I'd been tricked. "You'll be tutoring me then? Calculus and science and stuff?"

She laughed, the sound of it like wind chimes. "Something cooler. Something much, much cooler. Henry wants you prepared in case you pass, and that means learning about people.

How they work, how they see themselves and each other, why they make certain choices—psychology, mostly. Some astronomy and astrology as well. Aside from that, more importantly, you need to learn about this world. Not just the Underworld, but all of it."

"Mythology?" The word felt heavy on my tongue.

"It's not mythology here," she said with a wink. "As long as you remember that, you'll be just fine." Seemingly out of nowhere she pulled a thick book and set it on the table, which groaned.

"I have to read that?" I said.

"Don't worry," she said. "It has pictures."

Somehow that wasn't very reassuring. "Why do I have to learn all of this?"

She didn't have the chance to answer me. Instead, the door with no handle burst open, and unintelligible shouts filled the room. I stood so quickly I nearly knocked over my chair. Irene looked annoyed, but she remained seated and didn't speak.

Ella, Calliope and Ava stumbled into the room, each seemingly determined to be the first one inside. Ava wore a pink dress that I would have rather burned than wear, and Ella stormed in behind her, irate.

"You can't just take things that don't belong to you!" shouted Ella, her face glowing with fury.

"Kate, tell her," pleaded Ava.

"I'm sorry," said Calliope, shoving her way to the front. "I tried to stop them, but they wouldn't listen—"

"*She's* the one who wouldn't listen," said Ella, pointing at Ava.

"*Excuse* me? You're the one who wasn't listening to me."

They looked like they were ready to rip each other's throats out. Overwhelmed, I finally found my voice and stepped forward. "Stop it, both of you. Is this about the dress?"

Both fell silent, and I could feel the waves of resentment rolling off both of them. Calliope was the one who answered. "Your friend went into your room looking for something to wear, and Ella said she couldn't. But your friend said you gave her permission, and she didn't have anything else to put on, but Ella said there were other things, and if she just waited a little while she could—"

"I was naked, and this little bitch wanted me to leave!" said Ava, moving to stand by my side. Out of the corner of my eye, I saw her glaring at Ella, whose expression was perfectly smooth now that she'd quieted.

"She was in your suite," said Ella coldly. "No one is allowed in there without my express permission."

"It's my suite," I said. "Seems logical that if I say she can be in there, she can be in there, right?"

Ella was silent. I sighed. "All right, fine, listen—Ava can come in my room whenever she wants, okay? But she needs her own, if there's one available for her."

Ava snorted. "The whole place is full of rooms."

I ignored her. "And she'll need things to wear. All of you be nice, okay? Please?"

The look on Ella's face made my blood run cold. "As you wish, Your Highness," she said stiffly before turning on her heel and walking away. If I wasn't sure whether or not she hated me before, now I knew. I was doomed to be stuck in corsets and hoop skirts for the next six months.

"Here," said Calliope in a small voice. "I'll take Ava and we'll find a room for her."

Ava bristled. "I'm not a child. You don't have to hold my hand."

"It's all right, Calliope," I said. "I can do it once we're done here. I need to explore this place anyhow. You can come if you want."

"It's fine," said Irene, sounding irritated. "Just read the pages I marked for tomorrow. I'll have someone deliver the book to your room."

I nodded, not knowing what to say. Looking at Ava, I felt a stab of guilt; it was my fault she was here to begin with and had to put up with all of this. Maybe Ella didn't get along with anybody, but I had to make sure Ava wasn't completely miserable. Just because I was trapped here didn't mean she had to pay the price, too.

The rest of the morning wasn't much better, and the afternoon was a hundred times worse. After lunch, Ella joined us, a silent shadow as we wandered around the manor, and the tension she caused made me want to tear my hair out. Thankfully after a few well-aimed snipes, she made a point of avoiding Ava completely, and Ava made a point of ignoring Ella.

It was comforting having Ava there. She was a familiar piece of reality that I used to anchor myself, the proof I needed that this wasn't all some elaborate hallucination. She made it easier to believe that I wasn't going crazy. Maybe that's what Henry was counting on.

As we wandered the halls, exploring the countless rooms, I stayed close to Ava. She didn't seem to mind, and she even took my arm and led me from place to place, describing each room we passed as if she were trying to sell me a home. Calliope joined in, but Ella continued to keep her distance. Despite the tension, the afternoon was actually fun. It wasn't until we were back in my suite that it became unbearable, all because of the news delivered by Sofia midafternoon.

"A ball?" I said, my heart sinking. "You mean like a dance?"

No one else seemed to mind. Calliope squealed, and even Ella looked excited. "A dance?" said Ava, clapping her hands together excitedly. "I don't have anything to wear—what am I supposed to do?"

"Raid another closet?" said Ella. Both of us ignored her.

"A formal ball tomorrow night," said Sofia, "hosted by the council in your honor. Most of the time it's planned for the winter solstice, but since you're the last and everyone's so eager to meet you, it's been moved up."

"You mean it has nothing to do with the fact that half the girls were killed at their ball and Henry wanted to make sure she'd survive it before investing more time in her?" said Ella innocently.

Sofia gave her a look and turned back to me. "Consider it your introduction into society."

I took a deep breath and tried to ignore what Ella had said. Henry wouldn't let that happen to me. Not if I was his last chance. "I don't need to be introduced to society. Society and I have gotten by without knowing each other for years, thank you very much."

"The whole council's coming this time?" said Calliope nervously.

"This is it for Henry," said Ella with a grimace. "Did you ever really doubt they'd all want to meet her?"

"Who's the council?" I said. "Why are they so terrifying?"

"They're not," said Ella as she sat down in an armchair,

keeping her distance. "They're Henry's family. His brothers and sisters and nieces and nephews, though he and his brothers and sisters aren't actually related by blood. More like they adopted each other since they share the same creator and are the original six gods, but it's what they call themselves. It's as good enough a description as any."

"Like Zeus and stuff?" said Ava from her spot on my bed. "The lightning bolt guy?"

I could practically see the smoke start to pour out of Ella's ears. "Are you crazy or just incredibly stupid?"

Ava sniffed. "Neither, thank you. Calliope? Is this the lightning bolt guy?"

"Yes, that's him," said Calliope from an armchair, where she'd collapsed at the news. "That's Henry's brother."

I bit my lip, not knowing what to say. I had a hard time believing all of this to begin with. Throw in the king of the gods, and any conceivable chance I had at taking this seriously flew out the window. Besides, I had no doubt that if I actually started to believe what they were saying, I'd have fainted on the spot, and that was the last thing I wanted. For now, they were Henry's family. A very scary, very intimidating, very large family, but still his family. I could ignore the part about lightning bolts in the meantime.

"New rule," I said, swallowing the lump in my throat. "No one talks about them unless I ask. You're freaking me out, and I can't do this if I'm freaking out, so just—let's not. Not until this ball is over. Okay?"

None of them seemed too unhappy with this, and they all nodded, even Ava.

"We're not allowed to tell you much anyway," admitted

Calliope. I scowled, but I didn't fight it. If Henry didn't tell me, then I'd just have to figure it out on my own.

"One thing," said Ella. "Last I'll say of it, but you really ought to know. The council will be the ones to decide whether or not you pass your tests. And if you don't pass, they'll be the ones who decide what to do with you afterward."

My head spun, and I said in a small voice, "What they do with me afterward? I thought Henry said I wouldn't be able to remember it."

"Oh, don't worry!" said Calliope, glaring daggers at Ella. "You won't. They won't hurt you or anything, or at least I don't think they will." She hesitated. "No one's really made it to that point before."

The way Ella glared at her made me think I wasn't getting the whole truth. My stomach churned violently, and for a moment I thought I was going to be ill. If they didn't like me, I was screwed, and there would be no one left to care what they did with me.

CHAPTER 9

THE BALL

"A ball?" My mother's tinkling laughter rose above the people
we passed on the crowded New York street, who bustled around
us on their way to home or work or other important places.
"They really don't know you at all, do they?"

"It's not funny." I shoved my hands into my pockets, staring
across the street at Central Park. "What if Henry's family hates
me?"

"It's always a possibility, I suppose." She tucked her arm in
my elbow and drew me closer. "I highly doubt it though. Who
could possibly hate you?"

I rolled my eyes, refusing to mention the part where apparently someone inside the manor wanted me dead. "You're my
mother. You're supposed to say that."

"True." She grinned. "Doesn't mean I don't mean it
though."

Nearby a car honked impatiently at the slow-moving traffic,
and my mother and I were constantly jostled as we made our
way down the sidewalk at our own pace, not the brisk walk
the other pedestrians used. I closed my eyes and tilted my head
upward, inhaling deeply. The smell was uniquely New York,

and it reminded me how much I missed the city. How much I missed being here with my mother. "He thinks he's a god."

"Does he?" My mother raised an eyebrow. "He brought back Ava, didn't he?"

Before I could reply, she spotted a hot dog vendor. I tried to tell her I wasn't hungry, but she wasn't having it. Two minutes later, we reentered the park, both holding hot dogs. Hers was laden with every topping the vendor had; I stuck with ketchup.

"He said he was married to Persephone," I said reluctantly. Even to me, it sounded crazy.

"Then that would make him Hades." She said this so matter-of-factly that I gave her a puzzled look. Unfortunately she noticed. "What?"

"You actually believe him?" I said.

"And you don't? What else does he need to do to prove it to you, sweetheart?" She leaned over and gave me a sloppy kiss on the forehead. "You've always been too practical for your own good."

"But—" I took a deep breath, trying to focus my thoughts. "But why? Why do you believe him?"

She made a wide, sweeping gesture to the park around us. "How else can you explain this?"

She was right. Even if I was skeptical about Ava or what Henry had done or what he'd told me, this—being with my mother, talking to her, getting another chance—it was too vivid to be a dream. It was too real to be my imagination.

"He gave me more time with you," said my mother, pulling me into a hug. "How could I possibly not believe him after that?"

We walked in silence, finishing our hot dogs and tossing the wrappers in the trash as we made our way to the center of the park. She kept her arm around my shoulders, and I wrapped my arm around her waist, not wanting to let go.

"Mom?" I said. "I'm scared."

"Of what?"

"Of the tests." I stared at the ground. "He said I have to pass them all—what if I can't? What happens then?"

"And what if you can?" She rubbed my back soothingly. "What if you're exactly what Henry's been waiting for all this time?"

It seemed absurd, but the way he'd sounded talking about losing his wife—Ava had been right. Maybe he was some almighty god with the power to raise the dead, but he was also a very lonely guy. I knew what that kind of loss and loneliness felt like, and if there was anything I could do to stop anyone else from feeling that way, I would do it.

Maybe choosing me hadn't been such an accident after all.

My dress for the ball wasn't just ugly—it was painful. Much to my horror, Ella had her way and stuffed me into a corset, and she spent nearly half an hour lacing it as tightly as she could. I wasn't a willing participant, breathing out when I should've been breathing in, but it took her no time at all to figure out what I was doing.

"I can wait until you take a breath," she said. "You have to eventually."

"Why do I need a corset?" I said. "Did you die in the eighteenth century or something?"

Ella scoffed. "Hardly. I think they look nice, and I enjoy torturing you. Now suck it up."

The only person Ella didn't force into a corset was Ava, who looked stunning in a blue dress that matched her eyes, and as she helped me through the corridors, I tried to breathe in as slowly and as deeply as my corset allowed. I could get through this. It was only a few hours, and then it'd be over.

"Ready?" said Ava as she bounced on the balls of her feet. We stood outside the ballroom, waiting to be announced. Ella and Calliope, who were already inside, had stumbled all over themselves that afternoon, giving me instruction after instruction on how to behave. Stand up straight, greet everyone with a smile, be polite, don't say anything that'd get me into trouble, don't mention the outside world, don't tell anyone how I really felt about all of this, and don't under any conditions be myself. Easy enough.

"Don't think I have a choice," I mumbled. I was supposed to walk into the room immediately after I was announced. Small steps, Calliope had said, making sure to point my toes as I walked. When I'd mentioned the fact that no one would be able to see my feet underneath the satin and lace, she'd ignored me. "What if whoever killed the other girls tries to kill me?"

"I'll be right there the whole time," said Ava. "So will Henry and the council. If anyone tries to kill you, they'll have to get through all of us. Now don't forget to breathe."

Fainting would be the perfect way out of this, but knowing my luck, they'd just hold another ball once I recovered.

Two men on either side of the doors pulled them open for us, and my heart pounded so loudly that they probably heard it on the other side of the room. For a moment I couldn't make anything out in the dim light of the ballroom, but soon I could see inside. The room was gigantic, bigger than Eden High School's cafeteria and gym combined, and the only sources of light came from ornate chandeliers. Everyone was dressed as fancily as I was, and I got the distinct impression that this was the social event of the century.

And hundreds of pairs of eyes were focused directly on me.

"Kate?" said Ava. I must've swayed, because she took me by the elbow, her grip stronger than I expected. "Kate, breathe."

In and out, in and out—why was this harder than it was supposed to be?

"Kate, do something!" hissed Ava. "Everyone's watching."

That was the problem.

Being the center of attention had never been my thing. Once, in elementary school, long before my mother had gotten ill, my so-called friends had talked me into performing in a dance routine for the school talent show. I couldn't even step onto the stage, I'd been so nervous, and when they'd pushed me out in front of all those people, I'd promptly thrown up right in the middle of the theater. Not my proudest moment.

This time, my only saving grace was the fact that there wasn't anything in my stomach to come up. I could do this, I thought. One foot in front of the other—that's all it took.

"Okay," I said, taking a step forward. The silence that had fallen over the crowd turned into nervous whispers, and with every move I made, I could feel the burn of their stares.

"Ladies and gentlemen," called the herald. "I present to you Miss Katherine Winters."

Wild applause filled the air, and if I hadn't felt humiliated enough before, now I wanted to die. At least Ava was still by my side and gripping my elbow. Every bad thought I'd ever had about her evaporated. "Look, Kate—the guards! Look at them," she whispered excitedly. "Aren't they gorgeous?"

Out of the corner of my eye I saw the two men I'd noticed at breakfast the morning before. Ella had said they'd go with me everywhere, but this was the first time I'd seen them since. The dark-haired man was giving me—no, Ava—a coy smile. The blond was just as still as before, watching the crowd diligently.

Much to my relief, I spotted Henry on top of a platform on the other side of the room. Under the low light, he looked as attractive as ever, but while he caught my eye, he wasn't what held my attention. Behind him stood fourteen thrones—actual, real-life *thrones*. None of them were occupied, but they didn't have to be. I understood immediately.

The council was here.

If Henry was right and the impossible was possible, then those fourteen people were the things myths were made of, and I was supposed to—what? Walk up to them, shake their hands, and introduce myself?

Somehow I kept moving. Before I could process what all was happening around me, we'd reached the platform, and Calliope was helping me up the steps under the guise of dealing with the long hem of my dress. Once I was standing upright on my own at the top, Henry approached me, bowing his head in greeting.

"Kate." His soothing voice did nothing to calm me. "You look beautiful."

"Th-thanks," I stuttered, attempting to curtsy. It didn't work too well. "I see they didn't make you wear a dress."

Henry chuckled. "Even if they had, I wouldn't have looked nearly as lovely as you do."

He held out his hand, and I took it, having no other choice if I didn't want to fall flat on my face. Henry led me to the center of the platform, our backs facing the audience.

"My family," he said with a vague gesture toward the thrones.

"Are they invisible?" I whispered.

He gave me a wry smile. "No, they are among us. They wish to remain anonymous."

I nodded and forced a grimace, hoping it would pass for a smile. So I wouldn't be meeting them face-to-face after all. That was infinitely more frightening; it meant every single person I met tonight would be a potential tester. Maybe passing out wasn't such a bad idea.

I spent the evening seated next to him on another smaller platform, watching everyone else enjoy themselves. I worried someone might jump out and try to choke me, and I didn't dare take any of the food or drink that was passed around, but as long as Henry was there, I felt safe. Or at least as safe as I could be. I stayed quiet, refusing to look over at the empty thrones. I could do this, whether or not they liked me. I had to.

I watched Ava dance with the dark-haired guard, who seemed to enjoy himself more than someone on guard duty should have. He was cute, but I had a sneaking suspicion that the only man I'd be allowed to date was sitting next to me, not making a sound. I shied away from the thought. Our agreement was that I'd stay here, not that I'd do something as ridiculous as marry him, queen or not. Though the more I thought about it, the more I wondered if being his so-called queen meant marrying him, too.

"Who is everyone?" I finally said. No one approached Henry and me, but occasionally someone would stop in front of the platform and bow. I was instructed to nod my head in return, once and as regally as possible. I was too scared to do anything else.

"My subjects," said Henry. "Some asked to come so they could meet you, and others have been good to me in the past."

"Oh. They're dead?"

"Yes, though obviously not in the way you define it."

I watched them, fascinated, trying to pick up any hint that they weren't exactly the same as the living. Some danced archaically, but other than that, I couldn't find a single difference. Looking around, my eyes fell on Ava. At least she looked happy to be there.

"And one of them wants me dead," I said. Henry stiffened beside me, and that was all the confirmation I needed.

"Do not worry," he said. "You are safe with me."

"Do you know who it is?" I said, and he shook his head. "What about the person who's supposed to take over for you if I fail? Could it be him? Or her?"

He grimaced. "Somehow I think not." And that was all he'd say on the subject.

It was nearly midnight when Henry stood and everyone fell silent. My backside was killing me, and even though I hadn't taken a step in hours, my feet ached from the heels Calliope had forced me to wear. I was ready for this whole thing to be over, but instead of leading me toward the door, Henry steered us back toward the stage. My legs shook underneath me, and it was a miracle I managed to stay upright.

"This will be easy," he said quietly. "All you have to do is say yes and accept the seeds."

Bemused, I followed him up the stairs, nearly falling flat on my face when we reached the top. Luckily he caught me, and I steadied myself, waiting for him to speak.

"Katherine Winters," said Henry in a booming voice that

made me flinch. "Do you agree to stay at Eden Manor for the autumn and winter, to take the tests as given to you by the members of the council, and should you pass, accept the role as Queen of the Underworld?"

Everyone inside the ballroom was silent. No pressure or anything. "Yes."

A small plate appeared in his hand, with six seeds arranged carefully in the center. I took the first one in between my fingers, looking at Henry for approval. He nodded encouragingly, and I put the seed in my mouth, trying not to make a face. I hated seeds—I didn't even eat watermelon because of them. Unfortunately mythical seeds didn't taste any better.

I swallowed them rapidly, trying to ignore the slimy feeling as they slid down my throat. I wanted to gag, but I managed to keep my mouth shut. After the sixth seed was down, the crowd erupted into cheers, but that was nothing compared to the way Henry was looking at me, his expression strangely gentle. Whatever this was, it meant more to him than I understood.

That's when they finally put me out of my misery. Ella and Calliope were at my side and helping me down the stairs before I realized what was happening. The crowd parted to let us through, and hands I couldn't trace back to bodies reached through the walls of shoulders and torsos to touch my hair, my dress—even a few managed to touch my face. Eventually my guards joined us, shielding me from them. It was humiliating.

"Oh, Kate, he's so cute!" said Ava excitedly as she, Ella, Calliope and I made our way back toward my bedroom. "He said his name's Xander, and he's gorgeous and smart and funny and cute—"

"You've already said that," I said, but she continued on like I hadn't said a thing.

"—and he said he'd show me some magic tricks sometime! I mean, I know magic's this geeky thing, but it's still sort of cool, you know? In a nerdy sort of way."

She blabbered on for so long that by the time we reached my room, even Calliope looked less than enthusiastic. Luckily Ella, who I was beginning to like more and more, came to my rescue.

"Kate needs to sleep," she said, blocking Ava's way into my room. "You can see her tomorrow."

Ava narrowed her eyes, and I sensed a fight coming. "Says who?"

"Me," said Ella, drawing herself up to her full height, which was a good six inches taller than Ava. "She has more important things to worry about than listening to you prattle on about Xander. And Xander has more important things to do than to listen."

Ella said the last bit a little louder than was strictly necessary, making her voice echo down the hall. I heard an embarrassed cough in the distance, and I managed to suppress a smile.

"I'm sorry, Ava," I said, torn between wanting to be a good friend and wanting my head to stop pounding. "We can talk about it tomorrow, all right? I really am tired."

She glared at Ella. "Whatever."

After Ava stormed off in a huff, Ella and Calliope turned to me expectantly. I sighed. "You, too, guys. I can undress myself, I promise. Learned how to do that years ago."

Ella snorted. "Good luck with that corset," she said, walking away without another word. Calliope offered to stay and help, but I shooed her off as well. Worst case, I'd take scissors to the damn thing. Maybe that would stop Ella from trying to force me into one for a while.

Relieved to finally be alone, I shut the door and locked it. Kicking my shoes into a corner, I unlaced my dress, more than ready to be able to breathe properly again. Feeling as if I were about to collapse, I pulled back the curtain on my bed and swallowed a scream.

Someone else was already in it.

CHAPTER 10

THE FIRST TEST

I gasped. Lying off to the side of my massive bed was Henry, dressed in a silk robe and pajama bottoms, a thick novel in his hand. Instead of saying hello or apologizing, he glanced at me like I'd interrupted a good part.

"What—this is my bed!" Since I was still wearing that corset, catching my breath was a problem. "What're you *doing* here?"

"Reading," he said, sitting up. "Would you like help with that?"

It was then that I realized I was practically clawing at my dress in an attempt to free my lungs from their prison. He didn't give me time to answer. By my side in an instant, his deft hands undid my laces faster than I'd have ever been able to.

"There," he said once they were finished and I could finally breathe in deeply again. "All done."

"I need to—I need to change," I said dumbly, clutching my dress to my front.

"I won't look."

He settled back in my bed and opened his book once more,

making it clear he wasn't going to leave anytime soon. I stumbled to the opposite corner of the room, where my dressing screen stood. Making sure to grab the darkest pajamas I could find, I changed quickly, ignoring the ripping sound as I yanked the dress over my hips.

I emerged less than a minute later, wrapped in a thick robe. This was insane—did he think he was going to sleep in here? This wasn't part of the deal. And if he was going to take that bed, then I'd find another one. I would sleep on the floor if I had to. Either way, I wasn't staying in here with him.

"What're you doing here? For real, I mean," I said, approaching the bed cautiously. "Not just reading. I know you're reading. I mean, I can see that, and—" I stopped. "Why are you here?"

Henry bookmarked his page and turned his full attention on me. It was still as unnerving as it'd been the day before in the garden, but this time I was too upset and exhausted to care.

"I am here because the council has decided I am to spend time with you each evening—as much as you allow. If you wish for me to leave, then I shall. Otherwise, if you do not ask, I will stay."

I stared at him, my stomach twisting into knots. "Stay the night? The whole night?"

He raised an eyebrow. "I am certain that tonight you will ask me to leave long before that becomes a possibility."

"What about other nights?" I squeaked. "Do you—am I supposed to—do *that?*"

I'd never done that before with anyone. I hadn't had time to date while my mother was sick, let alone get serious, and I had no intention of starting now. If he thought making me eat a few dumb seeds meant he controlled me now, he had another thing coming.

He chuckled, and I flushed. The least he could do was not treat me like an idiot. "No, *that* is not a requirement, nor will it ever be."

I had to stop myself from sighing with relief. He was beyond attractive, but no amount of good looks was going to make me compromise on that. "Then why are you here?"

"I am here because I wish to know you better." He eyed me. "You intrigue me, and if you succeed in passing the tests the council puts before you, you will one day be my wife."

I opened and closed my mouth, trying to come up with something to say. "But—you said I wouldn't have to marry you."

"No," he said patiently. "I said I was not proposing marriage to you. I am still not. There is no need unless you pass. If you do, then yes, you will be my wife six months of the year."

I fidgeted. "What if I don't want to be your wife?"

He stilled, his smile disappearing. "Then it would be a simple enough thing for you to purposely fail."

The hollowness in his voice immediately made me feel guilty. "I'm sorry, I didn't mean—"

"Do not apologize." His tone was still void of emotion, and it only made me feel worse. "This is your choice. If at any time I ask too much of you, then you may leave."

And my mother would die.

I clenched my fists so hard that my nails dug into my palms, and it was several moments before I managed to come up with something to say—a peace offering, if nothing else. Maybe if I pretended that marrying him was a possibility, he wouldn't look so empty.

"What about then?" I said. "If we get—*married*—will I have to—you know?"

"No." Henry thawed slightly as he focused on me again. I was sure he could see right through me. "You will be my wife in name and title only, and I would not ask it of you if it were not necessary for the Underworld to recognize you as its ruler as it recognized Persephone. I do not expect you to love me, Kate. I do not dare hope that you would think of me in any way other than as a friend, and I know I must earn even that much. I understand that this is not your ideal life, and I do not wish to make it more difficult for you than it already is. My only desire is to help you pass these tests."

And to stop whoever it was from killing me. I cautiously perched on the edge of my bed. There was still enough distance between us that I felt safe, but even the air that separated us seemed to crackle. "What about love? Don't you—you know, want someone? Want a family and stuff?"

"I have a family," he said, but before I could correct myself, he continued. "If you mean children, then no, I have never believed that to be in my future."

"But is that what you want?"

He smiled faintly. "I have been alone for a very long time. To expect anything else in the years to come would be foolish."

Despite the fact that he looked only a few years older than me, I couldn't imagine how old Henry might actually be— wasn't sure I wanted to know, really. But how could someone live for so long and be alone? I could barely handle the few nights I'd spent at home without my mother. Multiply that by eternity…I couldn't fathom it.

"Henry?"

"Yes?"

"What happens to you if I don't pass?"

He was silent for a long moment, his fingers idly running across the silk lining of his robe. "I will fade," he said quietly. "Someone else will take over my realm, and therefore I will have no reason to exist any longer."

"So you die." The gravity of the situation hit me hard, and I stared off to the side, unable to look at him. It wasn't just my mother's life that was riding on my ability to pass these tests.

"I fade," he corrected. "The living die, and their souls remain in the Underworld for eternity. However, my kind do not have souls. We cease to exist completely, without a shred of our former selves remaining. One cannot die if one was never alive to begin with."

I clenched my fist around the blanket. It was even worse than dying then. "Who?"

He gave me a puzzled look. "Who what?"

"Who gets your job if you give it up?"

"Ah." He smiled sadly. "My nephew."

"Who is he? What's his name? Is he on the council?"

"Yes, he is on the council," said Henry, "but I am afraid I cannot tell you his name."

"Why not?" It seemed no one was willing to trust me with the truth in this place, and while I could understand Calliope not giving me the whole story, Henry knew. Henry should've told me.

He cleared his throat and at least had the decency to look me in the eye. "Because I fear it would upset you, and you are unhappy enough as it is. I do not wish to make it any worse."

I fell silent as I tried to think of who it could possibly be that would upset me. No one came to mind. "I don't understand."

"You will."

There was nothing I could say to that, and he must've known it, because instead of looking at me expectantly, he returned to his book. I watched him, searching for any sign that he wasn't human. The angles of his face were too symmetrical to be normal, his smooth skin devoid of even a hint of stubble, the thick, jet-black hair that hung an inch above his shoulders, and the unnerving color of his eyes—it was his eyes that did it, swirling pools of silver that seemed to constantly be moving. In the low light, they almost glowed.

It wasn't until he cleared his throat that I realized I was staring. Even though I was still annoyed that he wouldn't trust me with the truth, I wanted to break the tension, so I said the first thing that came to mind. "What do you do during the day? When you're not here, I mean. Or are you always here?"

"I'm not always here." He slid a bookmark between the pages again and set his novel aside. "My brothers and sisters and I all have duties we attend to. I rule the dead, so most of my time is spent in the Underworld, overseeing decisions and making sure everything runs smoothly. It's far more complicated than that, of course, but if you pass, you will learn the ins and outs of what I do."

"Oh." I bit my lip. "What's the Underworld like?"

"All in good time," he said, reaching over to briefly set his hand over mine. His palm was warm, and I fought the urge to shiver at his touch. "What about you? What do you enjoy doing with your time?"

I shrugged. "I like reading. And drawing, though I'm not very good at it. Mom and I used to garden together, and she taught me how to play cards." I eyed him. "Do you know how to play?"

"I'm adequate at a few games, though I do not know if they are still popular."

"Maybe we could play something sometime," I said. "If you're going to be in here every night, I mean."

He nodded. "That would be pleasant."

We fell into silence again. He looked comfortable, lounging on the bed as if he'd done it a hundred times before. For all I knew, he had, but I didn't want to think about that. I wasn't the first, but I would be the last. Rejecting him wouldn't do either of us any good—my heart thudded loudly in protest at the thought—and since I was stuck here for six months, I had no intention of getting on his bad side. I was, however, exhausted.

I grappled with myself for several seconds, going back and forth between what was right and what I wanted. I should've talked to him, asked him more questions, gotten to know him, but all I wanted to do was to sleep—which I would never get to do if he stayed, even if he didn't make a sound. No matter what he said about duties and expectations, that kind of anxiety wasn't going to go away overnight.

"Henry," I said softly. He'd gone back to reading his book, but in an instant his eyes were on me. "Please don't take this the wrong way, but I'm really tired."

He stood, taking his book with him. Instead of looking angry or hurt, however, his expression was as neutral as always. "It has been a long day for both of us."

"Thanks." I gave him a grateful smile, hoping that'd smooth over any wrinkles I wasn't sensing.

"Of course." He walked to the door. "Good night, Kate."

It was such a small thing, but the hint of affection in his voice made my cheeks warm. "'Night," I said, hoping he couldn't see my blush from across the room.

"So you like him." It wasn't a question, and I glared at my grinning mother as we sat on a bench, watching joggers and people walking their dogs pass.

"I didn't say that," I said, slouching. Beside me my mother sat poised, as if she were dining with royalty instead of spending the morning in Central Park. "I just—don't want him to die, that's all. No one else should have to die because of me."

"No one has died because of you," she said, running her fingers through my hair and brushing it out of my eyes. "Even if you don't pass, it won't be your fault. As long as you do your best, everything will be all right."

"But how can I do my best when I don't even know what the tests are?" I shoved my hands between my knees. "How am I supposed to do this?"

She wrapped her arm around my shoulders. "Everyone believes in you except for you, Kate," she said gently. "Maybe that should tell you something."

Even if everyone believed in me, that didn't mean they were right, and it didn't mean I would succeed. All it meant was that on top of everything else, I had to worry about disappointing them, too. Or in Henry's case, forcing him into early retirement from his entire existence.

"But you do like him, don't you?" said my mother after several minutes passed. I craned my neck to look up at her, surprised to see real concern on her face.

"He's nice," I said warily, wondering where she was going with this. "I think we could be friends."

"Do you think he's cute?"

I rolled my eyes. "He's a god, Mom. Of course he's cute."

A wry smile spread across her face. "It's about time you admitted that he's a god."

I shrugged and looked away. "Kind of hard to pretend otherwise now. But he's nice, so I guess as long as he doesn't try to turn me into a pile of ash, I could get used to it."

"Good." She hugged me and gave me a kiss on the temple. "I'm glad you like him. He could be good for you, and you shouldn't be alone."

I sighed inwardly, not bothering to correct her. If it made her happy to think I liked Henry like that, then so be it. She deserved a little happiness before I became such a disappointment.

I expected the days in Eden Manor to drag, but instead their repetition made them go by quickly. Calliope and Ella helped me get ready in the morning; Ava always sat on the edge of my bed, talking animatedly about her latest conquest. After a few short weeks of dating the guard, Xander, she'd moved on.

"His name's Theo," she said, so excited that she could hardly sit still. "He's gorgeous and tall and smart, and he says I have the prettiest eyes he's ever seen."

In the mirror, I saw Ella's expression harden. "Stay away from him," she snapped. I tried to turn around so I could see them both, but Calliope held my shoulders down, not yet finished with my hair.

"Why?" said Ava haughtily. "Is he your boyfriend?"

Ella narrowed her eyes. "He's my twin."

I sighed. If I had to put up with this for the next five months, I was going to do something drastic.

"So?" said Ava, crossing her arms. "He likes me, and I like him. I don't see the problem."

How Ava could look at Ella's face and not cower, I had no idea. But Ava was going to be Ava no matter how long Ella glared at her.

"If you hurt him, I will hunt you down and kill you all over again, and this time I'll make sure you won't have some pretty little afterlife to come back to," snarled Ella.

I opened my mouth to tell Ella exactly what was going to happen if she even tried, but Ava cut in before I had the chance. "And what if he hurts me?"

"Then I'm sure you'd have done something to deserve it."

From then on out, Ava and Ella could barely stand to be in the same room together. I couldn't blame them.

Slowly I adjusted to my new reality, and Henry was right. Once I accepted that maybe this all wasn't just one big crazy joke, things got much easier, and I didn't constantly exhaust myself trying to rationalize the incomprehensible.

While I still didn't like the idea of the guards or Calliope testing my food—a job which Ella strongly encouraged Ava to take over—pretending I was stuck in the eighteenth century helped me come to terms with everything that was happening around me, with the exception of my strange relationship with Henry. As the weeks passed, the evening quickly became my favorite part of the day, aided by the fact that I didn't have to listen to Ella and Ava bicker all the time. We talked about what I'd done that day, though even when he tried to distract me, it never escaped my attention that we never talked about how his day had gone. I taught him how to play my favorite card games, and he seemed to enjoy learning, asking me polite questions and not interrupting my rambling responses. Sometimes

I worked up the courage to ask him questions as well, which he would answer vaguely, if at all. He still refused to tell me what the tests were, but to his credit, he seemed eager to keep me as comfortable as possible.

Everything about my day was timed. Half an hour for breakfast, which was always full of my favorite foods. I didn't gain weight, and that only gave me an excuse to eat as much as I wanted. After breakfast, I had five hours of lessons, where I studied mythology, art, theology, astronomy—anything Irene thought I needed to know. Daydreaming wasn't an option either, being her only student, and she seemed to develop a distinct lack of compassion about what I was and wasn't interested in learning. Still, there was one plus: at least Calculus wasn't on the curriculum.

We spent an inordinate amount of time on the Olympians, the Greek gods who ruled the universe and who would decide my fate.

"Most people typically think there were only twelve," said Irene. "But if you look carefully throughout history, there are fourteen."

The significance of that number wasn't lost on me. Fourteen Olympians and fourteen thrones. They would be the ones deciding my fate, and because of that, I paid extra attention to my lessons about them, as if knowing everything I could would somehow give me a leg up.

I learned about Zeus and Hera and their children; the children Zeus fathered with other women, as well as Athena, who sprang fully-grown from his head; about Demeter and her daughter, Persephone; and about the role Hades played. This was Henry, as my mother had mentioned, and it was strange to balance mythology with the knowledge that to these people, this was history. That apparently Henry had really done all these things. But the more I learned, the easier it became to accept it, and once Irene was sure I knew as much as I could about the members of the council, we moved on to other myths. But the Olympians were always present in those stories, too, and it did nothing to help calm my nerves.

In the afternoons, I was allowed to do whatever I wanted. Sometimes I stayed inside and read or spent time with Ava, and sometimes I went outside and explored the grounds. Past the edge of the elaborate garden was a forest that grew wild, and it extended through the other end of the property, hiding the river I knew was back there. I stayed within eyesight of the manor, not wanting to get anywhere near the water. I'd had enough excitement there to hold me for a very long time.

At the end of October, I ran across Phillip, head of the stables. He was a brusque man who didn't speak very often, and his hair was wild, making him look intimidating, but he seemed passionate about his horses.

"Horses have as much personality in them as people," he said gruffly as he introduced me to the fifteen horses in the stables. "If you don't connect with any of them, don't try to force it. S'like forcing a friendship—awkward and useless, and it'll make both of you miserable. Long as you remember that, you should be all right."

His stallions were powerful and fast, and with my luck I'd have fallen and broken something, so even though I liked spending time grooming them, I never asked to ride them. At first Phillip refused to let me anywhere near them with a brush, but I didn't take it too personally. He didn't let anyone near them; even allowing me inside the stables to see them was more than Ava got. On my third attempt, however, he grudgingly gave me permission to help groom them, as long as he was supervising. I had a sneaking suspicion Henry had something to do with his change of heart, but I didn't ask. For the rest of the autumn, it was how I spent my afternoons, and though the weather grew colder, it remained warm in the stables.

As the weeks passed, I grew more and more comfortable in my new home. The rest of the staff stopped staring as I went by, and slowly we all got used to one another. It was almost peaceful, with my days spent with Irene, my afternoons with Phillip and Ava, and my evenings with Henry. And my nights— I lived for my nights, when I told my mother everything that was happening, and she was there to listen. Past the hedges, she was dying, but inside my dreams, she was still very much alive, and I wanted to keep her that way as long as possible. I knew I wouldn't be able to escape the dark reality waiting for me once this was over, but for now, I could pretend that living in Eden meant remaining untouched by the real world.

It was mid-November when Irene announced that my first test would be given the following Monday. By the time I left the room, I was nearly sick with anxiety, and it must've shown.

"Kate?" said Calliope in a concerned voice as I shut the door behind me.

"There's a test," I said shakily. "On Monday."

She seemed less than concerned. "Have you never taken a test before?"

I shook my head. She didn't understand. *"Test,"* I repeated. "The kind where my whole future's on the line. If I fail…"

Calliope's eyes widened. "Oh. That sort of test."

"Yeah." I started walking in the direction of my bedroom, not interested in lunch. My appetite had vanished.

"Uh, Kate? Dining room's this way. They made fried chicken for you."

I could hear her trotting to keep up with me, but I didn't slow down. "I need to study." If I failed, everything I'd done so far would be pointless. My mother would die, Henry would lose his place as ruler of whatever it was that he did, and Ava's death would have been for nothing. I wasn't about to let that happen.

I spent the next two days with my nose buried so deeply in Greek mythology—or "history," as everyone seemed to call it, and Irene made sure I knew it when a story really was just a myth—that even Henry left me alone at night. Instead of going to the dining room, my meals were brought to me, but I ate so quickly that it was tasteless. I slept for exactly eight hours and not a minute more, but even while I was sleeping my mother quizzed me on the material I studied. I memorized the twelve labors of Hercules, the names of the nine Muses, and the plagues released when Pandora opened her box, but there were still hundreds of other stories. King Midas, whose touch turned everything, including his daughter, into gold. Prometheus, who stole fire from the gods, gave it to the humans, and was punished for it. Icarus, who flew to escape his prison, only to fly so high the wax that held his wings together melted. Hera's jealousy, Aphrodite's beauty, Ares's rage—it was never-ending, and I became so immersed in it that it all started to blend together, but I had to pass.

"You're hurting yourself."

I jumped when I heard Henry's voice behind me. It was Sunday evening, less than twelve hours before I was due to take the exam, and I still had a few tricky chapters to review. If I didn't use every last minute I had—and skip breakfast the next morning—I wasn't going to make it.

"I'm fine," I mumbled, sparing him only a glance before looking back at the massive book Irene had given me. I was trying to read about the Minotaur, but the words swam in front of me, and I had to squint to focus. My head was pounding and I felt sick to my stomach, but I had to do this.

"If I didn't know any better, I would mistake you for one of the dead," said Henry, his voice in my ear. I shut my eyes, not daring to move, not when he was so close. I could feel the heat radiating off his body, much warmer than the cool air of my room, and the desire to close the distance between us overwhelmed me. I shivered. Usually, when I wasn't so tired, I was better at ignoring it. I was here for my mother, not for Henry.

Instead of Henry touching me, I heard pages rustle. When I looked, the book was closed and pushed to the side, and Henry sat across from me.

"If you do not know it by now, you will not learn it in time for your test." His voice was gentle. "You need to sleep."

"I can't," I said miserably. "I have to pass."

"You will pass, I promise."

I slumped in my seat. "What, can you predict the future now, too? You can't promise me that. For all you know, I'll fail so spectacularly that they'll come halfway through the test and take me away. You might never see me again."

He chuckled, and I huffed indignantly. "I have never seen anyone study so hard for a test as you have done this weekend. If you do not pass, then there is no hope for the rest of us."

Before I could point out exactly how bad my luck was, the door to my room burst open. Ava skipped inside, followed closely by Calliope and a man I didn't recognize.

"Kate!" she said, bouncing over to me. I gave Henry an apologetic look, but he didn't seem to mind. Instead he was watching the man, who was dressed in a black uniform and stared at the floor, as if he wanted to be anywhere but here.

"Ava, I'm supposed to be studying," I said, but this didn't deter her at all.

"C'mon, you've been studying all weekend. You have to come out to play sometime." She stuck out her lower lip in a pout. "Everyone's in the garden having fun. There's music and swimming and all sorts of stuff. I still need to teach you how, you know."

The prospect of being forced to swim was enough to put me off the whole idea, and I wasn't even sure I'd be able to make it down there anyhow, let alone enjoy myself. The fact that it was a party pretty much guaranteed I wouldn't. "I'm really tired," I said, glancing between Ava and Calliope, who was lingering at the door and eyeing Henry.

"So what? You can sleep later," said Ava. "You're smart, you'll pass. Besides, you have to meet Theo—"

"You two have not yet met?" Henry sounded surprised. He stood, beckoning for the man in the background to come forward. Theo moved crisply, and he had a look about him that made it clear he took himself very seriously. "Kate, this is Theo, my Master of the Guard. It is his job to keep an eye on everything that happens within the manor. Theo, this is Kate Winters."

"A pleasure," said Theo, dipping his head in a bow. I flashed him a tired smile and stuck out my hand. He shook it gingerly, as if he were afraid I'd break. His palm was smoother than mine.

"Nice to meet you, too," I said. "Ava talks about you a lot."

"I do not," protested Ava. She looked at Theo and frowned. "I don't."

"She does," I said, and Theo grinned. There was no resemblance between him and Ella at all, as far as I could see.

"C'mon, let's go," said Ava in a huff, tugging on his arm.

Sensing I'd wounded her pride, when she glanced back at me on her way out, I gave her an apologetic shrug. "I'll come to the next one, promise."

"Whatever," she said, pulling Theo away. He managed a quick bow in Henry's direction before exiting, leaving me alone with Henry and Calliope, who still lingered by the door.

"I guess I'll see you tomorrow then," she said, her cheeks bright red.

"Tomorrow," I said, forcing a smile. I wasn't fooling anyone. Even I could hear the nervousness in my voice.

Once Calliope was gone and the door closed, Henry stood and crossed the room to the large bay window. As he stared out into the inky night, he beckoned for me to join him.

"Henry, I can't," I said with a sigh. "I've got to study."

"I will ask Irene not to quiz you on the last hundred pages," said Henry. "Now come and sit with me. Please."

"I don't think she'll agree to that," I mumbled, but I did as he asked. My feet dragged against the carpet and my head felt too heavy for my body, but somehow I got to the other side of the room without collapsing.

Once I was there, he wrapped his arm securely around me, and another pleasant shiver ran down my spine. It was the most physical contact I'd had with him since arriving, and it was easy enough to lean against him, letting him support my weight.

"Look up," he said, his arm tightening around my shoulders as I rested against him. I turned my head toward the ceiling, but in the candlelight, it was too dim for me to see. He chuckled. "No, the sky. Look at the stars."

My face flushed with embarrassment, and I focused on the black sky through the window, just able to make out the pinpricks of light. "They're pretty."

"They are," he said. "Did you know they move?"

"Stars? Sure." Was this part of a lesson, too? "You see different stars during different times of the year."

He eased us both down onto the bench, so close that I was practically sitting on top of him, but being near him was much nicer than I wanted to admit. I wasn't willing to give it up yet.

"Not through the seasons," he said. "Through the millennia. See that star there?"

He pointed upward, and I could barely see the direction he was pointing in, let alone tell which one he was talking about. "Yeah."

If he knew I was lying, he indulged me anyway. "When I met Persephone, that star wasn't part of that constellation."

"Really?" My oversaturated mind barely processed this information, let alone what it implied. "I didn't think they did that."

"Everything changes with time," said Henry, his breath warm against my ear. "One must simply be patient."

Yes, I thought, everything changed with time. That was the problem, wasn't it?

But whatever Henry was trying to do to take my mind off

the test worked. That night, instead of worrying about nymphs and heroes, my mother and I wandered through Central Park, visiting the zoo and riding the carousel round and round until we were both dizzy from laughter. I slept better than I had in days, and when I woke up, I was smiling.

The next morning I was too nervous to eat, but Calliope made me swallow a piece of toast covered in strawberry jam anyhow. Even that threatened to come up as I walked to the classroom, and it was through sheer willpower alone that I managed to keep it down.

I could do this. Henry was depending on me, and he would never let them purposely make me fail without giving me a fair shot. I'd studied, and this wasn't rocket science. It was mythology. How hard could it be?

"Ready?" said Irene once I was seated.

"No," I said flatly. I'd never be ready for this. Instead of showing me the tiniest bit of sympathy, she laughed and set the test down in front of me. A knot of horror caught in my throat when I flipped to the final question. Twenty pages.

"Two hundred questions," she said, as if reading my mind. "You can only miss twenty."

"How long do I have?" I choked.

"As long as you need."

Her kind smile wasn't the least bit reassuring. Summoning every last ounce of determination I had, I picked up my pencil and began.

Three hours later, I sat anxiously in the corner as Irene went through my exam. I'd gone through every question in my mind over and over again, constantly second-guessing my answers.

What if I'd mixed up Athena and Artemis? Hera and Hestia? What if I'd studied too much and accidentally mixed up places and stories and the intricate timelines?

What if I'd failed?

Irene set down her pen, her face passive as she crossed the room and silently handed me the test. My hands shook so badly that I was afraid I'd drop it, and nothing in her expression gave away my score. I forced myself to look down. For a long moment, my eyes wouldn't focus on the number scrawled on top.

173.

"I'm sorry," she said, but I didn't hear her. Instead I stumbled toward the door and out of the room, my vision too blurry for me to see where I was going. Flying past Calliope and Ella, I barely noticed them, instead dashing through the first door I saw and bursting into the garden. Ignoring the voices calling my name, I kicked off my shoes and ran toward the forest, the biting wind numbing my skin.

I'd failed.

CHAPTER 11
FAILURE

I couldn't breathe.

My lungs burned and my body ached with the effort of running. I was in the middle of the forest now, though still within the confines of Henry's property. The hedge walls were nowhere in sight, but those weren't what I was looking for. I wanted to find the river.

Seven points below what I'd needed—seven questions that were the difference between success and failure, staying and leaving, life and death for my mother. Life and death for Henry. It didn't matter how comfortable I was here or whether or not I liked being around him. If he'd just wanted someone to spend time with, he could've chosen anyone, but he'd chosen me—he depended on me—and now I'd failed him. The only reason I was here was to pass those tests, and I couldn't even manage that much.

I don't know how long it took me, sprinting through the woods. My feet were bleeding and bruised, and more than once I stumbled, hurting my ankles and elbows and knees, but still I pushed on.

I'd failed. It was over, and I wouldn't have another shot.

I needed to see my mother before she died. I needed to tell her goodbye, even if she couldn't hear me in that body anymore. It would have to do though—I'd broken my side of the bargain, and therefore Henry had no reason to uphold his. There was no guarantee I would see her if I fell asleep, and I needed to say goodbye before it was too late.

Finally I found it, the river where this whole mess had started. Limping on a twisted ankle, I followed it upstream until the opening in the hedge appeared. It seemed smaller than I remembered, and I had no idea how I was going to get to the other side, but I had to do this. I would apologize to Henry later.

Wiping my dirty, tear-stained cheeks with the back of my hand, I set my bare foot in the water and gasped. It was freezing. The current was strong, and I knew if I slipped, I wouldn't be able to swim my way to safety. Not this time. Still, I had to try. One foot in front of the other, that's all it took.

"Kate."

I nearly pitched forward at the sound of Henry's voice. I was a few feet away from shore, balancing precariously on the same slippery rocks that had killed Ava, and I barely managed to catch myself. "Leave me alone." I didn't sound nearly as vicious as I'd intended.

"I'm afraid I can't do that."

"I failed." I didn't dare risk turning to look at him.

"Yes, Irene told me. That still does not explain why you're risking life and limb to get through a hole in the hedge. If you want to leave, the front gate is much more convenient."

My feet were numb, making me even clumsier than before. "I need to see my mother."

Without warning, Henry's arm wrapped around my waist, pulling me against him. Before I could protest, my feet touched land.

"Let me *go!*"

He held on long enough for me to regain my balance. I pulled away from him, trembling, though whether it was from the cold or from how furious I was, I didn't know. "If you leave," he said patiently, "your mother will die. I did not think you wanted that."

I opened and shut my mouth. "But—but I failed."

He gave me a curious look. "I am not so strict that I punish failure with death."

"But our deal—you said you'd keep my mother alive while I was still here. I can't stay here anymore, not when I failed the test."

Henry was still, and then his expression softened, as if he finally understood. "Kate…is that all this is about?"

"You said yourself I couldn't fail any of the tests," I said uncertainly.

"You cannot fail any of the seven tests the council will place before you. The exam Irene gave you was not one of those." He smiled hollowly. "So far, you are doing beautifully."

My mouth went dry. "So far?"

"Yes." He seemed amused, and I wasn't sure whether to be relieved or to wipe the smug look off his face. "So far, you have faced three. Only one is complete, but you were impeccable."

How was it possible that they were testing me without my knowledge? When I opened my mouth to ask, he neatly cut me off.

"You must be freezing—here." He draped his coat over my

shoulders, and I clung to it, soaking in its warmth. "Let's go back, shall we?"

I nodded, my hysterics coming to an end. Henry wrapped his arms around me delicately, as if he were afraid I'd break. "Close your eyes," he murmured, and I did.

This time, when I opened them, I was only marginally surprised to find myself in my bedroom. Henry stood beside me. "I see you are adjusting to the way I travel."

"Uh-huh." I swallowed. It was still disorienting. "I should… um…" I gestured down at my dress. It was torn and caked with mud.

"It seems that one is ruined. Perhaps we ought to find a replacement."

"I have tons, really." I glanced at my wardrobe, blanching. "Ella probably won't even notice."

"Do not argue," said Henry. "Change and ice your ankle for a few minutes. I will return shortly to fetch you."

Sighing inwardly, I decided it was useless. Just like Ella, he seemed to be determined to keep me up to my ears in itchy dresses. I couldn't wait for summer to arrive, if for no other reason than to finally be able to wear jeans again.

Before walking out the door, Henry turned. "Kate?"

I scowled down at the maze of buttons that lined the ruined dress, my fingers still shaking as I tried to undo them. "Yeah?"

"I only scored 164."

In the end, I'd needed Ella's help to unbutton the monstrosity she'd forced me into that morning. While she seemed sad to see it go, I couldn't have been happier—until I saw what she intended to replace it with.

Limping down the corridor of an unfamiliar wing, I leaned on Henry for support and tried my best not to scratch at the rough fabric. It was completely unfair. Henry got to wear pants—even Ava had the option, if she wanted—but with Ella in charge of my wardrobe, I was stuck in costumes from the dark ages. She may have thought they were beautiful, but I would have preferred a toga to those instruments of torture. No amount of wearing them was going to make me like them. Ever. And Ella knew that. It was why she did it, I was sure of it.

While I wondered whether or not it'd be a mark against me if I ran around in my underwear, Henry opened the door to a room I'd never been inside before. At first I couldn't make much out from behind him, but when he stepped aside, my jaw dropped, and the cloud of misery that had plagued me since seeing my score dissipated.

The suite was stuffed with clothes hanging off of racks, arranged by size and color and God only knew what else. They spanned so many eras that it looked like a costume shop, and there were dresses and shoes and shawls and—

My knees went weak.

Sweaters and *jeans*.

"Ella mentioned you did not feel comfortable in the outfits she chose for you," said Henry. "As a reward for failing a test with a higher score than my own, I believe a new wardrobe is in order."

I stared at him and then at Ella, who gave me a rare smile. Were they for real?

"Oh, my God!"

I wasn't the one to say it. Instead the high-pitched squeal came from behind me, and when I whirled around, Ava stood there, her mouth hanging open. Calliope lingered nearby, looking as excited as I felt.

"Are these all for *you?*" blurted Ava, moving past Ella to stand with me.

"I think so," I said with a grin. "Want some?"

She stared at me like I'd grown another head. "Do I *want* some?"

I laughed and looked at Henry. "Can she?"

"Of course."

That was all she needed to hear. In an instant she'd disappeared, sorting through the archaic dresses I had no intention of touching. Instead of joining her, I turned to Calliope and Ella. "You two can have whatever you want, too," I said, glancing at Henry. "If that's all right with you, I mean."

He nodded. Just like Ava, Ella and Calliope rushed into the room, leaving me behind with Henry. He gestured toward my ankle. "Are you able to make it through the room without assistance?"

"I'll be fine," I said, eyeing the piles of sweaters. Even from a distance, they beckoned. As much as I liked being near Henry, I was still embarrassed about my breakdown, and I didn't want him to think I was incapable of getting through the day without him, even though he did seem to know exactly how to make things better.

I'd limped halfway across the room before I realized he was trailing a few feet behind me. Glancing over my shoulder, I frowned. "Henry, really, I'm fine. It doesn't even hurt."

"I have no intention of helping you walk," he said in an innocent voice I wasn't buying. "I was merely going to offer to carry your things."

"If you say so." I raised an eyebrow, but while I didn't want him to know it, I was grateful he was there.

That night, long after Henry left, I was on the edge of sleep when a soft knock on my door pulled me away. Groaning, I rubbed my eyes and rolled out of bed, hobbling to the door. I'd spent all evening looking forward to telling my mother that I'd passed a test and hadn't disappointed Henry yet, so whoever was on the other side of the door had to have a damn good reason for interrupting.

"What?" I said as I cracked open the door, squinting against the light from the hallway.

It was Ava. "Are you still awake?" she whispered, and I glared at her.

"No, I'm sleepwalking."

"Oh." She eyed me as if she were trying to figure out if I was telling the truth or not. "As long as you're up, c'mon—I want to show you something."

She reached out to take my hand, and I stood my ground. "The only place I want to go is back to bed."

"Too bad." Ava gripped my hand so hard that trying to pull away would've likely resulted in broken fingers, and I was having enough trouble with my ankle already. "I'll get you back to bed before the sun comes up, I promise."

Not the most comforting reassurance, but she wasn't giving me much of a choice. Finally, huffing loudly so she couldn't miss it, I followed her, the carpet rough against my bare feet.

"Where are we going?" I said, but Ava shushed me as we turned the corner. There were guards stationed up and down the hallways leading to my rooms, and at least three of them had seen us so far, so I had no idea why she felt the need to sneak around.

The dull ache in my ankle turned into sharp pain, and I struggled to keep up with her, but she didn't slow down. At last, when we reached a dark corridor, she stopped and pointed to a door ten feet away.

It was different from the others in the manor, made of dark wood with ornate carvings that created a scene I couldn't quite make out. Light spilled out from the other side, and Ava tiptoed toward it, gesturing for me to follow.

This time I didn't ask any questions. I moved with her clumsily, keeping a hand against the wall to keep myself from tripping and announcing our presence to whoever was behind the door. The closer we got, the clearer the scene on the door became, and soon I realized what it was. On the top half of the door was a beautiful meadow, with tiny flowers carved into the wood and trees on either side. Somehow the artist had managed to make it look sunny, and it reminded me so strongly of Central Park that a lump caught in my throat.

But underneath it, the scene changed. A layer of earth separated the meadow from a dark river that flowed underneath, and beside it there was a delicate garden. Instead of growing from the soil, it grew from jagged stone. The trees weren't trees; they were made of something solid, and even though it was only a piece of art, I could tell they weren't meant to be alive. And in the center of the picture stood pillars of jewels forming an arch above a single flower, tiny and weak in its surroundings.

As spellbound as I was by the beautiful carvings, I overheard voices leaking through the crack in the door. At first I couldn't make them out properly, but Ava nudged me closer, and gathering my courage, I peeked into the room.

Henry stood with his back to me, his shoulders hunched as he stared at something I couldn't see. He turned enough so I could make out his profile, and something inside of me ached when I saw that his eyes were red.

But he wasn't the one talking. The second voice was higher than his, but still masculine and familiar, and whoever it was spoke in hushed words laced with urgency and frustration.

"You can't keep her here." I couldn't see who was talking, but I was certain I recognized his voice. "That was part of the deal. You can't force her to stay if she doesn't want to."

I inched closer. Underneath me, the floorboard creaked, and I froze. From my vantage point I could see Henry also still, and my heart beat so loudly I was sure he must've been able to hear it. But after a few tense seconds, he spoke, and I exhaled.

"She did not want to leave," he said tiredly. "She thought our deal had finished because she failed the exam."

"You still stopped her," said the second voice. It was achingly familiar, but he spoke so low it was hard to place. "She told you twice to leave her alone, and you ignored her."

"Because she did not understand." Henry glared over his shoulder to a spot behind the door where the other stood.

"It doesn't matter." He spoke viciously, and I glanced at Ava, but she lingered by the corner now. "You prevented her from leaving."

"I can argue semantics with you all night, but the fact remains that she has not left the property," said Henry. "You have no right to ask the other members of the council to terminate the deal."

"I do, and I will." A shadow passed over me, and I shrank back. "I won't let you force her to stay like you did Persephone. She isn't your prisoner, and you aren't her keeper. You can't manipulate her into this situation and then act surprised when she hates you so much she wants to leave."

Malice dripped from his words, and his voice was filled with venom. Across the room Henry tensed, but he said nothing. The urge to speak up for him was overwhelming, and I badly wanted to tell whoever it was that he was an idiot and I stayed because I wanted to help Henry, not because he was forcing me, but the words died on my lips. I'd gone for months without answers. I couldn't give up any chance I might have at finally getting them.

"Let her go," said the voice, quieter this time. "Persephone didn't love you, and you can't replace her no matter how hard you look. Even if you could, Kate isn't that person."

"She could be." Henry's words came out choked. "My sister thinks she is."

"My aunt is too blinded by guilt and determination to see the situation clearly. Please, Henry." The floor creaked again as he stepped toward Henry. I could make out his arm now, and he wore a black jacket that looked far too thin for November. "Let her go before she dies, too. We both know it's only a matter of time, and if you care about her at all, you'll let her go before she becomes another victim." He paused, and I held my breath. "Eleven girls are already dead because of you. Don't turn Kate into the twelfth because of your selfishness."

The sound of breaking glass exploded inches away from me. I gasped and stumbled backward, and my ankle twisted underneath me again. I cried out, falling to the ground. The door opened, and the blood drained from my face when I saw who was on the other side.

James.

CHAPTER 12
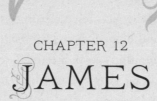JAMES

"You're in on this, too?" My voice was hoarse, and I stared at James in disbelief. He looked exactly like I remembered him from school—ears sticking out, his blond hair a mess, and his massive headphones wrapped around his neck.

"Kate—" he started, but Henry appeared in the door, and he pushed James aside. When Henry offered me his hand, I took it, glaring at James.

"What's going on?" The words came out strangled, and I could hardly see straight, but I wasn't going to give either of them a way out. "Tell me. First Sofia, then Irene, now you—"

"Perhaps it would be best if we continued this conversation inside," said Henry with a grimace. I gritted my teeth and nodded, leaning on him as he helped me into the room.

Inside, I realized it was a bedroom. While it wasn't dusty, it had the feeling of disuse, and as Henry helped me maneuver around the broken glass on the hardwood floor, I saw a mangled frame lying on the ground, its picture bent and torn. Smiling up at me was the photograph of a girl who couldn't have been much older than me, with freckled cheeks and strawberry-blond hair. Next to her stood Henry, and he looked much happier than I'd ever seen him, all of the tension from his body gone.

"Who's that?" I said, but I had a sinking feeling I already knew.

Henry glanced at the picture, and pain flashed across his face. He waited until he'd helped me to the bed before answering, and even then he wouldn't look me in the eye. "Persephone," he said in a fragile voice that threatened to break. "A very long time ago."

"Not too long ago," I said, eyeing the image. "Not if you had cameras around."

"It is not a photograph," he said, bending down to retrieve it. "It is a reflection. Look."

His hands shook as he handed me the picture, and as I examined it, I noticed it had a depth to it that photographs didn't. It seemed to shimmer, as if it was a pool of water, and Persephone and Henry were moving. Not so much that it looked like a home movie, but she blinked, and I could see his arms tighten around her.

"She's beautiful," I said softly. Part of me was jealous, knowing I could never live up to her memory, but I was so consumed by sadness for what Henry must have gone through that I pushed it aside. "I'm sorry."

He waved dismissively, as if it were no big deal, but when I handed the picture back to him, he took it gently and passed his hand over the surface. It smoothed out as if it had never been damaged. "As I said, it was a long time ago."

A cough tore my attention away from him, and I looked up to see James lingering near the doorway. My eyes narrowed. "What?"

"You asked why I was here." He crossed his arms and leaned

against the door, shutting it firmly. Behind it I heard a squeak. Ava was still out there, but this wasn't something I wanted her to overhear.

"And you still haven't told me." I winced as Henry gently touched my ankle.

"He is my successor," said Henry, and I looked at him sharply. "He will take over my duties if I fade."

A wave of horror washed over me, and I stared at James, disgusted. "Is that why you tried to stop me from coming here? You knew I was his last chance, and you thought if you stopped me, you'd have a clear shot at the winner's circle?"

"There is no winner's circle," said James. "It isn't some competition, all right? This is hard on all of us. We've been trying for a century to find someone to take Persephone's place, and if we don't—"

"If you don't, then you get to take Henry's place," I snapped. "Yet here you are, trying to ruin it for him."

"Because I thought you wanted out," he said, his jaw clenched so tightly that I could see a muscle twitch. "You *said*—"

"Henry was right. I didn't understand, and I'm not about to walk away and kill him if I can help it."

James shifted awkwardly from one foot to the other. "I never thought you would. But the terms of the agreement are final, and if you want to leave, there isn't anything we can do to stop you. If Henry holds you here against your will, then we have every right to step in."

"Wait," I said as what he was saying slowly dawned on me. "What do you mean, *we?*"

Next to me, Henry frowned, his brow furrowing so deeply that for a moment he didn't look like himself. "James," he said, a warning.

James straightened, his arms falling to his side. "I don't care if she knows."

"The others will," he said, but he made no move to stop him.

James took a hesitant step toward me, as if he wanted to reach out to me, but I gave him a cold look, and he fell short. "I'm a member of the council."

My heart nearly stopped. "You're on the council?" I sputtered. "You can't be. You're—*you*."

"Astute observation," he said, more to himself than to me. "Listen, Kate—I don't care if you believe me or not. Well, no, I'd like it if you did, but I don't expect you to. You can hate me all you want for trying to take you away from Henry, but I'm only trying to do what's best for you."

"And you think what's best for me is to live the rest of my life knowing I'm the reason Henry dies?" Hot tears threatened to spill out of my eyes, but I blinked them back, forcing my voice to stay steady. "Not to mention what's going to happen to my mother."

"You wouldn't remember any of this if you decide to leave," said James. "That's also part of the deal."

"*Enough* about this stupid deal." My voice broke, and my cheeks turned hot. "This is my decision, not yours. You can't go behind my back and end this just because you think you know what's best for me. I get to say when this is over, not you."

I looked back and forth between Henry and James to make sure they were both paying attention, but Henry was concentrating on my ankle, his head bent and his eyes closed. A thick warmth spread out from my knee to my toes, and Henry wrapped his hands around the joint, gently moving it in a circle.

"Does this hurt?" he said, and I shook my head. He set my leg down, and I gingerly pulled it toward me, wiggling my toes. It didn't ache anymore.

"How did you—" I started, my anger momentarily forgotten, and Henry shrugged.

"You're not supposed to heal her," said James from across the room. Henry righted himself, and even from the side, I could see the deadened look in his eyes.

"It seems we are breaking all sorts of rules tonight." He stood. "If you will excuse me."

Before I could protest, he was gone, leaving me and James alone in the room together. I stood as well, testing my ankle. It was solid.

"It wasn't my choice, you know," said James quietly. "Taking over for him if you fail. I'm the only member of the council who knows the Underworld as well as he does."

"But you still wanted it," I said.

He looked away, out a dark bay window and on to the grounds. The moon was nearly full, and I could see the tops of the bare trees rustling in the November wind. "We last as long as what we represent does. Minor gods fade all the time when they're forgotten, but the council isn't minor. As long as humanity exists, there will always be love and war. There will always be music and art, literature and peace, and marriage and children and travelers. But humanity won't last forever, and after it fades, so will we. Only death will remain."

"And if you control the Underworld, you get to survive even after everything else is gone?" I said it as a question, but I already knew the answer, and a knot formed in my throat. "That's what this is about?"

"No. This right here, this is about making sure you survive. I don't want you to die, Kate—please. None of us do, and Henry gave up a long time ago. Maybe he's trying for you, but not because he wants to continue—he just doesn't want you to be killed, that's all."

I paused. "Is there a good chance of that?"

James looked at me, and I could see the naked fear in his eyes. "No one's survived past Christmas. Please. Henry doesn't want this. He's always going to be in love with Persephone, not you. Look around you—look at where you are. This was her bedroom."

There was nothing unusual about the room, only the picture that Henry had thrown at James. But the more I studied my surroundings, the more I really saw it. It was like a child's room that a parent didn't dare touch after tragedy struck. There were old-fashioned hairpins on the vanity in the corner, and the curtains were drawn to let the sunlight in. There was even a dress lying out in the corner, waiting to be worn. It was like it was frozen in time, lying untouched for centuries until Persephone returned.

"That reflection—" James gestured to the image of Persephone and Henry together, looking so happy. "It isn't real. It's a wish, a dream, a hope, not a memory. He loved her so much that he'd have torn the world apart if she asked him to, but she could barely stand to look at him. Ever since she died, he's been begging the council to release him and let him fade. Do you really think you can compete with that?"

"It isn't a competition," I said roughly, echoing his words from before. But even as I said it, I knew it was. If I couldn't make Henry care about me, he would have no reason to continue, and in his mind, I would always be pitted against Persephone. But that was no reason to stop fighting for him. He deserved a chance at happiness just like I did, and I wasn't ready to tell yet another person in my life goodbye.

James's expression softened. "He'll never love you, Kate, not the way you deserve to be loved. He gave up a long time ago, and all you're doing is prolonging the pain for him. It would be kinder to leave him be."

I stepped closer to James, torn between anger and a pressing need to touch him, to make sure my James was still there underneath the cunning god he'd suddenly become, saying all the words he thought I needed to hear to convince me to leave. To steal eternity from Henry and hand it to him. "And you think I should?" I said. I was barely a foot away from him now. "You think I should give up and leave him, just like Persephone left?"

"Persephone had her reasons," said James. "He took her away from everything she ever loved, and he forced her to stay with him when she didn't want to. You'd have done the same."

I was silent. The difference between me and Persephone was that she'd had something left to lose. James reached forward timidly, and I let him wrap his arms around me, burying his face in my hair. I heard him inhale deeply, and I wondered if he could smell the lavender of my shampoo, or if it was my fear and guilt and determination he sensed instead. After a tense moment, I returned the embrace.

"Please don't do this to yourself, Kate," he mumbled into my ear. I closed my eyes, and for a moment I pretended that he was just James again. Not Henry's rival, not the god poised to gain everything from my failure, but my James.

"Will you do something for me?" I said against his chest.

"Of course," he said. "Anything."

I let go of him. "Get the hell away from me, and don't come back until spring."

His eyes widened. "Kate—"

"I mean it." My voice shook, but I stood firm. "Get out."

Stunned, he stepped back and shoved his hands in his pockets. For a moment he looked like he was going to say something, but then he turned away and walked out, leaving me alone in Persephone's bedroom.

I'd spent four years refusing to let my mother give up, and I wasn't about to let Henry do the same. If he wouldn't keep going for himself, then I'd come up with a way to make him keep going for me instead.

Hours later, long after the moon had risen so high in the sky that I could no longer see it from my window, I lay in bed and stared up at the ceiling. I wanted to sleep and tell my mother everything I'd learned, to ask her what I could possibly do to convince Henry to try, but I knew there was nothing she could tell me that I didn't already know. It wasn't up to her to fix this; I was the one who'd made the deal, and I wasn't going to give up so easily.

In the small hours of the morning, I heard a soft knock on my door, and I buried my face in my pillow. Ava was gone when I'd crept out of Persephone's room, and I wasn't in the mood to tell her what had happened. I needed a day or two to figure things out for myself before the entire manor knew, too, if they didn't already.

Even though I stayed silent, I heard the door open and shut, and soft footsteps fell against the carpet. I remained as still as possible, hoping whoever it was would go away.

"Kate?"

I didn't have to turn around to recognize Henry's voice. Something thrummed inside of me, a familiar note that sent a wave of comfort through my tense body, but I still didn't face him.

He moved so quietly that I didn't know he was close until I felt the mattress give way. It was a long moment before he said anything. "I'm sorry." His voice was hollow. "You shouldn't have seen that."

"I'm glad I did."

"And why is that?"

I refused to answer. How was I supposed to tell him that I didn't want him to give up? I was risking everything for him— and I would gladly do it, but I wouldn't let it be for nothing. I couldn't make him fight, but I would find a reason for him not to fade.

I heard Henry sigh. Forcing silence was only hurting things, so finally I said into my pillow, "Why didn't you tell me about James earlier?"

"Because I thought you might react this way, and I wanted to keep you from this pain for as long as possible."

"Knowing it's him doesn't hurt," I said. "What hurts is that no one trusts me with anything around here."

I felt his hand on my arm, but it only lasted for a moment. "Then I will make the effort to trust you with more. I apologize."

His apology was hollow to my ears whether he really meant it or not. "If I pass, things are going to change, right? Life won't be one big game of keep away from Kate anymore? Because if the answer to that is anything but a resounding yes, I don't think I can do this."

He brushed the back of his hand against my cheek, but it,

too, only lasted a second. "Yes," he said. "A resounding yes. It is not that I don't trust you now. It is only that there are some things you simply cannot know yet. As frustrating as it may seem, I promise you that it is for your own good."

For my own good. Apparently that was their go-to excuse when they did something I didn't like. "And Persephone," I added, glad I was turned away and couldn't see the pain I knew was in his eyes when I said her name. "I'm not her, Henry. I can't be her, and I can't spend eternity trying to live up to your memory of her. I'm nobody to you right now, I get that—"

"You are not nobody," he said with surprising strength. "Do not think that."

"Let me finish." I hugged my pillow tighter. "I get that I'm not her and won't ever be. I don't want to be her anyway, not with how badly she's hurt you. But if this works—if I pass, I need to know that when you look at me, you're going to see *me,* not just her replacement. That there's more in this future for me than standing in the shadows while you wallow the rest of your existence away. Because if James is right and I can walk away if I want to, and if you're doing this knowing full well that spending half of the rest of eternity with me is going to make you miserable no matter what I do, then tell me now and I'll spare us both."

The seconds ticked by, and Henry was silent. It was unfair that he was so willing to throw away forever when there were others out there—my mother included—who wanted to live, but couldn't. As I stared out the window resolutely, my anger built, but short of yelling at him before he had the chance to respond, I had no release.

"I brought you a present."

My head turned toward him a fraction of an inch before I could stop myself. "That isn't an answer."

"Yes, it is," he said, and I could hear his small smile in his voice. "I would not have brought you something like this if I did not want you to stay."

I frowned. "What kind of present is it?"

"If you roll over, you will see."

Before I had the chance, something nudged my shoulder. Something cold, wet and very much alive.

Flipping around, I sat up and stared at the black-and-white ball of fur sitting next to me on the bed. It looked up at me with liquid eyes, its tiny tail wagging. My heart melted, all of my anger and frustration temporarily forgotten.

"If I did not truly feel that you could change things, I would not have risked your life to begin with," said Henry. "I am sorry you feel you are nobody to me, Kate, because the very opposite is true. And I could never expect you to be Persephone," he added, that same hint of pain in his voice. "You are you, and as soon as I am able, I will tell you everything. I promise."

I stared at the puppy, too afraid to say anything and make him change his mind. Was he just like James, saying what he thought I wanted to hear? Or did he really mean it?

"You lost a friend today because of me, and I did not want you to be lonely," he said as he stroked the puppy, and its tail thumped against the mattress. "It is my understanding that one does not get a pet with someone if one does not expect—" He hesitated. "If one does not hope to spend quite a bit of time with that person in the future."

Expect. Hope. Which one had he really meant?

I wanted to tell him exactly where James could shove our so-called friendship, but it took me a moment to remember how to speak. I'd spent my entire childhood bothering my mother for a puppy, but she'd always put her foot down. After she'd gotten sick, I'd given up, unable to take care of both her and a dog at the same time.

How had Henry known that? Or had he simply guessed?

"Is it—a girl or a boy?"

"A boy." The corners of his lips twitched upward into a faint smile. "I do not wish for Cerberus to get any ideas."

I hesitated. "He's mine?"

"All yours. You can even take him with you in the spring, if you would like."

I scooped the little dog up, cradling him to my chest. Standing on my arm, he licked my chin, barely able to reach.

"Thank you," I said softly. "This is really nice of you."

"It is my pleasure," said Henry, standing. "I will leave you be and allow you the chance to get to know one another. He is quite friendly, I assure you, and very much alive. He is still learning etiquette, but he is an eager pupil."

The puppy jumped higher, managing to reach my cheek. I grinned, and as Henry placed his hand on the door, I said, "Henry?"

"Yes?"

I pressed my lips together, trying to come up with the right combination of words to make him want to stay. To make him want to try for more than just my sake. Nothing came, so instead, after a moment that seemed to stretch out far past the point of politeness, I said in a small voice, "Please don't give up."

When he finally responded, his voice was so low that I could barely hear him. "I will try."

"Please," I said again, this time urgently. "After everything that's happened—you can't. I know you miss her, but—"

Silence lingered between us. "But what?"

"Please just—give me a chance."

He looked away, and through the dim light I saw his shoulders hunch, as if he were trying to make himself as small as possible. "Of course," he said, opening the door. "Sleep well."

I nuzzled the top of my puppy's head. I didn't want him to leave. I wanted to play cards or talk or read—anything that didn't remind him of Persephone. After the night he'd had, he deserved that much. We both did.

"Stay," I blurted. "Please."

But when I looked up, he was gone.

CHAPTER 13

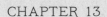CHRISTMAS

For the next several weeks, my time with Henry was almost unbearable. While we still spent our evenings together, it was no longer easy, and every conversation and accidental touch felt strained. He never looked me in the eye, and the closer we got to Christmas, the more he seemed to pull away. The more he pulled away, the more I wanted to tear my hair out and tell him in no uncertain terms that either he shaped up or I would walk. Problem was, it was an empty threat and he would know it. Worse, I was afraid he would take me up on it.

"I don't understand," I said, pacing up and down the sidewalk. "He acts like he wants nothing to do with me anymore."

My mother and I were near a playground in Central Park, and despite the deep snow that surrounded Eden Manor as the winter solstice arrived and the first half of my stay was over, it was midsummer here. In the distance I could hear children shouting, but I was too focused on Henry's behavior to enjoy myself.

"Why do you think that might be?" said my mother. She sat on a bench and watched me, looking wholly unconcerned.

"I don't *know*," I said, frustrated. "What if he really has given up? What am I supposed to do then?"

"Keep trying until you have no more chances left," said my mother. There was a hint of steel in her voice that made me wonder if she were really as passive about this as she seemed. "And even then, you keep going."

I shoved my hands into my pockets. It wasn't that easy and she knew it. "James said none of the other girls had survived past Christmas—do you think maybe that's why he's avoiding me? He thinks I'm going to drop dead at any moment?"

"Perhaps," she said. "Or perhaps he realized he does care about you, and he's afraid of losing you as well."

I snorted. "Fat chance of that. He won't even look at me."

She sighed. "You're the one spending time with him, Kate, not me. I can only go off of what you tell me, and if Henry really is as miserable as he sounds, then I doubt anyone else is going to be able to pull him out of it."

"And how do you suggest I do that?" I said, not meaning to snap, but it slipped out anyway. I immediately felt guilty, and I slouched toward her. She scooted over, making room for me on the bench, and I sat down next to her.

"Any way you can," she said, pushing a lock of hair out of my eyes. "If you want to do this for him, then it isn't going to be easy. It won't be easy passing the rest of the tests, but it won't be easy giving him a reason to continue, either."

I frowned, racking my mind for the umpteenth time in the past few weeks, trying to come up with something, but nothing came. My one flash of brilliance had gone into his Christmas present, and even that was a risk.

"You are being careful though, aren't you?" said my mother, concern etched into her features. "I don't want anything to happen to you, and if what he says is true and there is a danger out there—"

"I'm fine," I said. "Really. No one's tried to off me yet, I promise. And if I can't convince Henry it's worth sticking around, then they might as well kill me anyway."

"Don't talk like that. I don't care what happens in the next three months, but you will not give up, do you understand me?"

She spoke so fiercely that it startled me, and I straightened up on the bench. "I'm not going to give up," I said. "But if Henry won't even try, then he'll die, and you—" And my mother would die as well. I knew it was inevitable, but I wasn't ready to say goodbye yet. I still had three more months until the spring equinox, and I intended on soaking in every moment of our time together. I wasn't going to let Henry get in the way of that.

"No matter what happens to me or to Henry, you will keep going," said my mother, though in a gentler voice. "Neither one of us is worth giving up like that, and if you do, you'll be no better than Henry. But I know you are, all right?"

I nodded mutely. If I had my mother's strength and certainty, I was positive it wouldn't be so hard to convince Henry of the same. "Maybe you should talk to him. Bet he'd listen to you."

"He probably would." Something flickered in her eyes, something I didn't understand. "But that's your job, sweetie, and I know you can do it."

It was either that or let everyone around me die. "I hope you're right."

She gave me a noisy kiss on the cheek. "I'm always right."

Before either of us could say another word, the sky darkened, and I looked up, confused. When I turned to my mother to ask what was happening, she was gone, replaced by the last person I wanted to see.

James.

"What the hell are you doing here?" I jumped to my feet. "What'd you do with my mom?"

"It's all right," he said, standing with me. I hurried down the path, searching for my mother, but he easily kept up. "Kate— listen. Your mother's safe. I want to talk to you."

"So you hijacked the only time I get to spend with my mother?" I turned around, and he stopped dead in his tracks, inches away from me. "Just because you're some kind of god doesn't give you the right to do this. I told you to stay away from me."

"I know." He stuck his hands in his pockets, and the look on his face was so pitiful that I momentarily forgot he was the bad guy. "I just need a few minutes, and I promise everything will go back to normal. Please."

I sighed irritably. "Fine. You get five minutes."

"More than enough." He grinned, but when all I did was stare, his smile slowly faded. "I'm not the one trying to kill you."

I blinked, taken aback. That was the last thing I'd expected him to say. "You're the most logical choice," I said slowly. "Deny it all you want, but I'd be stupid to take you at your word without a shred of proof."

He tilted his head in a strange, almost archaic kind of nod. It was a jarring reminder of who and what he was. "I wouldn't ask you to. But if you'd like, you can ask Henry. I've never been involved in the testing process for obvious reasons. You're my friend, and I'd never hurt you."

"Is that why I've survived so long?" I said waspishly. "Because we're friends?"

His expression darkened. "I told you, I'm not the killer. You should know me well enough for that."

"Lately it doesn't seem like I know you at all," I snapped, and he at least had the decency to look sheepish.

"You've survived so long because everyone's gone to extraordinary measures to keep you safe," he said. "The guards, the escorts, the food tasters—you have no idea how closely you're being watched."

A shiver ran down my spine. "After a century, you people really have no idea who's doing this? I thought gods were supposed to be omniscient."

He laughed, but it was hollow. "Wouldn't that be nice? It'd solve a whole host of problems. But no, we're not. We've followed leads, changed out the staff, interrogated everyone involved, but nothing's come up. Henry's even gone down to the Underworld to interview the girls who were murdered, but they never saw it coming."

I frowned. As difficult as me being in danger was for Henry, I couldn't imagine how much it must've hurt him to talk to the girls who had died because of this. Whom he undoubtedly thought had died because of him.

"So what?" I said exasperatedly to mask my fear. "If you guys can't come up with something, there's no hope for me figuring it out, so why are you telling me this?"

"Because I want you to be safe," he said. "You don't have to trust me in order to at least listen to what I'm saying and do what you have to do to protect yourself. Henry's cut off every method the killer's used to attack before. All that means is they'll try something else. Henry knows it, we all know it, and you should as well."

"Great," I said, rolling my eyes. "So instead of poisoned food, I should be on the lookout for a swarm of killer bees? An anvil that's about to fall on my head? What?"

"Anything," he said. "Anything out of the ordinary. And if you ever suspect something might be up, get out of there, okay? I don't care how much they seem to like you. Someone in that place wants you dead, and if you want to have any chance of survival, you can't ever forget that."

I didn't respond. I'd adjusted to living in Eden Manor, and while it wasn't perfect, at least I wasn't miserable anymore. But the thought that the person who was trying to kill me might've been someone I knew—and knew well—shook my confidence more than I wanted to admit. For the first time, I really understood that it wasn't just my mother's life and Henry's life on the line. Mine was, too.

"Why are you telling me this?" I said quietly as thunder shook the air. "If I die, Henry will fade, and you'll get everything you want."

He stared at the ground. "Not everything."

Before I could contemplate whether he meant losing Henry or losing me, the sky opened up, and for the first time in my dreams, it started to pour.

"Promise me you'll stay safe," he said over the rain. "Promise me you won't do anything reckless."

I nodded. No matter how desperate I was to find some small piece of happiness in the remaining shreds of my life, I wasn't willing to die for it. For my mother, yes; but not myself.

"Thank you," he said, his shoulders sagging with relief. "I'll see you in the spring. And Kate?"

I looked at him, silent as the park began to fade.

"I am sorry," he said, and it was the last thing I heard before the darkness closed in around me.

Even though I was still furious with James, when I woke up gasping alone in my bed, I couldn't help but think that while I was fighting so hard to save my mother's life and Henry's, maybe all James was trying to do was fight to save mine.

Christmas was the one holiday my mother and I celebrated, and it was always festive. Back in New York, our tiny apartment could barely hold a tree, but we'd shoved one into the corner of the living room anyway and spent hours decorating it. A little piece of nature in a metal jungle, she would say as we stood back to admire our efforts after we were done.

The towering Christmas trees spread throughout Eden Manor made our apartment trees look like twigs. Almost overnight they seemed to crop up all over the manor, and for weeks the smell of sugar cookies lingered in the corridors. The staff was giddy with excitement, and there was a sense of joy in the air that I couldn't shake, even on my bad days. I'd expected them to celebrate the winter solstice instead, but Ella made it clear they would celebrate Christmas for me.

It didn't escape me that none of the other girls had survived past Christmas, and despite how angry I was with James, I made an effort to never be alone. But the closer Christmas came, the scarcer Henry became, and that made it difficult. During the autumn, he occasionally joined me around the manor, but now the only time I saw him was in the evenings. Even then, things were as bad as ever, and despite my mother's advice, for the life of me I couldn't figure out how to give him the purpose he needed. Survive past Christmas, I hoped, but there was no guarantee that would work. I didn't allow myself to consider the possibility that I might not make it.

But I did know I wanted him to have a happy Christmas. The entire household was supposed to have dinner together, and while that was a nice start, I wanted to show him the kind of Christmas my mother and I had together. Maybe if I invited him into a private part of my life, he would return the favor— or at the very least not scowl at me anymore. And, selfishly, I didn't want to spend Christmas alone.

On Christmas Eve day, a giant tree showed up in my room while I was eating breakfast, along with two large boxes of decorations. My lessons were canceled due to the holiday, so I dragged Ava into my room to help me before we both had to get ready for dinner. When Henry wasn't around, she was the only one I trusted enough to be alone with for any length of time. After all, she hadn't been there for the other girls, and I was reasonably sure she wasn't going to try to kill me for not accepting Henry's offer on the autumn equinox.

Come early afternoon, however, I was beginning to regret inviting her.

"If I'm late for my date with Xander tonight, I am personally blaming you," said Ava grumpily as she tugged at a tangled string of lights. Nearby, my puppy, now called Pogo, watched us both with interest.

"Don't pull so hard," I said, bounding over a pile of tinsel to save the lights from Ava's brutality. "They're delicate. And you won't be late—I thought you were dating Theo?"

"Not anymore," she said in a singsong voice. "I got back together with Xander, and he invited me to his room for our own private party instead of the banquet."

I didn't ask. "Here, help me with this." I offered her one end of the lights and deftly undid the knot. "Now go around to the back—don't step on the ornaments! Yes, just like that."

She held still as I arranged the lights, though I had to use a hook to decorate the highest branches. "What are you and Henry going to do tonight anyway?"

"My secret," I said, and when I walked around to see the look on her face, I rolled my eyes. "Not *that*. What are you and Xander going to do?"

"That." She gave me an impish look, and I scowled. "What? I'm dead. It's not like it matters anymore."

"Don't screw with them, Ava." I bent down to collect some of the delicate glass ornaments and ignored the image of Henry and Persephone that rose to the forefront of my mind. I needed to believe that Ava wouldn't do that to someone she loved. "I mean it. This isn't a game. Henry doesn't react well to people messing around like that, and the last thing you want to do is piss him off. Please. For me." I was already teetering on the edge of failure as it was. "Here, take some of these."

Ava took the ornaments and started hanging them haphazardly, clustering them together or placing them on branches that bent dangerously with the added weight. I grimaced and started to rearrange them. We continued on like that for a few minutes, until finally Ava whirled around to face me. Startled, I dropped the ornament I was holding, and it landed on the bit of carpet I'd put down for exactly that reason.

"You think I'm a slut, don't you?"

"What?" I said, taking in her flushed cheeks and red eyes. She was seconds away from crying. "Why do you think I think that?"

"Because." She turned back to hanging ornaments, shaking the whole tree as she tugged. After another ornament fell, she sat down heavily on the floor. "I think Xander only likes me 'cause I'll sleep with him."

"Why do you think that?" I said carefully as I knelt down beside her. Chances were good that she was right, but that didn't mean it was the only reason. Except for Henry, all of the guys eyed her everywhere she went, so I wasn't sure what else she'd been expecting.

"I don't know," she said. "He never talks to me. He'll talk at me or show me things or kiss me, but if I don't sleep with him, he suddenly finds other things to do. Or he'll try to make me jealous with other girls."

"Then he's a jerk," I said flatly. "And you're better off without him."

She sniffed. "You think?"

"Yeah, I think." I paused. "What about Theo? He was nice, wasn't he?"

Ava rolled her eyes. "He was so protective, it was like he never let me breathe. But yeah," she added softly, "he was nice. Sensitive, but nice."

"Then why don't you break up with Xander?" I said. "Especially if you'll be happier without him."

"But I wouldn't be." She looked at me tearfully. "It's lonely here, Kate, you know that. You're so busy all the time, and Ella doesn't like me, and I don't like Calliope, and—if I don't have Xander, who else do I have?"

I tried to think of the right words to say, but nothing came. Ava was as alone here as I was, and while we had each other, sort of, she'd suffered just as much of a loss as I had when she'd died. She'd lost her parents, and even though she was hiding it well, it was moments like these that reminded me.

"I'm sorry," I said, hugging her. "Even if I'm busy sometimes,

I'm always here for you, and you'll always have me. I promise. Just be careful, okay?"

She didn't react for several seconds, but when she did, she buried her face in the crook of my neck and wrapped her arms around me. Her shoulders shook and her breath came in gasps as she started to cry properly, and I rubbed her back as soothingly as I could, wishing I were better with this sort of thing. No one I'd known back in New York had ever broken down like this in front of me. But it seemed to help, so I stayed still, waiting for her to cry herself out.

Finally she loosened her grip and pulled back enough to look at me. When I saw the pout on her face, I knew that the worst had passed. "How can we be friends when you won't even let me teach you how to swim?" she said, delicately wiping her eyes.

"That doesn't work on me, Ava," I warned. "I don't care how much practice you've had on your boyfriends."

Her shoulders slumped again, and I sighed.

"I don't want to learn how to swim—not because I don't like you or want to spend time with you, but because I'm afraid of the water. It isn't some easy thing for me to jump on in and learn, okay?"

Her eyes widened. "You're afraid of the water? Honest to God afraid?"

She was determined to make this as embarrassing as possible. "Terrified," I said. "When I was four or five, I thought it'd be fun to swim in the lake at Central Park, and I jumped in and sank like a rock. My mother had to jump in and save me. Ever since, I can't bring myself to try."

Speaking about my mother so casually made my throat

tighten, but luckily Ava didn't seem to notice. Instead she eyed me calculatingly, and I knew I was in trouble.

"Tell you what," she said, straightening up. "When the weather gets warmer, I'll teach you how to swim, and you can…I don't know. I'll owe you a huge favor, how about that?"

"There isn't anything you could possibly offer me that would make me willing to get in the water." I stood again and picked up the ornaments. There were only a few left, and nestled underneath was a small, heart-shaped box wrapped in delicate pink tissue paper. On a tag in flowery script was my name. Frowning, I picked it up. "Is this from you?"

Ava eyed it. "No. Where'd you find it?"

"With the ornaments." I untied the ribbon, but Ava snatched it out of my hand. "Hey—"

"Don't touch it," she said, setting it on the bed as if it were a bomb about to go off. "You don't know where it came from."

Irritated, I turned back to the ornaments. "It's a Christmas present, Ava. Ever heard of them?" James's warning rang in my head, but all I'd tried to do was unwrap it. I wasn't stupid enough to eat something or put it on without knowing where it came from. Besides, maybe there was a signed card inside. "Yours is under the bed, if you want it."

She ducked underneath the bed and pulled out a jewelry box wrapped in blue with her name on it. I watched her open it and reveal the gold hoop earrings inside, but while she made an effort to look excited, her eyes kept darting over toward my unexpected gift.

"Thanks," she said, putting them on. "They're beautiful."

"You're welcome." I walked toward the bed. "Really, Ava, it's just a present. I'm sure it isn't going to try to bite me or—"

"Stop."

Henry's voice cut through the room, and my hand froze inches away from the pink wrapping paper. He stood framed in the doorway, half a dozen guards behind him, each with their hands on their weapons. Power radiated from him in waves, and the temperature dropped so low I thought I could see my breath. For the first time I understood why everyone seemed to keep a respectful distance from him, especially when he was angry.

I swallowed my unease. "It's a present—"

"Kate," said Henry coldly. "Step away."

I did as he said, but I wasn't happy about it. Crossing my arms over my chest, I watched as he picked up the present. A shimmering bubble formed, enclosing it completely, and my mouth dropped open.

"How did you—"

"I need to open it," he said. "This is the safest way."

Without anything to guide it, the lid rose from the box. Nestled inside was a collection of chocolates, each a different color and shape. One with a purple flower rose above the others, and it broke in half.

Instead of nougat or strawberry filling, there was green liquid inside, and as it dripped onto the pink tissue, it made a hissing noise I could hear from several feet away.

"Cancel dinner," said Henry to the guards. "Make sure everyone is in their room. I want a complete search of the manor."

It took me a moment to regain the ability to speak, and

when I did, my voice came out as a croak. "You can't cancel Christmas dinner."

"I can, and I will," he said. "And you will stay in your room tonight, do you understand?"

Did I understand? Was he crazy? "I'll stay in my room under two conditions," I said sharply. "One, after you're done searching the manor, you let everyone have Christmas dinner. There should be plenty of time for both."

His mouth twitched in annoyance, but he nodded. "Fine. Your second condition?"

I hesitated. There was more on the line than a happy holiday, and if he rejected it—but I had to at least try. "Two, you spend the evening with me. And enjoy it as much as you can. And," I added, "stop acting so damn cranky all the time. It's getting on my nerves."

He didn't answer for several moments, and when he did, he simply nodded again. But for a split second, I thought I saw the barest hint of a smile. "I will be here after the manor is secured. In the meantime, do not open any strange packages."

As he walked out the door, he gestured for Ava to follow. Shrugging apologetically, she touched her new earrings and winked before following after him, leaving me alone in my suite. I sighed and collapsed on the bed, trying not to think about how long it would take them to search the manor—or how Ava had known to be suspicious of the poisoned present in the first place.

I spent the rest of the afternoon decorating my room in order to keep my mind off of what had happened. With the lights down low, the tree looked magnificent, and I'd even managed to get a star on top. But the best part was the strings of twinkling lights stretched out across my bedroom, and as I walked through it, I could see the colors reflected on my skin. It even smelled like sugar cookies, and all that was missing was music.

By the time I'd finished, I was convinced Henry wouldn't show. It was dark out and so late that my stomach was rumbling, and no matter how many times I asked my guards, no one seemed to be willing to tell me when he was coming.

Expecting to spend Christmas alone, I changed into my pajamas and constructed a nest of pillows and blankets in the middle of the floor. As I settled down, however, I heard the door open. Henry entered, carrying a silver tray laden with savory food, and Cerberus and Pogo were hot on his heels. Silently he offered me a cup of hot chocolate.

I took the mug from him and sipped, spotting what looked like baklava on the tray. It smelled exactly like my mother used to make, and my mouth watered.

"As you missed dinner, I thought you might be hungry." His tone was painfully neutral, as if he was making every effort to be polite, and he glanced uncertainly at my makeshift pile of blankets. "Is there room for one more?"

"Plenty," I said, trying to sound inviting. "If sitting on the floor isn't your thing, you can pull up a chair. It works almost as well."

After hesitating, he sat down next to me, and I scooted over to make room. He shifted around, looking awkward, but finally he settled.

"Do you and your mother do this every year?" said Henry. "Gather your pillows and watch the lights?"

"Usually." I took a sip of my cocoa. "She's been in the hospital for Christmas for the past three years, but we always made do. Did you find anything while searching the manor?"

"No," he said. "But the staff had their festivities, as promised."

I nodded, and Henry was silent and tense beside me. But at least he was there. I stared at the tree until the lights burned into my eyes, and when I looked away, I could still see the pattern of colors. "What's it like to be dead?"

I flushed when I realized what I'd blurted out, and the way he didn't answer right away only made it worse. "I would not know," he finally said. "I do not know what it is like to be alive, either."

I pressed my lips together. Right. Kept forgetting that.

"But if you would like," he said, "I could tell you about death."

I glanced up at him. "What's the difference?"

"Death is the process of dying. Being dead is what happens after death has occurred."

"Oh." I'd purposely ignored thoughts of my mother actually dying—whether it'd be painful, if there was a bright light, or if she'd even be aware of it. But Henry wouldn't be speculating. "Please?"

He tentatively stretched out his arm, and to my surprise, he settled it around my shoulders. He was still stiff, but it was the most contact we'd had in weeks. "It is not as bad as mortals tend to think. It is much the same as going to sleep, or so I have been told. Even when a wound causes pain, it is very brief."

"What—" I swallowed. "What happens after the going to sleep part? Is there a—a bright light?"

Henry at least had the grace not to laugh. "No, there is no white light. There are gates, however," he added, giving me a meaningful look. Whatever he was trying to get me to understand didn't sink in, however, and he gave up and told me. "The gates at the front of the property."

I blinked. "Oh." And then thought about it. "*Oh*. You mean this—"

"Sometimes, when they may be useful," he said. "The vast majority of the time, they are sent into the beyond."

"What's the beyond?"

"The Underworld, where souls stay for eternity."

"Is there a heaven then?"

His fingers slowly wrapped around my bare arm, and I automatically leaned against him. Maybe my mother had been right—maybe he'd been so distant because he was afraid I wouldn't make it past Christmas. Or maybe he was just trying to comfort me. Either way, the contact was warm, and I craved it.

"Initially there were many different beliefs, so the realm was undefined," he said, his voice taking on a clinical tone. "Then came more substantial religions, and with it formed Tartarus and the Elysian Fields, among others. From then on, as religions grew..." He paused, as if choosing his words very carefully. "The afterlife is whatever a soul wishes or believes it to be."

The endless possibilities swam through my mind, making me dizzy. "Doesn't that get complicated?"

"It does." This time he smiled back. "Which is why I cannot rule alone. James has been helping me temporarily."

My mood immediately turned sour. "If you can't rule alone, then how is he supposed to if you fade?"

Henry shifted, and for a moment I was afraid he was going to pull away. I set my hand on his, and he stilled. "I do not know. If it comes to that, it will no longer be my concern. Given how he has acted about you, I would speculate he intends to ask you, but once the council rules, it will be final. If you do not pass for me, you will not pass for him."

The possibility of James liking me enough to put up with me for eternity just like Henry was offering had never occurred to me, and I took a breath, trying to keep myself from fidgeting. Henry wasn't necessarily right—James and I were just friends, if even that anymore. He knew that. They both did. "What would I do? I mean, if I pass—how does this work?"

"It is a job, as most else is," said Henry, and I could see the lights from the tree reflected in his eyes. "Much of it is making rulings in disputes, or when a soul is undecided, we help them come to a greater understanding. We do not interfere unless the soul believes it will be judged."

"And what happens to them?" I said, trying to remember what my mother was. Methodist? Lutheran? Presbyterian? Would it matter?

"It depends solely on their belief structure," said Henry. "If they believe they will be walking around in a human form, then that is what occurs. If they believe they will be nothing more than a ball of warmth and light, then so be it."

"What if what they believe and what they want are two different things?"

"That is also where we come in."

I was silent. The prospect of spending the rest of forever ruling over the dead seemed impossible, like a faraway thing I would never reach, and I wasn't so sure I wanted to. I wasn't doing this for the job or even for immortality. After seeing Henry, I couldn't imagine how lonely forever could be, and I wasn't looking forward to experiencing it.

"What if I can't handle it?" I said. "What if I fail miserably and you have to find someone else?"

It was a long moment before he responded. "That is what the tests are for. I have already done my part in choosing you, and I believe you are capable of handling it. My brothers and sisters test you because with this task comes a great amount of responsibility, and there is no room for error. If you cannot do it, then you will not. It is simple."

There was nothing simple about it, but I couldn't focus on what would happen afterward while I still had to make it to spring. Even if I passed all of the tests, if the council didn't like me, all of this speculation was pointless. I already had one vote against me with James. If they needed a unanimous ruling, it was already over.

"Henry?" I said quietly. He stared straight ahead at the tree. "You know I want to pass, right?"

"I concluded as much, yes, given you are still here."

I ignored his sarcasm. His hand was warm underneath mine, and I squeezed it. "It isn't only because of my mother. It's because of you, too. I know you've been trying for a really long time, and I know I'm just another silly little girl trying to help out, and I know you think I'm going to fail, but—I like you, Henry, and I'm doing this for you, too, okay? I don't want you to fade."

Even though he wasn't looking at me, I could see his lips twist into a mirthless smirk. "You could never be just another silly little girl," he said. "I do not wish to influence you or make this more difficult on you than it already must be, but do not think I do not care about what happens to you, Kate. Perhaps it is impossible that anyone takes Persephone's place, but if that is the case, it is out of no failure of your own. But if anyone is capable of it, I am certain it is you."

"Then please don't give up," I said. "I'll never be Persephone, and I know that, but—we could be friends. And you wouldn't have to be alone anymore."

Henry looked away, hiding his face completely from my view. But when he spoke, his voice was tight, as if he were struggling to keep it steady.

"I would very much like that," he said, and I released a breath I hadn't realized I'd been holding and wriggled out of his grip. He didn't look at me, but he did set his hand back in his lap.

"Can I give you my present now?" I said. "I promise it's not poisoned."

He rewarded my tasteless joke with a wry half smile. I untangled myself from the blankets, ducked underneath my bed to retrieve a large package wrapped in gold, and carried it over to him. To my surprise, there was a present where I'd been sitting moments before.

"Your gift," he said. "Also not poisoned."

"Thank you," I said. I sat down and handed him his, but he set it aside as he watched me open mine. I pushed the silver wrapping paper away, revealing a plain box. Squinting in the low light, I pulled off the lid and pushed away the tissue paper, exposing a framed black-and-white photo.

I froze. It was my favorite picture of my mother and me, from when I was seven years old. We were in the middle of Central Park on my birthday, the exact spot where we met every night in my dreams, and we'd spread out an entire picnic, only to have it ruined by a large dog that had gotten loose from its owner. The only things that had survived were the cupcakes I'd helped her make.

In the picture, we sat in the middle of the mess that'd been our lunch, each holding a cupcake. Chocolate with purple frosting, I remembered, a smile tugging at my lips. She had her arms around me, and while we were both smiling, we weren't looking at the camera. The owner of the dog had taken a number of photos of us to make up for ruining our picnic, and in the end, this had been the one that had spent the past eleven years framed on my bedside table.

But as I stared at it, I realized it wasn't the same. It had depth to it, like the picture in Persephone's room. A reflection, Henry had called it, but unlike the one with him and Persephone, this one wasn't a hope or a wish. It was real.

I wiped my eyes with the back of my hand. "Henry, I don't—"

He held up a hand, and I fell silent. "Not until I've opened yours as well."

I waited, my vision blurry, as he unwrapped the large box. It'd taken me four tries to get the wrapping right. Lifting the lid, he paused. "What is this?" he said, puzzled as he examined the blanket I'd meticulously decorated. I'd refused to let anyone else help me, even though I knew it would've taken days instead of weeks if I had.

"It's the night sky," I said, hugging my picture to my chest. "See the dots? They're stars. I remembered what you said about the stars moving. You said they were different when you met Persephone, and—this is how they are now. When you met me."

Henry studied the constellations I'd painstakingly arranged on the blanket, and he gently brushed his fingers across the one I recognized as the Maiden. Virgo. Kore.

"Thank you." He looked at me with his eyes made of moonlight, and something had changed. The barrier that had been there all this time was gone, and for a moment he almost looked like a different person. "For everything. I have never received such a wonderful gift."

I raised an eyebrow. "I'm not so sure I believe that."

"You should." He continued to run his hand across the fabric. "It has been a very long time since I've received a gift as extraordinary as you."

Unable to look away, I stared at him, absorbing every detail of his face. With that barrier gone, it was almost as if I could see who he was underneath, someone kind and lonely and scared, who wanted nothing more than to be loved. "Can I try something?" I said. "If you don't like it, I'll stop."

He nodded, and I took a deep breath, trying to keep my stomach from doing somersaults. Gathering what courage I could find, I leaned forward and pressed my lips to his chastely. I'd only ever kissed a few boys in my life, and it felt unfamiliar, but not awkward. Nice, I thought. It felt nice.

He seemed surprised, but he didn't resist. It was a painful few seconds, but finally he relaxed and kissed me back, his hand cupping my neck. The heat of his skin against mine was almost unbearably hot.

I don't know how long it was before I forced myself to pull away. While I caught my breath, I watched Henry warily, afraid he would bolt. He sat still, his expression blank, and finally I couldn't stay silent any longer.

"That—" I hesitated and offered him a smile. "I liked that. A lot."

After what felt like ages, he returned my smile with a small one of his own. "As did I."

Nervously I reached out to thread my fingers with his, looking down at our hands instead of directly at him. Mine was so small that it looked lost in his. "Henry? Don't take this the wrong way—"

I could feel him tense, and I immediately felt guilty, though I made an effort to mask it with a teasing look.

"Let me finish," I said. "Don't take this the wrong way, but since it's Christmas and all...would you stay with me tonight?"

His eyes widened a fraction of an inch, and I quickly shook my head, my cheeks flushing with embarrassment.

"Not like *that*. You've got to earn that, and it costs more than just a picture, y'know." My weak attempt at a joke managed to break the tension enough to get him to crack an apologetic smile. "But could you just...stay for tonight?"

Several seconds passed, and I mentally kicked myself for asking like I had—like I was some hormonal teenager who only wanted *that*. But I didn't want *that* at all. I wanted his company. He made me happy, and tonight of all nights, I didn't want to be alone. Most of all, I didn't want him to be either.

"Yes," he said. "I will stay."

Nothing happened.

We spent the rest of the evening talking and watching the lights on the tree. When it was time to go to sleep, I curled up next to him and unashamedly used his chest as a pillow, but that was it.

I didn't kiss him again, too content to risk screwing things up. He didn't deserve to be pushed like that, and while taking the next step opened a whole new set of doors, for now I wanted to appreciate his company. We both deserved to enjoy Christmas, rather than fumble through a lot of awkward moments.

My mother and I walked through Central Park, the haze of the city in the summer bearing down on us. She looked pleased as I recounted what had happened between Henry and me, and she hugged me to her when I told her that I'd kissed him.

"That's my girl," she said, sounding happier than she had in ages.

We spent our last Christmas together eating ice cream and wandering through the gardens in the hot summer sun, and she pointed out the kinds of flowers that grew wild. She never took her arm from my shoulders, and when I felt myself begin to wake up, I wished her Merry Christmas for the last time.

My contentment didn't last for long, however. The first thing I heard when I awoke was pounding on my door. Confused, I sat up, my hair sticking out every which way, and I ran my fingers through it as Henry stood and walked toward the door.

In that moment, I hated him. He looked impeccable, not a hair out of place, and he moved as gracefully as ever. Meanwhile, I'd be paying for sleeping on the floor for the rest of the day.

"Yes?" he said, opening the door. To my surprise, Ella dashed in, closely followed by Calliope. Ella was crying, her face beet-red, and Calliope looked crushed with her slumped shoulders and her face drawn.

"I want her gone!" cried Ella furiously, looking back and forth between Henry and me.

"Is that a request," said Henry, moving back toward the nest of pillows and blankets on the floor, "or a demand?"

"She hurt him!" said Ella, now focusing on Henry. "She hurt him, and he tried to find her, and now—"

"Wait, who?" I said as I struggled to my feet. "What's going on?"

Ella dissolved into tears. Now standing next to me, Henry looked expectantly at Calliope. She stared at the floor, not meeting his gaze.

"Ava," she said. "She spent the night with Xander, and this morning Theo found them. They fought, and—"

Henry tensed, and my blood ran cold. "And?" he said.

"Xander's passed into the beyond."

CHAPTER 14

JUDGMENT

Ava sat huddled in the corner of her chamber without so much as a scratch, but on the bed, bloody remains were all that was left of Xander's body. A putrid stench filled the room, and I clasped my hand over my nose, but it didn't seem to bother Henry as he examined the corpse.

Ella and Calliope didn't come with us, opting instead to stay in a separate wing of the manor with Theo. He was injured, but it wasn't fatal, from what Calliope had described. Seeing him could wait.

Apparently for the people living in Eden Manor, passing into the beyond was the same as death in the outside world. It was as much an ending for them as it was for the living, never getting to see their loved ones again until they passed into the beyond as well. Xander was gone, lost to the Underworld, and the only person who could find him now was Henry. I struggled with the knowledge that this wasn't the real end of things, that I could lose Ava all over again, along with everyone I'd befriended since September, and this time they wouldn't reappear. This death was the final step for the people at Eden

Manor; this time there would be no in-between for Xander. Despite the painful void Xander's loss left in the manor, I took a small amount of comfort from knowing that this place was still part of the world I understood. A knife to the back meant blood, and too much blood meant death.

"Ava?" I said as I approached her. She looked like a frightened animal, ready to bolt at the slightest movement.

"I didn't mean it," she whispered, tears streaming down her face. There were smears of blood underneath her eyes, where she must have wiped her cheeks. "I—I thought he didn't want to see me again, and Xander was right there, and I—"

"It's all right," I said, although it was anything but. I was queasy and barely able to keep from being sick at the sight of all the carnage, but I turned away from it, focusing on Ava. "We should get you cleaned up."

I helped her to the bathroom while Henry continued his inspection. Once I was sure she wasn't going to pass out, I found her a robe to wear and busied myself with washing the blood off her skin and out of her hair. We were both quiet. I didn't want to know the details, and she was too shaken to say anything. By the time she was dry, I poked my head back in the bedroom, averting my eyes from the horrific scene on the bed.

"What do you want me to do with her?" I said.

Henry hadn't moved since I'd left. "The guards will escort her to another room, where she will stay until we have decided if she deserves punishment."

I paled. "Is this—is this another test?"

He was by my side in an instant, faster than anyone could possibly move. "No," he said. "Xander has passed. Now come— Ava will be taken care of."

Shielding me from having to look at Xander's body, Henry led me toward the door. As we left, a woman dressed in a uniform entered, but I hardly noticed her.

"Where are we going?" I said, breathing in a lungful of clean air once we reached the hallway.

"To see Theo." He guided me around the corner, and I followed without protest. My stomach lurched with the thought of what condition Theo might have been in, but I refused to think about it. For all I knew, he was fine.

But the moment we stepped into his chamber, it was obvious he was anything but. Ella stood at her brother's bedside, her face drawn and her hands trembling. When Henry and I entered, she glared at me, and I stopped a foot into the doorway.

"How is he?" said Henry, standing at the end of Theo's bed. He was unconscious.

"There's a shallow wound in his chest that worries me, but everything else is superficial. He's lost a lot of blood though," said Ella, her voice rough.

"Will he wake up soon?" There was no compassion or worry in Henry's voice. Instead it was hollow, and that emptiness scared me more than anything else had that morning.

Ella shook her head. "I don't know."

"Will he be able to handle the pain if I wake him up?"

Both of us stared at him. I searched for any trace of the Henry I'd kissed the night before, but he was no longer there. A very large part of me was relieved; this cold shell wasn't someone I wanted to fall for. But another part wondered which one was really him.

"Y-yes," said Ella, averting her gaze after several seconds. "He'll manage."

Even I could hear the uncertainty in her voice, but apparently that was all the confirmation Henry needed. He let go of my hand and took a step closer to the bed, towering over it.

A moment later, without any pretense or sign that something had changed, Theo groaned. His eyes were so swollen he could barely crack them open, and he coughed weakly. There was a rattling sound in his chest that made me wince.

"What happened?" said Henry coolly.

Theo struggled to reply, opening and shutting his mouth several times. "Ava?"

"She's gone," said in Ella with a surprisingly tender voice. "You'll never have to see her again."

Instead of being comforted by this, Theo's eyes widened, and he struggled to sit up. "No," he gasped, and even from across the room I could tell how much pain it caused him. "I didn't—I didn't mean to—"

"She is still here," said Henry, and Ella whirled around, stricken. "Xander is gone."

Theo slumped back on the bed, his eyes squeezed shut. "He attacked me," he mumbled. "I came in to wish Ava a Merry Christmas, and I found them together. Xander—he must've forgotten the rules. Thought I was going to fight him. He pulled out his sword and swung at me, and—I had to fight back."

He was wheezing. Why Henry was putting him through this when he could have easily questioned him once he was feeling better, I didn't know—better yet, why couldn't Henry heal him like he'd healed me? Somehow I doubted his abilities were limited to ankles.

"Calm yourself," said Henry, nodding to Ella, who put a cup to Theo's lips. He drank, although most of it splashed on his chest. Ella mopped it up methodically with a towel, as if this were something she was used to doing, though her brow was furrowed deeply. Regardless of how little he'd swallowed, whatever it was worked quickly. A few seconds later, Theo relaxed again.

"Is that your story then? That you had no ill intentions toward Xander, and that he was the aggressor? You were merely protecting yourself?"

"And Ava," said Theo, his eyes fluttering shut. "I thought he was going after Ava."

Henry waited while Theo fell back asleep. Once his breathing had steadied, Henry moved toward me and set his hand on my back, guiding me out of the room.

"Is he telling the truth?" I said.

Henry looked at me, his expression still void of any trace of the humanity I'd seen the night before. "What do you think?"

I swallowed, feeling as if I'd suddenly dived headfirst into the middle of a deep lake, the surface nowhere within sight. "I think I need to talk to Ava."

Henry let me go into the room alone, although he and two guards stood immediately outside the door, undoubtedly able to hear everything we said. I didn't care though—getting the truth out of Ava was my top priority, not her privacy. If Theo was being honest, then she hadn't really done anything wrong, had she? But Xander was gone, and that was something that couldn't be ignored.

She lay in the middle of a large bed, her knees drawn to her chest. I gingerly sat on the edge of the mattress, reaching out to touch her hand.

"Are you okay?" The answer was obvious, but it was the only thing I could think of to say.

"No," she said in a choked voice. "Xander's dead."

"He was already dead," I said as gently as I could. "He just passed into the next level of things, that's all."

Ava was silent. I ran my fingers through her wheat-colored hair, still damp from washing out the blood. "Did they hurt you at all? Do you need to see a doctor?"

"No," she mumbled. "I'm fine."

It was clear that she was anything but, but the pain of losing Xander didn't negate the possibility that she had something more to do with it. "What happened?"

She hesitated, and for a second, I didn't expect her to say anything. When she did, she spoke so softly that I had to strain to hear her, even though the room was silent. "I don't know. I just—woke up, and Theo was there, staring at me and Xander like—I don't know."

I bit my lip. "Was Theo the one to attack Xander, or did Xander attack Theo?"

"I don't *know*. I woke up, saw a sword, screamed and ran into the corner. I wasn't looking. I just—" She rolled over onto her back and stared up at me, her eyes red and full of tears. "There was blood and I was screaming and they were swearing and I don't know what happened, all right?"

I nodded. My fists were clenched, and my nails dug painfully into my palms. "Is there anything else you can tell me? Anything else you saw or heard or—"

"No." She rolled away from me. "It doesn't matter anyway, does it?"

I wasn't sure what happened, but something inside of me must've snapped. I'd spent months—*years* trying to stop the people I cared about from dying, and Ava couldn't muster up enough compassion about someone she claimed to love to figure out what had happened.

I stood quickly, and suddenly the room seemed much smaller than before. "Don't you get it, Ava? Xander is dead. Really, truly, never coming back here *dead*. And right now, everything points to Theo murdering him because he caught you in bed with him."

That got her attention. Twisting around, she stared at me, her mouth open.

"Here's how it goes," I said heatedly. "Either Theo is innocent and Xander was the one who attacked him, or Theo is guilty and Xander was defending himself. Do you even care, or are you just upset because you lost a toy?"

Seething, I began to pace up and down the room. I couldn't remember ever being this angry in my life.

"I get it, you're dead, your life is over and you're having fun while you can. But this isn't fun anymore, not for anyone but you—you're playing with these guys like they're only here to entertain you. You act like no one else matters except in relation to you getting what you want, and now Xander is dead because of you."

"You're blaming me?" she said. "But I didn't kill him—"

"You didn't hack him into little pieces, but you're the reason it happened." I stopped in front of the bed, running my fingers through my hair. "Ella wants you gone. Frankly, if all you're going to do is waste your time sleeping with every guy in the manor and acting like the world revolves around you, then so do I. You're useless here. The only things you've done are bicker with Ella and get Xander killed."

The moment I said it, I regretted it, but I couldn't take it back. It was the truth, or at least an exaggeration of it. But when I looked at Ava, I saw a scared girl who was my friend, not the heinous, selfish whore I'd painted her as. My stomach twisted, and guilt flooded through me so fast that I felt like I was choking.

"Henry let you stay here because we're friends," I managed to say, and while I was calmer, my voice held the chill of accusation. "And we are, Ava, or at least I thought we were. But he risked that for me, and all you've done is get one of his men killed and the other branded a murderer. Do you have any idea how awful that makes me feel?"

Ava stared at me, her lower lip trembling. "You're just jealous," she whispered. "You're stuck with Henry your whole life while I get to be with anyone I want. Admit it—the only reason you're acting like this is because I get a choice and you don't."

I glowered at her, trying to ignore the way her words echoed through my mind. Hadn't I been thinking the same thing a few months before? But I wasn't going to give Ava the satisfaction of thinking she was right. She wasn't, not anymore. "Don't try to turn this back on me," I said. "I had a choice, and I made it. More important, I'm happy with my decision, and I'm doing everything I possibly can to live up to it. I'm not jealous of you, Ava. I'm ashamed."

The hurt in her eyes was painful to see, but I forced myself to continue. She had to understand there were limits, and until she stopped hurting others, I couldn't stand by and watch anymore.

"Stay in Eden as long as you want, but don't you dare come near me or Ella or Theo or any other man in this place again, do you understand? You leave them alone. You leave *me* alone.

I have enough to deal with right now without having to make sure you don't get anyone else killed."

I would have buckled if she'd looked at me, so I stormed out of the room and past Henry, who wordlessly followed me to my suite. I wanted to slam the door, but he was behind me. Pogo and Cerberus were still curled up together on the floor, and the pillow I kicked missed them by inches.

"Now what?" I said, turning on Henry. "Do we sit here and talk about what happened? Are we the judge? The jury? What happens now?"

"Nothing," he said, giving Cerberus a scratch behind the ears. "You have already made your decision."

I paused. "What?"

"Ava will not have any romantic contact with any men, nor will she have any contact with you or Ella," said Henry, and I sat down heavily on the bed. "As for Theo, that is not a judgment I could possibly ask you to make. Not yet."

"Why not?" I said, my throat dry with the realization that I wouldn't see Ava again. After everything we'd both been through since September, I felt like I'd failed her. But in a way, hadn't she failed herself? I knew it wasn't her fault, not really— she couldn't have predicted this would happen. She'd still been careless though, and I'd stood by and let her. This was on my shoulders, too. But no matter who was to blame, Xander was still dead.

"Because you do not yet have the ability to see past a lie." He moved to my wardrobe and began to pick through clothing as if we were talking about the weather or something equally as mundane.

I raised my eyebrows. "And you do?"

He ignored me. "Nor do you have the power to go into the

Underworld and question Xander. Fortunately, that will not be necessary. I already know what happened."

I cuddled Pogo to my chest, finding comfort in his warm body. I didn't want to ask, dreading the possibility of Theo's guilt, so I didn't. Henry couldn't search through my closet forever, and he would tell me sooner or later whether I wanted to hear it or not.

A minute passed, and finally he set a clean pair of jeans and a white sweater on the bed. "Theo is telling the truth, and therefore he will not be prosecuted. Your punishment for Ava is appropriate, and there is no need for me to intervene. I will instruct the others to ensure she follows your restrictions, and that will be the end of it."

I nodded numbly. Setting Pogo down, I took my clothes to change behind the screen in the corner. There wasn't anything else to talk about, and the weight of my judgment fell heavily on my shoulders. Had I done the right thing, or had I reacted in anger? And how would Ava, who was already so alone in this house, survive being cut off from me and Theo as well?

"I will see you down at breakfast then," said Henry, though the thought of food was enough to make me nauseous.

I heard the door open, but not close. Still distracted by the thought of what I'd done to my only real friend in Eden Manor, I buttoned my jeans and stepped out from behind the screen, only to see Henry still standing there. His shoulders were weighed down by some invisible load, and he shoved his hands into his pockets, looking so similar to how he had in Persephone's room that a jolt of fear ran through me. But his eyes weren't deadened as they had been so many weeks ago—he was weary, but he hadn't given up again.

"What you did today is never easy," he said, "but it was

necessary. I cannot imagine how difficult it was for you, especially considering Ava is your friend."

"Was my friend," I whispered, but I wasn't sure he heard me.

"Do not feel guilty for it. Her actions are not yours. I do not regret inviting her here, knowing she has, up until now, been good company. Your safety and happiness are what matter most to me."

I nodded, and he left. Glancing at the reflection he'd given me, which now sat on my nightstand, I felt even guiltier than before. No matter how at fault she was, if I couldn't even protect Ava, how was I possibly going to do the same for Henry?

Even if this hadn't been a test, I still had several to go. The wrong word, the wrong thought, the wrong action and this would all be over. Henry's life was no less fragile than Xander's or even my mother's, and I felt myself start to crack under the burden of fighting for him on my own. Henry stood on the sidelines because I had dragged him there, forcing him to pay attention, but I couldn't make him care. I was the only one fighting for him, and I was no longer sure I was up for the challenge.

CHAPTER 15
POISON

One unfortunate side effect of Ava's banishment and the risk that she might try to take revenge was the towering guard that was now with me everywhere I went. Measuring in at six and a half feet tall, he was the large blond I'd spotted at the ball back in September. He walked with a limp that didn't seem to affect his speed, and I was too afraid to ask how he'd gotten it. While he didn't say much, Calliope called him Nicholas, and he was nice enough for a guy who could easily kill me with his pinkie.

I was never alone anymore. When Nicholas wasn't with me, Henry was, and he had more guards stationed outside my room while I slept. They were only for show; after Christmas Eve, Henry spent every night with me, a complete turnaround from how he'd acted before Christmas. It was as if I'd broken through an invisible barrier, and now instead of avoiding me and hoping I'd keep myself alive, he seemed determined to do the job for me.

Nothing ever happened in the evening except for the occasional kiss or brush of his hand in my hair, and he never pushed for anything more. I was simply grateful for the company, and the more I saw of his human side, the more I hoped I was enough to make him want to stay.

It wasn't a charade. I wasn't returning his kisses to fool him into thinking I cared about him or because I pitied him. I was falling for him, a little more every day, even though a very large part of me knew that this was a bad idea. There was no guarantee I would pass and nothing that gave me reason to think that any kind of relationship would last more than the remainder of winter. But if I did somehow miraculously succeed, Henry would need a reason to stay, and I would be that reason. So for the first time in my life, I shoved aside the worries and the doubts, and I let my barriers down. The afternoons were a burden now, a time I had to endure in order to get to the evenings we spent together, and every time I saw him, no matter how short a time he'd been away, my heart raced. Now that I had survived Christmas, I dared to hope, and with that hope came possibilities.

When I woke up before him, I watched him sleep as the early morning rays filtered through the curtains, and I tried to picture waking up to him like this for the rest of eternity. It was strange to think that if the impossible happened and I managed to pass the tests without getting myself killed, he would be my future. My entire future, with no threat of death lurking around the corner any longer. My husband.

The word was foreign to my thoughts, let alone on my tongue, and I was sure I'd never get used to the idea. But as much as I resisted it—I was too young, too alone, too not even remotely ready for that sort of life—I began to see that it wouldn't be so bad. Henry was broken, but so was I, and spending my life with him was hardly the hell I'd thought it would be in the weeks after he'd saved Ava's life. And in time, maybe we would be able to fix each other. I could give him what he needed—a friend, a wife, a queen—and in return he could be my family.

As the days until spring grew fewer, my dreams with my mother grew more solemn. Every moment was precious, but most of the time I had no idea what to say. We walked hand in hand through the park most days, and she led the conversation as we talked about everything and nothing. She told me every night how proud she was of me, how much she loved me, and how badly she wanted for me to be happy without her, to not need her to continue as Henry needed me, but the most I could give her in return was a tight nod and a squeeze of the hand. The things I couldn't say gathered in my throat, forming a knot I could never swallow. As the days passed and my chances to tell her dwindled, I knew I would have to force them out eventually, but not yet. As long as there was a tomorrow in the manor, I could pretend there was still hope she would never have to die.

The closer I got to Henry, the further removed from the real world I became. Even though it was beginning to feel like I would never go back, like those six months would somehow find a way to stretch into eternity, I knew they wouldn't. There was an end, and we were rapidly approaching it.

Despite Henry's company and constantly being shadowed, I was lonely. Ella spent all of her time with Theo now, and while Calliope stayed with me when Henry wasn't there, even she seemed subdued after the incident at Christmas. And though James was the enemy now, I thought about him often. It couldn't have all been fake, our friendship, and I missed being able to miss him without feeling angry. He wasn't the one trying to kill me, I was sure of it now, and something about knowing he was on my side even though I wasn't on his was comforting.

I missed Ava most of all. Every time I came across something I wanted to show her or thought of something I wanted to tell her, it took me a few seconds before I remembered that I would never see her again, at least not as friends. Occasionally I caught glimpses of her leaving a room as I entered or at the other end of a hallway I turned down, but she was never there for more than a moment.

Henry never made me talk about the pain and guilt I felt at the separation, even though it sometimes kept me up at night. He let me work my way through it on my own, and I wasn't sure if I were grateful or resentful. Knowing that Ava must've felt as badly as I did only made me feel worse. Maybe she wasn't the best friend in the world, and maybe she was a little too selfish sometimes, but I wasn't perfect either. With each day that passed I regretted my judgment more and more. Ava was allowed to make mistakes—we all were. And what gave me the right to punish her for them when all she'd been trying to do was make the loneliness a little easier to bear?

To try to fill the empty hours, I spent more and more time in the stables with Phillip. It was quiet, and he didn't press for conversation. He seemed to understand what I was going through, and he offered to let me spend as much time with the horses as I wanted. It was a generous offer, considering how protective he was of them, but it wasn't enough to make me forget what I was losing.

It was near the end of January when one afternoon, Henry found me in the garden, wrapped in a cloak and kneeling next to a dormant, snow-covered rosebush. The memory of how I'd gotten there was hazy at best, but I didn't particularly care.

Once Irene had told me the date in the middle of our tutoring session, everything became fuzzy, and it was Henry's voice that brought me crashing back down to reality.

"Kate?" Dressed in a heavy black coat, he stood a few feet away, sticking out like a sore thumb against the snow. I didn't look up.

"It's my mother's last birthday."

He stood still. Part of me wanted him to keep his distance, but a much more insistent part wished he knew me well enough to know when I desperately needed a hug.

"She always hated being born in January," I continued, my voice blank as I stared at the lifeless plant in front of me. "Said she never felt like celebrating when there weren't any flowers and all of the trees were dead."

"Sleeping," said Henry. "The trees are only sleeping. They will return when the time is right."

"My mother won't." I sat down heavily in the snow, not caring if my jeans got wet. "We've been celebrating her last birthday ever since she was diagnosed. This time it's really it."

"I'm sorry." He sat down beside me and wrapped his arm around me, and the warmth from his body stopped mine from becoming numb. "Is there anything I can do?"

I shook my head. "I don't know what I'm going to do without her."

Henry was silent for a long moment, and when he did speak, his voice sounded distant. "May I show you something?"

"What sort of something?"

"Close your eyes."

Fairly certain of what was about to happen, I obliged, expecting the change in climate. Instead of going from the cold outdoors to the warm indoors, however, I felt sunshine on my face and a warm breeze. We were still outside.

When I opened my eyes, half expecting to still be in the garden, I had to steady myself against Henry as I looked around. We were standing in the middle of Central Park on a summer day, exactly as my mother and I did in my dreams, except now the park was empty. My mother was nowhere in sight.

"Henry?" I said uncertainly, looking around. The lake was nearby, and I heard the strains of a familiar song being played somewhere in the distance, but we were alone. "What are we doing in New York?"

"We are not in New York." He sounded wistful. I inched closer to him, both afraid and fascinated by this place. "This is your afterlife."

I stared at him, his words taking several seconds to settle properly in my mind. "You mean this is—we're—"

"This is your corner of the Underworld." He raised an eyebrow at my expression. "Do not worry, it is only temporary. I wanted you to see it."

Wildly I looked around, hoping my mother would appear, but it was just us. "Why?"

"I wanted you to see it so you would know—" He stopped, but he didn't need to finish for me to understand what he wasn't saying. He wanted to show me where I would go when I died. My stomach twisted into knots, and I glared at an unoffending patch of grass. So he wasn't really fighting after all.

But he continued, his eyes lowered to the ground. "I am showing you so you will have some firsthand experience if you pass the tests." A lie, but I tried to believe it. "Once you become immortal, when you are here, the Underworld will take on the shape as the mortal sees it." Several seconds passed, and he added in a quieter voice, "I also wished to know you will be content in the end if the council does not rule in your favor."

My favor, not his. Not ours.

I whirled around to face him. "Why are you letting them walk all over you like this? The council, your family, whatever they are—if you think I'm good enough, then why don't you tell them to put a sock in it and respect your decision?"

Henry's expression was unreadable. "I am not omnipotent," he said, taking a cautious step toward me. I didn't move away. "It is within the council's power to make those sorts of decisions, not mine."

"But you could at least try, and I don't see you doing much of that lately," I snapped. He flinched, but I kept going. "Aren't you a member of the council?"

"Yes and no." He gestured for me to sit down on the grass, but I refused, standing with my arms crossed. "I spend most of my time separate from them. When they desire my input, or when it is a decision that directly affects my duties, I join them. But their decisions deal with the world of the living. That is not my realm."

"So why don't you tell them to shove it and get this whole thing over with? If they rule over the living and you're not living, why do they get to say whether or not you're doing a good job?"

Henry gazed off into the distance toward the sparkling lake. "They are the ones who are able to grant you immortality, not I. Perhaps in the beginning they would have trusted me with this decision, but the mistakes I made with Persephone have colored the council's opinion of my judgments."

I gritted my teeth at the mention of Persephone, and hatred

gnawed at my insides. Even if it was his actions that caused her not to love him, she was the one who'd hurt him. "Can I ask you something?"

He made a wordless sound in the back of his throat, and I took that as a yes. I settled on the grass beside him.

"Why did you kidnap Persephone?"

He pulled away enough to look me in the eye, and the pain on his face made me regret my question.

"I'm sorry," I said quickly. "You don't have to tell me if you don't want."

"No, no." He shook his head. "I am not angry. I am only trying to understand how it is possible that the truth of the matter could have gotten so lost in time."

I waited for him to continue, ignoring the dampness of the grass that was starting to seep through my jeans. He looked pensive, as if he were looking for the exact way to tell me something he didn't often get to say.

"I did not kidnap her," he finally said. "It was an arranged marriage that she accepted, as her parents were the ones to set it up."

I hesitated, trying to remember the details of the mythology I'd learned. "Zeus and Demeter?"

"Very good." His smile didn't reach his eyes. "You must have figured out by now that my family is a strange one. We call ourselves brothers and sisters, but in truth we are not. We have simply been together for so long that the words to describe the bond we have do not exist. Family is the only comparison we can draw, though it is a weak one."

"Ella told me you weren't actually siblings."

"Did she?" He seemed darkly amused by this. "We all have the same creator, but we are not strictly related. In fact, my brother—who is, of course, not actually my brother—is married to my sister. And their son is married to our other sister as well."

Making a face, I tried to wrap my mind around that. "Not related, right?"

"Not even remotely." He pressed his lips to my forehead, a silent apology. Or maybe he was trying to alleviate my anger. "Persephone's mother is my favorite sister, and she was the one to suggest the match. Persephone and I got along well when we saw each other, and her mother insisted she wanted us both to be happy. While I was used to being alone, I enjoyed the prospect of spending so much time with Persephone. When she didn't object, things were finalized, and she became my wife."

Wife. What I would be to him if I succeeded. As often as I thought of what a future with Henry might bring, the idea of being his wife—anyone's wife—still hadn't settled well with me. Maybe it was because I was eighteen, or maybe it was because my mother had never married, but I couldn't imagine it. Then again, maybe that was a good thing. No expectations. And my desire to be married wasn't stronger than my desire to be with Henry, like I suspected Persephone's might have been.

"She helped me rule," he continued, "doing as you will hopefully be doing soon enough. But she was young when we married, and..." He averted his eyes. "Eventually she saw me as her captor rather than her husband. She resented me greatly, and while in the beginning she was fond of me, I do not believe she ever loved me, not like I love her."

Love, not loved. I exhaled.

"History takes her side, of course, and I have my suspicions about that, but in truth I never forced her into a marriage. I love her dearly, and it was agony for me to see her so miserable. After several millennia, she fell in love with a mortal and chose to give up her immortality for him, and I let her go. It hurt a great deal, but I knew it would hurt more if I made her stay."

I was silent for the space of several heartbeats as I digested what he was telling me. Unrequited love was one thing, but spending an incomprehensible amount of time in that sort of pain—I couldn't imagine it. I didn't even want to try.

"I'm sorry," I said, my anger dissipating as I wished there was something else to say.

"Don't be." Henry's lips curled up into a smile that held so much self-hatred that I wanted to reach over and smack him upside the head for it. "She made her decision. You have made yours. It is the most you can do."

Again I nodded, still at a loss for words. James was right. He would always be in love with Persephone no matter what I did; I had to accept that. But part of me wanted him to love me, too. Even if it was only enough to get him through the spring, it would do.

"Henry?" I said, my throat tightening as I gathered the courage I needed. "Do you think you could ever love me? Even a little?"

He looked stunned at my question, his brow furrowed and his mouth slightly open. But I needed to know—I couldn't expect a fairy-tale ending, but I never had anyway. My fairy tale was one where both my mother and Henry were still alive, and since it was too late for my mother, all of my hope rested on Henry's shoulders.

Finally he pressed his lips to the corner of my mouth in a chaste kiss, and he then said softly, "As much as I am capable of loving anyone else, yes."

My heart sank, but while it wasn't the answer I'd hoped for, it would have to do. He took my hand in both of his and looked at me, as if daring me to look away. I didn't.

"You have fought for me, and do not think I have not seen that. You believe in me when few others will, and I cannot tell you how much that means to me. I will always treasure your friendship and affection."

Friendship and affection. The words hit me like a rock, but I struggled to remember that they were better than the alternative—so much better. But something inside of me felt empty, as if he'd stolen something precious from me. Maybe it hadn't been all romance and rainbows between us so far, but I'd hoped for more, and I didn't know how else to show him what I wanted. Not without offering myself to him completely, and I couldn't, not yet. Not when I didn't know if he felt the same.

When he continued, I wanted to look away, but I couldn't. "If you are not deemed worthy, then I will step down, and it is my hope that if you wish, we might spend time together before I fade completely."

A rush of surprise filled me, and I blinked back the stubborn tears that had formed in my eyes. "How long would that be?"

"I do not know," he said. "But I suspect I will last until your death, if it comes to that. If you will still have me when this is through."

I forced a small smile. "That would be nice," I said. "To—to be your friend."

"You are my friend," he said, and I said nothing. Friends. Just friends—nothing more. I tried to feel relieved, to remind myself that I hadn't wanted any of this to begin with, but all I could feel was mind-numbing hurt.

He said he would love me, and I believed him. But it would never be in the way I wanted. I didn't know when I'd decided I wanted more—maybe the moment I'd kissed him at Christmas, or when I'd lost Ava all over again and couldn't bear to lose anyone else—but all I knew was that I did. It was something he could never give me, and that hurt more than I could stand.

Most of February slipped by in the same monotonous pattern as before. I took my meals alone, and I had classes with Irene nearly every day. After that first exam, she never gave me another test again, although whether it was because she'd never intended on it or because Henry had asked her not to, I didn't know.

The one thing that was not monotonous was my time with Henry. Our conversation in the Underworld had been a silent turning point, and while spending the evenings with him was always the best part of my day, there was an underlying hurt now that I couldn't justify. He'd laid out what he wanted, and I knew I had to respect that. I couldn't have him, but with each evening that passed, I felt myself falling deeper and deeper for him, spiraling downward into a place where the word *love* was synonymous with pain.

Every look, every touch, every brush of his lips, as innocent as they may have been—how could he say he only wanted friendship when he was treating me like his partner? When he wanted me to be his wife? I didn't understand it, and as time passed, I grew more confused. I didn't know what this sort of love felt like, but by the time winter started to come to an end, with the exception of my mother, I felt closer to him than

I had to anyone in my life. It hurt to be away from him, but sometimes, when he told me stories of his life before me, his life with Persephone, it was agony to be with him. Still, our friendship was so strong that it felt like the most natural thing in the world. There was no one I'd have rather spent my time with, no matter how much it hurt.

Finally, despite there still being so many tests remaining, it was March, the last month I was required to stay in Eden Manor. On one hand, I was reluctantly excited at the thought of getting to leave and seeing the world again; on the other, I knew what was waiting for me when I left. If I were lucky, I would have one last day to sit by my mother's side and talk to her, whether or not she could really hear me. Then, once I'd said my goodbyes, she would die. I began to prepare myself for that reality, though I struggled with it as I always had. How was I ever supposed to tell her goodbye?

A few days into the month, Henry met with the council. I wasn't allowed to go—didn't want to go and face James—and I busied myself with entertaining Pogo in the green-and-gold drawing room while he was gone. I suspected it had something to do with my tests and how they'd seemed to stop in the months that followed Christmas, but I hadn't asked him before he'd left. The only thing I was certain of anymore was that no girl had gotten as far as I had, and with each day that passed, the danger grew. Unless it really had been James who'd killed all those girls—and as angry as I was with him, I refused to believe he was capable of murder—whoever had done it was still out there, waiting for the right time.

"Do you think he'll grow much bigger?" said Calliope as we waited for Henry to return, and she scratched Pogo's pink belly. His tongue lolled out to the side, and he seemed to be enjoying himself.

"Doubt it," I said. "He hasn't really grown much lately."

"Are you going to take him with you when you leave?"

I shrugged. "Maybe. I haven't decided. He'd probably like it here better, wouldn't he?"

Before she could respond, the doors opened and a chill fell over the room. Calliope scrambled to her feet, still awkwardly holding Pogo, and I twisted around to see who was there. Henry stood framed in the doorway, anger rolling off of him in waves.

"I—I have to go," said Calliope, shoving Pogo in my arms and rushing out of the room. As she passed Henry, she gave him a strange, lingering look, though she didn't say anything to him.

Several tense seconds passed before Henry finally spoke. "I need you to stop eating."

Cuddling Pogo to my chest, I sat down on one of the couches. "Why? I like eating. Eating's sort of important to staying alive, y'know, and unlike the rest of you, that's something I happen to be."

"You do not need to eat here." Henry closed the door and moved toward me, but he didn't sit down. "It is unnecessary, and you must adapt."

Slowly I set Pogo down, and he at least had sense enough to run behind the couch. I, on the other hand, stupidly stayed put. "I like eating. I'm not overweight, and I don't see what the big deal is."

Henry's eyes were a stormy shade of gray that made me shiver. "What about Calliope?"

"What about her?"

"Every time you sit down to a meal, you put her in jeopardy."

I stared at him. "That's a horrible thing for you to use against me. What am I supposed to say to that?"

"It is true," he said harshly. "And I would prefer that you say it is enough incentive to make you stop eating."

I clenched my jaw. "Why are you bringing it up now?"

He closed his eyes, a crease forming in the middle of his brow. I'd never seen him so upset, even when Xander had been killed. But it was *food*. What was the big deal?

"It is a test," he said softly, as if he didn't want anyone to overhear. "If you don't stop eating before the council makes their judgment, you will fail."

Eating was a *test?* "How can that possibly be a test?" I blurted. "What's the point? To see if I can starve myself until I'm so skinny that I'll die the instant I leave?"

"Gluttony," he said sharply, and I shut my mouth. "And to see how well you adapt. That is what it tests. Do not yell at me, Kate. I am not the one who decided what the tests would be."

Gluttony. I had to think for a moment, but once I realized where I'd heard the word before, I froze. "The seven deadly sins? That's what I'm being tested on?"

Henry wrung his hands together. "I cannot answer that. If the council discovers I have told you this much, there is a very good chance that we will automatically fail."

We. The way he said it in a thick voice tugged at something inside of me, and with a start I realized he was finally doing it. I pressed my hands together, hardly daring to hope.

"You care?" I said. "I thought—"

He stood and started to pace, refusing to look at me. "You have been unhappy with me. Why?"

I opened my mouth to protest, but nothing came out. He was right. "Because," I said in a miserable voice and hating myself for it. "I don't want to just be your friend."

Henry stopped and turned toward me, though he didn't look surprised. Instead he looked like he was trying to put the pieces together. "I thought you did not wish to act as my wife."

I made a face. "There are steps between friend and wife, you know. I mean, I know you're ancient and all, but you must have at least heard of dating."

He didn't smile, but his expression softened. "If you pass, you *will* be my wife. Is that something you are willing to accept now?"

I nodded, trying not to look too nervous. Or think about the whole thing too much.

"Because you care for me?"

"Yes," I mumbled, embarrassed. "And if you hold that against me—"

I didn't have time to finish. One second he stood across the room, and the next he crouched down beside me, kissing me so deeply that by the time he finally pulled away, I was almost gasping for air. "What—" I started, but he pressed his finger against my lips.

"I care," he said in a trembling voice. "I care so much that I do not know how to tell you without it seeming inconsequential compared to how I feel. Even if I am distant at times and seem as if I do not want to be with you, it is only because this scares me, too."

I stared at him. He leaned in and kissed my swollen lips again, and this time I kissed back. Time seemed to fall away around us, and all I could see, hear, taste, smell, feel was him. A delicious kind of warmth spread through me, but this time it wasn't my ankle he was healing.

When he pulled away a second time, I let my hands fall from his hair to my side, and I watched him, unsure of what to do now. He straightened and stood, though he didn't take his eyes off me. "Please," he said. "Stop eating."

I nodded, too disarmed to come up with anything to say in protest.

"Thank you." He reached out to brush his fingers against my cheek, and then stepped toward the door. Before I could form any kind of coherent thought in my head, he was gone.

I licked my lips, still able to taste him, and smiled. Finally, after nearly six months, he was trying.

That night, as he always did, Henry slipped into my room an hour after I finished dinner. I'd spent the afternoon wondering what would happen, if it would all go back to normal or if there would be more of those heart-pounding kisses, but by the time he arrived, I'd decided it didn't matter. It was more than enough to know I was no longer alone in the fight for his existence.

"I am sorry," he said, lingering near the doorway. I was on my bed playing with Pogo, who had a new assortment of toys to keep him entertained. I looked up in time to see Henry close the door. "My actions earlier were uncalled for."

For one horrible moment, I thought he was apologizing for kissing me. It wasn't until I felt my face drain of color that I realized he was sorry for getting angry I was still eating, and by then, all I could manage was a nervous laugh. "You were just trying to warn me. I had one last meal tonight, but I'm done now, I promise."

The Greek seafood pasta, which usually made me delirious with hunger, had tasted like sawdust in my mouth, and I'd only managed a few bites. But there would be no more food now. I'd made a promise to Henry, and I wasn't going to break it any more than I already had.

He took a tentative step toward me. "Still, I should not have yelled as I did. You did nothing to deserve it."

"You were worried." I shrugged. "I want to pass, and I wouldn't have stopped eating if you hadn't told me. So thank you."

He crossed the room and took a seat next to me on the bed, picking up one of Pogo's toys. Yipping happily, my puppy dropped the bone I'd given him and went after Henry, tugging and growling relentlessly at the piece of rope.

"He is quite determined," said Henry with a tiny smile.

"Stubborn as a mule," I said. "Thinks he's the size of one, too."

Henry chuckled, and I was so relieved to see him happy again that I almost didn't hear the soft knock on my door. "Kate?"

It was Calliope. "Come on in," I said, and she pushed the door open as she carried a tray with the two mugs of hot chocolate she brought us every night. I glanced at Henry, silently asking for approval, and he nodded. When she set the tray down on the nightstand, he held up his hand to stop her. Even though she was staring at the carpet, she froze.

"You're sure it's safe?"

It was the first time he'd ever questioned her in front of me. Since the incident at Christmas, nothing else had happened, no threats or suspicious packages, but Calliope still tried everything I ate.

"I'm sure." Calliope spoke so softly I could barely hear her, and a blush stained her cheeks. "May I please go?"

He nodded, and she left the room so quickly that I didn't have time to thank her. I eyed the door, wondering what was wrong, but the scent of cocoa reached my nose and distracted me. After handing a mug to Henry, I picked up my own and took a sip. Henry watched me closely, and my pulse increased, though I wasn't sure whether it was because I thought something might happen or because of the way he stared. Maybe both.

I rolled my eyes playfully. "I'm not going to die today, Henry, I promise. Now, are you going to tell me why Calliope's terrified of you?"

He grimaced and drank, undoubtedly a stalling technique. "I am afraid she has been like that for a number of years. The ease you have while spending time with me is quite rare. Most are afraid of me."

"That's ridiculous." Though part of me knew it wasn't. I was sure he held back when he was around me.

"When you are the ruler of the dead, it is not so difficult to see why others do not like you." He waved dismissively. "It is the same with most of the staff. Those who will look me in the eye when I speak to them are few and far between."

"I'm not afraid of you." And to demonstrate that point, I leaned forward and kissed him like he'd kissed me in the drawing room, careful not to spill my drink. My heart pounded in my chest as I waited for him to respond, hoping he wouldn't pull away and declare everything that had happened a mistake.

To my relief, he finally returned it. His lips were warm against mine, and he tasted like chocolate.

Eventually he broke the kiss and took my mug from me, setting both of them on the nightstand. "I do not think Pogo appreciates being ignored."

Pogo was on his belly and watching us both intently. When he saw that I was looking at him, he wagged his tail. "Pogo, off," I said, tossing a few of his new toys from the mattress onto the pillow that served as his bed. He obeyed and scampered down, leaving me and Henry on our own.

I turned back to Henry, feeling more relaxed and content than I had all day. "There," I said, leaning toward him again. "All better."

The way he kissed me—I could've drowned in him and never been happier. Each time he touched me, I expected sparks, and the heat of his palm against my bare neck was almost too much to take. Crawling into his lap, I wrapped my legs around his waist, deepening the kiss. While I was leading, he seemed as eager as I was, and it felt as if all of that pent-up emotion was finally spilling out of both of us. Several moments later, I pulled away.

"Henry?" I ran my hands through his hair as I caught my breath. "Can I tell you something and have you promise not to laugh at me?"

"I would never laugh at you." His eyes reflected the ache I felt, and I knew I could trust him on that.

Swallowing, I said in a low voice, "I'm not very good at this. The whole—falling for someone thing, being with them...even with the kissing, I'm not very good."

He started to protest, but I kept talking. Now that I knew he cared for me like I cared for him, I had to tell him. Maybe

I should've given him more time to adjust, but there was an urgency that seemed to spread through me, making the words fall from my lips without anything to stop them.

"I'm not, even if you think I am. But no matter what this started out as…an accident, fate, whatever—I'm glad you found me that night. Not because of what happened, but because of now. Because I get to be here with you. And I'm scared, too, but—but thank you for telling me today. Thank you for trusting me with that. I've never…" I pressed my lips together, trying to find the right words. "I've never felt like this for anyone. And I'm not really sure what falling in love feels like, but I think—I know I have. With you."

It wasn't the most eloquent speech ever, but Henry didn't seem to care. For the first time since we'd met, he looked bowled over, and I worried that I'd said too much.

"Did you know," he said, his breath warm on my cheek, "that that is the first time anyone has ever told me they loved me?"

Startled, I did the only thing I could think of—I kissed him again. "You'd better get used to hearing it more often, because I plan on saying it to you an awful lot."

He returned my kiss, and my head spun as my hands drifted down to unbutton his shirt. This time we didn't stop.

The next morning I awoke in a tangle of limbs. My head pounded and my body ached, but I couldn't find it in me to mind too much. The warmth and drowsiness I felt wrapped in Henry's arms was more than enough to make me happy. The previous night came flooding back to me, and I distinctly remembered skirting the topic of Henry with my mother, too embarrassed to tell her I'd slept with him, but I didn't regret it. It simply wasn't the kind of thing I wanted to tell her until I had no choice. Better she assumed that sort of thing happened after the wedding, if it happened at all.

"Mm, morning," I said, forcing my eyes to open. Instead of smiling, Henry was staring at me as if I'd grown another limb. Confused, I struggled to prop myself up on my elbow, but even that little movement felt like a knife being thrust into the side of my head. Wincing, I gingerly lay back on the pillow. One look at Henry's face told me I'd made things worse.

He was standing before I realized he'd gotten out of bed. Producing a black silk robe out of nowhere, he quickly wrapped it around his body, never taking his eyes off of me. But it wasn't the loving look he'd given me the night before. "Does your head hurt?"

It seemed like a stupid question, all things considered, but I nodded—and immediately regretted it.

"Do you feel achy?"

"A bit," I admitted, squeezing my eyes shut. "What's wrong?"

He didn't answer. Forcing myself to open my eyes once more, I saw him standing over the mugs, sniffing what remained of the hot chocolate.

"Henry?" I said, my voice rising. "What's going on?"

Without warning, he threw the mugs across the room. They smashed against the wall, staining the wallpaper.

"Dammit!" he roared, and then proceeded to curse in another twenty languages I couldn't name. Struggling to sit up again, this time I pushed past the pain. I clutched the sheet to my chest and stared at him, too shocked to say anything.

"Calliope!" he yelled, his voice booming, but there was no

reply. Instead Nicholas opened the door, making a point of not looking at me.

"In bed," he said gruffly. "She is ill."

Henry clenched fists so tightly that I was afraid he might hit something and destroy the whole manor in the process. "Look after her," he said, storming toward the door. "No one comes in or out of this room without my permission, do you understand?"

Nicholas nodded, his expression impassive. He wasn't helping.

"Henry?" I said in a small voice, my heart pounding in my chest. "What's going on?"

"I'm sorry," he said, staring at me in a way that made my blood run cold. "I am so very, very sorry."

And with no other explanation, he left.

CHAPTER 16

THE RIVER STYX

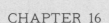

I spent the rest of the morning in bed crying. My head ached and my entire body was so sore that getting up didn't seem possible, but all I could think about was the way Henry had looked at me before he'd left. As if he would never see me again.

It wasn't fair, and for the life of me I didn't understand why he was doing this. Was it because I'd said I loved him? It'd been quick, and I hadn't given it much thought, but after I said it, I knew it was the truth. I was willing to do anything it took to give him another chance, even if it meant giving up any choice I had in my life, and if that didn't equal love, I didn't know what did. But it wasn't like I expected him to love me in return.

The more I thought about it, the more I put the pieces together. The confession that fell off my tongue in a shower of words I couldn't stop—the sudden need to be with him—the warning not to eat. I'd been poisoned. Except this time, so had Henry and Calliope, and we'd all survived.

It hadn't been designed to kill me. It was an aphrodisiac.

Once I understood, everything seemed much clearer to me. The only question was who? Was someone trying to give me and Henry a push in the right direction, or was there something else to it? And if there was, who hated me enough to even try?

The only person I could think of was Ella. She hated Ava, and maybe if she thought I was on her side…or maybe she thought that getting rid of me would mean getting rid of Ava, too. With the way Ava had behaved lately, I almost couldn't blame her. But what did Ella have to gain?

James? I dismissed the thought as quickly as it appeared. The last thing he wanted was to push me and Henry closer together. It was possible that this was his intention, for Henry to storm out and ignore me for the rest of my stay, but it was a risk I was sure James wouldn't take. Giving Henry any excuse to fall for me and to fight for his realm would be dangerous. Besides, the only surefire way to stop it was to make me fail a test, and—

My blood turned to ice in my veins. Of course. The tests. Gluttony, the seven deadly sins—lust.

Despair filled the pit of my stomach. I'd failed, hadn't I? Even if it wasn't my fault, even if it had been an aphrodisiac, it didn't matter. That had to be why Henry was so upset. Anything else didn't make sense, unless he really had been forcing affection for my sake.

I didn't want to think about that. I didn't want to think about possibly failing either, so instead I dragged myself out of bed, grateful that Nicholas was stationed outside my room instead of inside. Without any painkillers, I had to deal with the aches and pains, apparent side effects of whatever drug I'd been given, but even those were duller now.

I dressed, and despite my protesting body, I picked up my clothes from the night before and remade the bed. The council had to see what had happened, that we'd been set up. If they were at all fair and just, they couldn't fail me because of this. I clung to that hope, that one last chance, and forced myself to push any other possibility aside. Everything would be okay. It had to be.

Calliope came by shortly before sundown, looking about as sick as I felt. She was pale and trembling, and instead of sending her away, as Nicholas had with every other servant who tried to check on me, he offered his arm to her and escorted her inside.

"Calliope?" I said from my spot near the window, curled up in one of the overstuffed armchairs. "Are you okay?"

"I'm fine," she said with a tired smile as Nicholas helped her into a chair. "The more important question is, how are you?"

I waited until Nicholas left to answer, even though I was sure he could hear everything through the door. "Tired," I admitted. "I ache a lot."

That had unexpected results. Calliope's face crumpled, and in less time than it took for me to haul myself out of my chair, she was sobbing. "Oh, Kate! I'm so sorry, I didn't know until after I'd dropped it off, and I tried to send someone to warn you, but it was too late, and I didn't know what to do—"

I knelt beside her chair, taking her hand. "Don't apologize. You had no way of knowing, and I'm sorry they got to you, too."

Her lower lip trembled, but she seemed to be making a valiant effort to keep herself in check. "I should have waited a few minutes. It was stupid of me, and it could have gotten you killed."

"But you didn't," I said. "We're both fine. All three of us are *fine*."

She stared at me, her eyes almost unnaturally wide. "But did you and Henry..."

I swallowed the lump in my throat. "It's fine, Calliope, really. If this works out, then that would've probably happened eventually anyhow. And if it doesn't, I won't remember it, so either way."

The dark look on her face told me she didn't believe me. I didn't believe myself either. His extreme reaction to the drug had distracted me from thinking about the fact that something major had happened the night before, and it didn't feel as if it'd totally sunk in. This was supposed to be a big deal; I was supposed to feel upset or dirty, or at the very least confused about what to feel about the whole thing. But at that point, I was far more concerned about Henry than I was myself.

"Why do you think it was inevitable that he go to bed with you?" said Calliope in a careful voice I couldn't read. "There are rumors that he has never...that he and Persephone didn't even..." She trailed off, clearly uncomfortable.

I opened my mouth, fully intending on saying something intelligent, but the only thing I managed to blurt out was, "*He* was a virgin?"

"No one knows for sure," said Calliope quickly. "He was very possessive of Persephone, but he did love her. She just didn't love him back, that's all. They had separate bedrooms and everything."

I frowned. "He doesn't have to worry about that with me."

"Which part?"

"The part where she didn't love him back. I mean, if we'd met on the street or something, I probably wouldn't have even bothered—I mean, he's gorgeous." I remembered what James had said so many months ago and managed a small smile. "He's a ten. A twelve, even, and I'm nowhere near that. I would've never worked up the courage to talk to him on my own. But getting to know him..." It was pathetic and hard for me to admit, but it was the truth. And maybe if Calliope understood, she wouldn't feel so guilty about letting it happen in the first place. "I love him. I don't understand how anyone could know him and not love him."

Calliope stared at the carpet, her cheeks red. "Me neither."

I was silent, not knowing how to respond. Had she even intended for me to hear it? But she didn't say anything else, so I didn't press her. Eventually I stood on my aching legs and eased back down in my chair, wincing when my head protested. It wasn't the end of the world, but it was bad enough to make me glad I didn't have to trek down to the dining room for dinner tonight.

"I have an idea," said Calliope cheerfully. Her bright mood, so different from what it'd been only seconds before, startled me.

"Yeah?" I said, not meaning to sound as suspicious as I did.

"A picnic—tomorrow, once we've both recovered. We can walk out to the river and bring a blanket and everything. It's supposed to be warm."

After getting a good look at the way she was beaming, there was no way I could've said no. She felt bad enough about getting Henry and me into trouble, and an afternoon away from the drama and confusion of the manor sounded wonderful. The thought of the river still sent a shiver down my spine, but I did my best to ignore it.

"That sounds great," I said, and Calliope grinned. At the very least it would serve as a nice distraction from the possibility that I'd already failed.

Henry didn't show up that night, and for the first time since Christmas, I slept alone. I tried not to think about it too much, but in the dark with Pogo curled up beside me, it was impossible not to. Was he mad at me because I'd made him sleep with me and subsequently failed because of it? But I hadn't made him, had I? He hadn't tried to stop me.

Was he mad because I said I'd loved him, and now that the drug had worn off, he realized how stupid it sounded? Or did he feel guilty about it? I didn't care if he still loved Persephone. While I didn't exactly like her, he was dedicated and loyal, and that he could still love someone who'd been so horrible to him—there was nothing to feel guilty about.

Unless he felt guilty *because* he loved his wife so much. Did he feel like he'd betrayed her?

It was an accident, not a mistake, unless Henry thought it was. Maybe it wasn't exactly how I'd envisioned it all happening, but it hadn't been bad enough to make him feel like he had to stay away. Had it?

Or maybe he felt guilty for giving in and helping me fail. Even if that was the truth, it didn't explain his absence. It hadn't been his fault, and if I really had failed, there was no point in me staying in Eden Manor anymore. But I was still here, and that had to mean something.

I slept badly, and even my dreams with my mother brought me no comfort. I was quiet and withdrawn, and while she asked me again and again what was wrong, I couldn't bring myself to tell her. I hated myself for it, not wanting to squander my last

few weeks with her, but even if I could talk to her about it, I
didn't know what I would say. She was placing all of her hopes
for my future in Henry, and I couldn't tell her how badly I'd
managed to destroy it. It would break her heart, and at least
one of us deserved to be happy.

Thinking of Henry hurt, and the morning brought no re-
prieve. I tried to leave my bedroom, but Henry's orders hadn't
changed: I was stuck in that room until someone Henry trusted—which seemed to be limited to himself, Nicholas and
Calliope—came to pick me up. There wasn't anywhere to go,
but I hated being caged.

But wasn't that exactly what I'd been for the past six months?
The small voice in the back of my head was surprisingly bitter.
Hadn't I been caged like some sort of animal, like I belonged
to him?

No. I'd walked into this willingly, and he'd made it clear I
wasn't being held against my will. It was terrible of me to even
think otherwise. I wasn't Persephone.

Calliope came to pick me up at noon, picnic basket in hand.
She looked so happy that it felt like the conversation we'd had
the day before never happened, and I didn't dare bring it up.
We linked arms, and while we moved through the corridors,
I kept my eyes peeled for any sign of Henry. He'd always been
there when I wanted him to be, but now there was no sign of
him.

As we left the house, Nicholas trailed a few feet behind us.
While being followed was still annoying, it was comforting
to have him there; limp or not, no one could've been crazy
enough to mess with him. Pogo also seemed fond of him as he
followed him through the garden, sticking close to Nicholas
instead of me.

"Kate?"

I looked up at the sound of my name, but that was as far as I got. In an instant, Nicholas was between me and Ava, who was standing on the other side of the fountain. It was the closest I'd been to her since Christmas.

I didn't want to ignore her, but between all that had happened with Henry, she was one more thing I couldn't find the energy to deal with. She made me feel guilty, and I felt enough things right now without piling that on as well.

"Kate—" Ava tried to move around Nicholas, but he was massive. "Please. They wouldn't let me into your room, and I need to—"

"Don't you get it?" said Calliope so viciously that I stared at her, surprised. "She doesn't want to talk to you."

I could see Ava's expression underneath Nicholas's left elbow, and she looked stunned. "Kate," she said, her eyes welling with tears. "Please. Just for a minute."

I stood there with my feet rooted to the ground. I'd never seen her look so scared in her life, and against my better judgment, I said, "What is it?"

She looked at Nicholas and Calliope nervously. "Can we talk alone?"

Nicholas scowled. "No one is alone with her."

"Please, Nicholas," said Ava in such a familiar way that made me wonder if she had gotten to him as well. "I just need a moment—"

Calliope cut her off. "We're leaving now." Tugging at my elbow, she led me toward the forest. I didn't fight her, though I would've insisted on speaking with Ava only a few days before. But someone had to have done this to Henry and me, and as much as I hated the thought, Ava had the motivation to do it.

All she would've had to do was slip into the kitchen and spike our drinks. Maybe she'd only been trying to help, to give me and Henry a push, not realizing what the consequences would be. Or maybe she'd been trying to ruin things for me so completely that I felt as alone as she did. Neither possibility was pleasant.

As we reached the edge of the trees, I glanced over my shoulder and saw Nicholas holding Ava's arm, stopping her from following us. She fought back, whirling around to face him and giving him a lecture I was glad I couldn't hear. But at least she wasn't following us.

"How embarrassing," said Calliope, stepping gingerly over a thick root that sprung from the ground. "It must feel awful to be in her position, but that's no excuse for acting like that."

I dared another look. Nicholas was following us now, and Ava sat on the edge of the fountain, her shoulders slumped. She was watching me.

I snapped my head around to stare straight ahead, not looking back the rest of the hike. I was silent, trying to sort through my thoughts, but my head was still a little muddled from whatever had been in my hot chocolate. Did I have it wrong? Was it possible that she'd heard about the poison as well? Was she concerned?

But the more I thought about it, the more I realized that she was the most likely suspect. After what had happened over Christmas, I couldn't blame her for being angry with me, and I had so many things she didn't. Life, opportunity—and at least for a day, I'd had Henry.

What was the next step? Did her jealousy give her motivation enough to try to kill me? Or had she heard about Henry's reaction, and was that enough to satisfy her?

"The river's this way," said Calliope, interrupting my thoughts as we picked our way through the forest floor. I looked down as I walked, not wanting to trip.

I struggled to come up with something to say that didn't involve Ava. "Does it run through the whole place?" I couldn't remember seeing any river on the other side of the hedge.

"It goes underground," said Calliope, as if this were perfectly normal. "I heard Ava almost drowned in it once. Is that true?"

"She didn't almost drown," I said, grimacing at the memory. "She did drown. I had to jump in after her. It's how she died— hit her head on a rock." I focused on the forest floor, not wanting to think about that night.

"What do you think you'd be doing right now if you weren't here? If Ava hadn't died?"

That was the very question I'd been avoiding asking myself for the past six months. "I don't know. I'd be back in New York, I guess."

"With your mother?"

I sighed. "No. She'd have died by now." That was much easier to say than I'd expected. "She wanted me to stay in Eden and finish high school, but I don't think I'd have been able to do that."

Calliope shot me a sympathetic look, but I didn't want her pity. "The clearing's just up here," she said, and peering through the trees, I saw it—a meadow about the size of my bedroom. I heard the river gurgling nearby. "What about your father?"

"What about him?" I said. "He's never been in the picture. I don't know where he is, and I don't care. We've always done fine without him."

"You're not so fine anymore," said Calliope softly. I ignored her. My mother rarely talked about my father, and I'd learned from an early age not to mention him. It wasn't that she'd seemed angry or bitter about him. There simply wasn't much to tell. They hadn't been married, I hadn't asked what happened, and that was that. Any fantasies I'd had when I was little about him showing up on the doorstep one day and embracing me, buying me ice cream and toys—they were long gone now. My mother and I were a team. We didn't need anyone else.

Calliope and I set up our picnic in silence, her laying out the blanket and me rifling through the food. Remembering my promise to Henry was difficult while staring directly into a basket stuffed with sandwiches and macaroni and fried chicken and the same luscious desserts I was served every evening, but I managed. Barely.

"I'm sorry—this looks delicious, but I can't eat," I said. "I'm really not very hungry."

"Sure you are," she said, straightening out a corner of the blanket and flopping down in the middle. At the edge of the clearing, Nicholas loomed, looking surly. "You didn't have breakfast. Besides, I'm eating, too, remember?"

"It's not—" I bit my lip. The last thing I wanted was to insult her, but I couldn't very well tell her it was a test. "After what happened...I promised Henry, that's all. I'm sorry. I should've told you that before you hauled all of this out here."

I waited for her to say something, but her expression was unreadable. Finally she smiled, though it didn't reach her eyes. "It's no problem at all. Would you mind if I...?"

"Not at all," I said. "Help yourself, really. And don't mind my growling stomach."

She started to unpack the basket, and I sat down across from her, folding my knees to my chest. We weren't very far from the spot where I'd first met Henry. It hurt to think about that, so I turned away, instead concentrating on Pogo as he pounced around on the grass. "Calliope? Can I ask you something personal?"

She didn't look up from unpacking. "Of course."

I glanced at Nicholas, who was still within earshot. "It has to do with the…um, the stuff that was in the hot chocolate."

"Oh." Her cheeks colored. "Maybe it'd be better if Nicholas…"

"Right." I cleared my throat. "Nicholas? Do you mind giving us a few minutes?"

He looked back and forth between us warily.

"I promise that no one's going to jump out and attack me in the middle of the forest," I said with a grim smile. "And if they do, I've got Calliope and Pogo to protect me. Just a few minutes, I promise."

"I'll watch out for her," said Calliope, and Nicholas caved, melting into the trees.

"How did you handle it? The thing that made me and Henry…" Now it was my turn to blush. Instead of doing the same, something unreadable flashed in Calliope's eyes.

"I'm not seeing anyone, and I didn't have enough of a dose to be climbing the walls, as you must have, so I rested." Her tone was flat and unfriendly, and I frowned. What had I said?

"Why aren't you dating anyone?" I said, figuring that was a safe enough question. "I mean, you're pretty and smart and funny, and you must know a lot about everyone here—"

"You're very kind," she said stiffly. "But I'm afraid I will never be good enough for the person I want."

My frown deepened. "Of course you are. Any guy would be crazy not to want you, you know."

"No, Kate." Her tone was icy now. "I'm not good enough for him, and I never will be. He's made it perfectly clear that the only person good enough for him is you."

Stunned, I stumbled over my words. "Calliope, I—I'm sorry, I didn't mean to—whoever it is, I'm sure I can talk to them and figure it out and—"

"Are you really that dense?"

I fell silent. Apparently I was.

"Your *Henry*," she spat. "I've been watching him weed through girls like you for decades. He doesn't care about me—all I am to him is someone to take care of his *guests*." Her eyes were bright with tears. "I told him once, you know, the first time he invited a girl here. Told him I'd be perfect for it, that I would love him and treat him a thousand times better than Persephone ever did. And you know what he did? He walked away and never said a damn thing to me again unless it had something to do with one of his spoiled girlfriends."

I didn't know what to say or think—what was I supposed to do? Was this why she was mad at me? Because I'd slept with him while under the influence of some stupid aphrodisiac?

"I'm sorry," I said, fighting to keep my voice under control. "I didn't choose this. Maybe if Henry never noticed you… maybe it was never meant to be."

"Of *course* it was meant to be!" she exploded. "How could it not be? I love him. I've loved him for longer than you've been alive."

Her expression flattened, and for a frightening moment, her eyes looked as dead as she was.

"And I will love him long after you're gone."

From the picnic basket, she withdrew something sharp and metallic. I didn't have time to run. She moved so fast that the knife was a blur, and I tried to move, to kick her legs out from under her and scramble away, but she grabbed my hair and yanked my head back so hard I was afraid my neck would snap.

"Nicholas!" I cried, but it was too late.

I felt the pressure first, a strange pushing against my side. The pain didn't blossom until she yanked the knife out, and that was when I screamed. Instinctively I thrust my elbow at her, feeling something crack as it found purchase, but that only gave her another opening. I gasped as she thrust the knife into my belly, the wound instantly white-hot. Already I could taste blood.

"How disappointing," she said, wiping the stream of blood from her broken nose. "Is that really the best you can do?"

With one last burst of adrenaline, I lunged at her, my hands closing around her throat. But I was losing blood rapidly, and I didn't have the strength to do the damage I wanted to do. Helpless, I squeezed my eyes shut as she delivered her final blow, stabbing me in the center of my chest. This time she didn't bother pulling the knife out.

She pried my hands from her neck and lifted me with ease. I could hear Pogo barking, the sound of it muffled and far away, and I tried to call out, but all I could manage was a sickening gurgle. Pain burned through me like fire. I grew dizzy, as if I were falling through a tunnel, but there was nothing I could do to hold on.

The splash of freezing water roused me enough to open my eyes. My vision was blurry, but I could see Calliope looming over me. Her body moved away from me, but she stood still. With my mind so sluggish, it took me several seconds to understand that I was in the river and floating away.

This was it. This was what death felt like. Cold and wet and numb and fire as I struggled to breathe, but no air filled my lungs. Instead of being scared, I was relieved. I wouldn't have to say goodbye to my mother after all. If Henry had any mercy in him, he would let her go the instant he realized I was dead.

Henry.

After letting him lower his guard and get his hopes up, I'd managed to get myself killed. And if I was dead, he would be, too. He hadn't given up on me, so what right did I have to give up on him?

I struggled weakly against the current, but it was futile. I could barely move, let alone try to swim to shore. The river would take me, and if I were lucky, eventually they'd find my body washed up on the riverbank somewhere nearby.

Above me the sun streamed through the bare branches, and I let myself drift down into the darkness, no longer cold. Instead I felt warm, as if Henry was embracing me, and I imagined him pulling me to shore. The cool air would hit my wet skin, and I would shiver. He would heal me, and in the end, everything would be all right again.

But it was too late for happy endings. I was already dead.

CHAPTER 17

DEATH

When I opened my eyes, I wasn't sure what I was expecting, but my mother wasn't it. Except there she was, looking as whole and healthy as she did every night when I fell asleep. Instead of greeting me with her usual smile, her expression was grim, and she stared at something in the distance.

"Mom?" I said, and when she looked at me, her eyes were so red and hollow that they couldn't have possibly been hers. Even in the worst days of her illness, she hadn't looked so empty. There had still been something inside of her, a spark or a smile or something that reminded me she was still my mother. Not this time.

I tried to take her hand, but the ground was unsteady, and I fell back down onto the bench. It was dark outside, nothing like the usual bright days we spent together, but the full moon and twinkling stars above us gave off enough light for me to make out where we were. We were still in Central Park, but for the first time since my dreams had begun, we weren't in Sheep Meadow. We were in a boat floating in the middle of the lake.

I froze. This was exactly how I'd nearly drowned when I was a kid.

"Mom, I—" My voice cracked, weaker than usual. I was exhausted and badly wanted to close my eyes and forget about all of this. To let it fade away with the rest of my life. "I'm sorry."

She stared out across the water, her misery painted so clearly on her face that I could feel it. "It isn't your fault," she said, her voice cutting through the eerie quiet that surrounded us. Even the things that usually made sounds, like crickets chirruping or leaves rustling in the breeze, were silent. All I heard was her voice and the sound of waves lapping against the side of the boat. It was as if we were the only living things in the city.

I was too exhausted to move, but I wanted so badly to cross the boat and touch her. To show her I was still here, even if it wasn't for much longer. "But it is. It was Calliope this whole time, and I never saw it. I should have—"

"There have been many others who have known her for much longer than you," said my mother. "If anything, they should have been the ones to see it, not you. You cannot blame yourself for something you could not have possibly known."

"But I should have," I said, my voice so strained I was afraid it might disappear. "I knew someone wanted to hurt me, and I should have tried to find out who it was, but I was so concerned about Henry, and I thought—I thought no one would dare when he was around. I thought I was safe."

"You should have been." I could see the moonlight reflected on her cheeks, a sure sign she was crying. "I should have done more."

I hesitated. "What do you mean?"

Instead of answering me, she stood and crossed the boat,

making it sway. I gripped onto the edges as hard as I could, but drowning was the least of my worries. If I wasn't already dead, I would be soon enough. She sat beside me and enveloped me in her arms, and it was all I could do to keep my composure. One of us had to be strong.

I don't know how long we sat there, listening to the boat bob up and down in the water. It could have been minutes or hours—time seemed to stop in this place, and her embrace was all the protection I needed against the cool night air. I ran through the events that had happened by the river, how one moment Calliope had been my friend and the next my killer. How had I not seen it? But looking back on it, what was there to see?

"Why do you think she did it?" I mumbled against my mother's shoulder. "She said she loved Henry, but why kill everyone? Why risk his life like that, too?"

She ran her fingers through my hair. I was sure she meant to comfort me, but it only reminded me of what I was losing. What we both were losing. I'd failed her just as much as I'd failed Henry, but at least she forgave me for it. I wished I could forgive myself as well. "Why do you think?" she said gently, and I shrugged.

"I don't know." My mind wandered from Calliope to Henry to Ava, who had been so desperate to find love. "Maybe she was as lonely as he was. Maybe she thought she could save him. But—if she really did love him, how could she risk his existence like that? I mean, if I were her, I would've rather seen him with me than not see him at all."

"There's more than one kind of love," said my mother. "Maybe that's the difference between you and Calliope. Maybe that's why you were chosen and she wasn't."

I closed my eyes as I tried to think about it, but nothing outside of the sway of the boat and the sound of my mother breathing made sense anymore. "I don't want to go," I whispered. "I don't want to say goodbye."

She buried her face in my hair. "You won't have to."

Before I could figure out what she meant, the boat glided toward the shore. When it came to a stop, I opened my eyes and saw a silhouette cast against the water, distorting as the water rippled. My mother's slender arms were replaced with muscle, and I felt myself being lifted out of the boat. I wanted to struggle, to insist on staying with my mother, but my tongue felt heavy and my thoughts sluggish.

"I've got her," said a pained voice. Henry.

"Thank you," said my mother, her voice weighed down with something I didn't understand. She brushed a hand against my cheek and leaned forward to kiss his. "Take care of her, Henry."

"I will," he said, but there was nothing beyond that. My mother bent down and pressed her lips to my forehead. I desperately wanted to take her hand, but she did it for me, and using the last of my strength, I managed a small squeeze.

"Mom?" Even to me my voice sounded foreign and twisted, as if I were only beginning to learn how to form words.

"It's all right, sweetheart." She pulled away, and I could see the tears in her eyes. "I love you, and I'm so proud of you. Don't you ever forget it."

Panic bubbled inside of me, but with no way of releasing it, I suffered through the heart-wrenching pain. She was leaving. This was the end. I was supposed to have weeks more with her, wasn't that our deal?

Stupid me. How could I possibly spend time with her when I was dead and she wasn't?

"Love you, too," I said, and though it came out as more of a gurgle than anything, she smiled.

As Henry turned away from her and carried me into the inky blackness of the night, I turned my head enough to watch her grow smaller and smaller in the distance. Finally she seemed to fade, and she was gone. I clung to her last words, the glue that held me together as I struggled to resist the deep lull of sleep. I would see her again when she passed, and there would be no end of sunny summer days we could spend together in Central Park.

But even though I knew this, even though Henry was carrying me to my own death, I couldn't help but form a single word on my lips, one I'd resisted saying for so many years. The one word I hoped I'd never have to say.

Goodbye.

I expected death to be cold. Instead the first thing I felt was warmth—incredible warmth that filled my body, or at least what was left of it, and spread through me like honey. Was this what Ava went through? Waking up warm? It seemed too easy.

And then the pain started. Overwhelming, agonizing pain in my chest and my side, exactly where Calliope had stabbed me. Gasping, I mentally kicked myself for thinking it'd be so simple. Ava hadn't shown any signs of her head wound, after all, and my body had to heal before I could get up and walk around.

Whispers filled the air, and I couldn't make them out. Other dead souls? Would my mother be there waiting for me already?

Would I open my eyes and see grass and trees and sun, or was there more to it? I should've asked Henry when I'd had the chance.

It seemed like ages before I forced myself to look. At first the light burned, and I closed my eyes again, but when I took it slowly, they adjusted. This time my gasp had nothing to do with pain.

I was in my bedroom in the manor, surrounded by familiar faces. Ava and Ella, Sofia and Nicholas, even Walter was there, and they all looked worried. And out of the corner of my eye, I saw him. Henry.

My heart skipped a beat, but I was already too confused to wonder why it was still pumping in the first place. This wasn't Central Park.

"Am I dead?" Or at least that's what I'd meant to say. It came out more like a croak, and my throat was on fire—but what did it matter? Henry was there.

He grimaced, and a block of ice filled my stomach. I was dead, wasn't I? He could barely even look at me. "No," said Henry, staring down at my hands. He was holding mine. "You are alive."

My heart managed to sink and soar at the same time. That meant it wasn't over, that we could still do this, that I might still pass—

But then I remembered my mother's last words, and I realized what she'd meant. It hadn't been my time to go; it had been hers. Horror filled me, and I couldn't help the rush of tears, too exhausted to hold them back. I struggled to sit up, but the pain in my chest was torture.

"Lie still," said Walter sternly, putting a cup of warm liquid to my lips. I drank the sweet medicine, my eyes still streaming.

Everyone watched me, but I never looked away from Henry, too devastated to be embarrassed. "Henry?" I slurred as the medicine took effect. "Why…" I couldn't get my question out. Fighting against the urge to close my eyes, I tried to wiggle my toes to keep myself awake, but even that hurt.

"Sleep," he said. "I will be here when you awake."

Having no choice, I let myself drift away, clinging to his words and the hope that he was telling the truth.

That night, I didn't dream of my mother, and I knew I never would again. Nightmares filled the hours instead, images of water and knives and rivers of blood, and no matter how loudly I screamed, I couldn't wake up. They were different from the ones before I'd moved to Eden Manor—those had been menacing somehow, a warning. These were memories.

After what felt like an eternity, I woke up. My eyes flew open, my body still aching and the tension in my muscles doing nothing to help it. I expected light, but for several seconds there was nothing but dark. As my eyes adjusted, I noticed Henry.

He'd pulled an armchair up next to the bed, and while the other three sides of the curtains were closed, there was enough space open on the fourth for me to see him. He was still holding my hand. "Good morning," he said. There was a distance to his voice that I didn't understand.

"Morning?" I mumbled, trying to move my head to look out the window, but the curtains were closed. Henry ran his hand over a candlestick on the nightstand, and the wick burst into flame. It wasn't much light, but it was enough for me to see.

"Very early in the morning. It is still dark out." He hesitated. "How are you?"

Good question. I considered it for a moment, surprised when I realized that the pain had lessened. But that wasn't what he'd meant, and we both knew it. "She's gone, isn't she?"

"She asked to take your place, and I allowed it," he said, his eyes trained on our joined hands. "It was the only way I could take you from the Underworld. A life for a life—even I cannot break the laws of the dead."

His words hit me hard, and I licked my dry lips. "She gave up her life for me?"

"Yes," he said, offering me a cup of water. I took it with shaking hands, spilling more than I got inside of me. Henry refilled it, and this time he held the cup to my lips for me. "You were dead, and I could not heal you. It was her last gift to you."

I let out a soft sob as grief washed over me. She was gone, all because of my mistake. Because I'd let Calliope get too close. Because I'd trusted the wrong person. I felt like a piece of myself had disappeared, like I'd lost something vital I would never get back. I was empty and full of heartache at the same time, and everything felt wrong.

Several minutes passed before I could look at Henry again, let alone talk. When I did, my vision was blurred and my voice hoarse and forced. "What happened after the river?"

His grip on my hand tightened. "Ava was the one to find your body. She spent a very long time trying to save you, but despite her efforts, there was no hope."

My throat closed. After all I'd done to her, Ava still tried to save me. "And Calliope?"

Henry's expression hardened. "Nicholas apprehended her. She will be tried and punished for her actions, and I promise you that as long as I am in charge of hell, you will never have to see her again."

I shivered, and Henry covered me with the blanket once more. I didn't have it in me to tell him I wasn't cold.

"She was the one to send those nightmares," he said. "And the one to try to run you off the road. She saw the potential in you as we all did, and it is my guess that she feared the only way to stop you was to get to you before you were in Eden Manor."

She'd almost succeeded, too. If I hadn't been sure before, I was now certain that the only reason the car hadn't crashed into the trees was because Henry had been there to protect us.

"What's going to happen to her?"

"I do not yet know. She must have known she could not get away with it, as she did not try to run or deny her involvement, but—" He hesitated. "I suspect she thought she would be above punishment. In light of all that has happened, I thought it appropriate that you have a hand in deciding her fate."

I started to ask why she thought she wouldn't be punished, but part of me already knew. "She loves you so much that she couldn't stand the thought of you being with anyone else. She thought she was the only person who could make you happy."

"And instead she is the one who almost ruined the rest of my existence." Henry bent down and kissed my knuckles. Another shiver ran through me, completely different from the first. "I am the one who failed, not you, and I will do what I must to spend the rest of our time together making it up to you."

"You didn't fail me." I tried to turn on my side to face him, but movement brought only pain. "I'm the one who failed you."

He must have known I meant the test, but he shook his head anyway. "You could never fail me. I should have seen the signs long before this and never allowed her anywhere near you, and for that, I am so very sorry."

I was silent for a long moment, and at last I said in a small voice, "Are we okay? Not—not this, but the drink and—"

"Yes," he said. "I apologize for the way I reacted that morning. I was not angry at you, I was angry—" He stopped, fury briefly contorting his face, but when I blinked, his expression was blank. "It was not your fault. It was a tainted drink, nothing more."

"Even if I failed, I still love you, you know." Several seconds passed, and when it was clear he wasn't going to say anything in reply, I closed my eyes and sighed. My body screamed for sleep, and with my mind numb from the loss of my mother, I was sure that any attempt to resist would be lost.

I couldn't be sure, but as I found the edge of consciousness, his voice reached me, gentle and warm and everything I so badly needed to hear.

"I love you, too."

CHAPTER 18

THE OFFER

For the next week, Henry stayed by my side. Whatever was in the sweet tonic Walter kept pouring down my throat worked, and I spent most of the time asleep. Eventually the nightmares faded, but I still woke up gasping, unable to forget what the freezing water of the river felt like as it closed in around me.

The pain of my mother's death didn't dull, but I slowly managed to accept that it would be there for a long time, and wallowing in misery when I was supposed to be healing would only hurt Henry. It would be an insult to the gift she'd given me to ignore what she wanted for me, and the past six months had prepared me for this. They'd given me the chance to say goodbye in a way I would have never been able to do without Henry. Even though it hurt just as much, there was a kind of peace inside of me that wouldn't have otherwise been there. I held on to the hope that if the council decided to accept me despite what had happened between me and Henry, that I would one day be able to visit her, to talk to her and walk with her again. Death wasn't the end; Ava was proof of that. But I still mourned her. I still missed her.

I had a steady stream of visitors. At first it was Henry and

Walter, but after I insisted, Ava was allowed into my room as well. The moment she saw me, she flew to the side of my bed, her eyes red and puffy.

"Kate! Oh, God, you're all right—they said you were okay, but I was afraid they were just saying that 'cause you know how people can be, but you're really here and awake and oh, my God."

She wrapped her arms around me so loosely that I could barely tell they were there, but I didn't care if it hurt a little. I hugged her as tightly as I could and then spent the next thirty seconds paying for it. Pain shot through me, reaching all the way to the tips of my fingers and toes, but it was worth it.

"I'm sorry!" she said, flushing deeply as I gasped. On the other side of the bed, Henry looked worried, but by now he was used to me overexerting myself. As long as my stitches didn't start to bleed, everything was fine.

"Don't," I said once I could talk again. "I wanted to hug you. I am so monumentally sorry for everything. For yelling at you about Theo, for saying all that awful stuff to you—you didn't deserve it, any of it."

She waved her hand dismissively. "It doesn't matter. You were right—I was being an idiot. But you're alive! You're going to make it, and I won't be stuck here without my best friend." She gave me a look she must've intended to be stern, but it made me smile. "You know, none of this would've happened if you had let me teach you how to swim."

"Yeah, you were right on that," I said, ignoring the part where I'd been stabbed before being thrown into the river. I doubted it'd matter much to Ava. "Tell you what—once Henry says I'm all right, we can find someplace on the grounds and you can teach me how."

The grin on Ava's face was more than worth whatever it would cost me to get into the water again.

After she left that afternoon, Henry and I played cards. Even though I was recovering, I was still destroying him, but he didn't seem to mind. Instead, he seemed to enjoy having his backside handed to him, and I was more than happy to oblige.

"I'm going to miss you over the summer," I said after winning my fifth game in a row. "And beating you at Jacks."

Henry eyed me as he shuffled the deck. "I will miss you as well." There was a note of finality in his voice that frightened me. I held out hope that the council would understand and see that sleeping together hadn't been our fault, but had he spent the past week preparing to say goodbye to me?

"Henry?" I said softly. "Can we play pretend for a little while?"

He didn't look at me. "Of course."

I took a deep breath. "Can I visit sometime? I mean, I know I'm supposed to be going out and exploring the world, getting an education, passing high school, all of that, but I figured maybe if I wind up staying in Eden, I could stop by every now and then before September."

Henry hesitated. "I meant to wait until after the meeting with the council to discuss this with you."

"Discuss what with me?"

"Your freedom." He looked up at me, and I stilled. "After all you have been through on account of me, I could not possibly ask you to return in the fall, no matter the council's decision."

I tried to hide my hurt, but there was a flash in his eyes that made it clear he noticed. "You don't want me to come back?"

"If I had my way, you would never leave. But that was not our bargain—and more than that, you have endured a great many hardships because of me. I do not wish to further make your life miserable by forcing you to return. So I am offering you your freedom, no matter what the council decides. Your permanent freedom."

It took me several seconds to understand what he was saying. He wanted me here, but he felt guilty—because of what? Because of what Calliope did? "But I want to come back," I blurted, the thought of never seeing him again making my heart race. Maybe he didn't get it, but Eden Manor was all I had left. "What am I supposed to do if you don't let me come back? You and Ava and Ella and Sofia and—and—"

I faltered, too choked up to continue, and wiped my eyes. Abandoning his cards, Henry brushed the back of his hand against my cheek. "If you wish to come back, then I would like that very much. It is your choice to make, and that you would choose staying here over living your life...I cannot tell you what that means to me."

"But I *am* living my life," I said miserably. "And I can live my life with you, too. Just because it's a little unconventional doesn't mean it isn't as good as everything else that's out there. Better, even. Tons better."

He hesitated. "You are very kind, and it means the world to me that you think that. But if I may say this and hope you do not take it to be any sort of slight...you were not living, Kate. Not with me and not in the real world. You were waiting for your mother to die, and now that that has happened—"

"Now that she's gone, the only thing I have left is this place, and the only person I have left is you," I said. "It'll take more than a knife-wielding murderer to make me give you up."

Instead of fighting me on it, his face broke out into the first real smile I'd seen from him since I'd died. "Good, then the feeling is mutual." He held up the deck of cards. "Shall we? I hear the sixth time is the charm."

I rolled my eyes. "Maybe you'll win when hell freezes over."

He raised an eyebrow. "That could easily be arranged."

When the council convened the day before the spring equinox, I still wasn't healed enough to walk on my own. It took both Ava and Ella to help me dress, and by the time we were done, I was so exhausted that I wanted to crawl back into bed.

"Maybe they could wait another day," said Ava, biting her lip as she eyed me. I sat in the armchair Henry usually occupied, cradling my head in my hands.

"No," I said with a grimace. "I'm fine. Just give me a minute, would you?"

They'd forced me to wear a white dress, and I was too afraid of popping a stitch to move. The only good thing about these injuries was that a corset was out of the question, but that meant there was very little padding between the fabric and my bandages. One wrong move and I'd be standing in front of the council with my chest covered in blood.

"Would you like me to fetch Henry?" said Ella. She was still keeping her distance from Ava, but since the river incident, she seemed to be making an effort to tolerate her. It probably didn't help that Theo and Ava were back together again, but Ella was putting on a brave face. I had to give her credit for that.

"No need," said a deep voice. I pulled my face away from my

hands enough to see Henry standing in the doorway. "Girls, you are dismissed."

They scattered quickly, although Ava paused to give me a quick kiss on the cheek. "Good luck," she whispered, and then she was gone.

Henry was by my side before I could sit up straight. "Are you well?"

"I feel like I'm going to puke."

The corner of his mouth twitched. "As do I." He offered me a hand and I took it, relying on him for balance as I stood. There was no way I was going to make it all the way to the ballroom, where the meeting would be held.

"Do I have to wear shoes?" I said, glancing at the heels Ava had picked out for me.

"Your gown is long enough that the hem should hide your bare feet," said Henry. He hesitated, then said in a low voice, "Kate, are you sure?"

"Sure I don't want to wear shoes? Yes. I can barely walk."

"No, I mean—are you certain that you do not wish to take me up on my offer?"

Never seeing Henry again or returning to Eden. I couldn't think of anything I wanted less. "Positive," I said, leaning against him. "If we don't leave now, we'll be late. I'm not exactly in any shape to be sprinting down the hallway."

"Do not worry about that." He brushed his warm fingertips against my cheek. "You understand the consequences of passing and failing?"

"If I fail, I go back to the real world with my memory wiped." And Henry would fade into nothingness. "If I succeed, I hang out here with you for six months a year."

"For eternity, unless you wish to end your life," said Henry.

"You will forever stay as you are today, and you will be granted immortality by the council. It is not an easy thing, immortality. You will form connections with mortals, and you will live well beyond their lifetimes. There will never be an end. Your life will be continuous, and eventually you will lose touch with humanity. You will forget what it was to be alive."

The thought of forever was daunting—it took away the one certainty in life, and that was death. But what good did dying bring? All it brought was pain, and I'd had enough of that to last me the next thousand lifetimes or so.

"Well, then I guess it's a good thing my best friend is already dead, isn't it?"

"Yes," he said dully. "You are quite lucky."

"No one ever said this was going to be easy," I said. "I know that."

"Indeed," he said, his eyes focused on something I couldn't see. "And you do understand that success also means that you and I will be married?"

I didn't know if the shiver that ran down my spine was out of excitement or nerves. "Yeah, I sort of picked up on that. You don't mind, do you? I mean, I know it's a little fast and all."

He cracked a smile. "No, I do not mind. Do you?"

Did I? I wasn't ready to be anyone's wife or queen, but it meant I would get to keep him. He'd said that I would be free to be with others and live my own life during my six months away if I wanted, and while I couldn't imagine finding anyone who could compare to him, it helped alleviate the feeling of being trapped. I shook my head. "Just as long as you don't make me wear a dress for the ceremony."

Henry gave me a look. "Why do you believe you are dressed in white?"

"Oh." I made a face. "That's not very fair, you know."

"Yes, I know." He wrapped his arm around me, the weight of it familiar and comforting. "Now we must leave, else we truly will be late. Close your eyes."

I did as I was told, wishing my stomach would stop doing somersaults long enough for me to get through this without ruining my gown. When I opened them, we were in the ball-room. It was empty, except for fourteen magnificent thrones arranged in a circle, all from the ball in September. Each was unique: some were made of wood, and others of stone, silver or gold. One looked like it was even made out of branches and vines, but I couldn't get close enough to get a good look.

Waiting for me in the center was a padded stool. We appeared only a few feet away from it, and Henry helped me to it and didn't let go of my hand until I was settled. "Comfortable?" he said.

I nodded, and he pressed his lips to my forehead for a linger-ing moment. "No matter what happens, I will always be there for you, even if you do not remember who I am."

As his eyes searched mine, I forced a small smile, too nervous to really try. Beneath me the lace of the cushion was irritat-ing, but I didn't trust myself to move. "There's no way they could make me forget you," I said. "No matter what they do to me."

I saw a glimpse of the sadness in his eyes before he looked away and stepped back. "I will see you shortly," he said. "Do not move."

I blinked, and he was gone. I examined the thrones to keep me busy, trying to figure out what the owners might be like. The largest one, looking like it was shaped out of glass, sat directly in front of me. Seeing all fourteen circled around me made my heart pound and my palms sweat, and I fought to keep myself as calm as I could. Instead I looked around, trying to figure out which one belonged to James. Not the one made of seashells. Silver or gold, perhaps, or maybe the one that glowed like an ember.

Thinking about James gave me a headache, so instead I closed my eyes. This was it. There were no more chances and nothing I could do to change the council's mind. The thought was strangely comforting, knowing that whatever they'd had in store for me was over. For better or for worse, I'd survived. Barely.

But my mother hadn't, and losing her darkened everything I did now. It felt wrong to be here knowing she was alone. She was the most important thing in my life, and to think about something other than missing her—it felt like a betrayal. I hadn't moved on, not after only a week, and I was afraid she thought I had.

It was stupid and I knew it—this was what she'd wanted for me, wasn't it? Would she still be proud of me if I failed? Would she still have given her life for mine if she'd known it wouldn't do any good?

Of course she would have. She loved me just as much as I loved her. Death didn't change that, and neither did failure. But I would pass if I could, if I had any chances left. For her and for Henry.

The sound of faint yelling pulled me away from my thoughts. A door on the left side of the ballroom burst open, and Henry stormed inside.

"No," he said, anger saturating his voice. "I made her a promise, and I have no intention of breaking it."

"It was not your promise to make." I tried to see the owner

of the second voice, but he was blocked by a throne that looked as if it were full of water. "She is one of us, and she will stay."

"She is not welcome in my home," said Henry with a growl that made the hair on the back of my neck stand up.

"Either she stays or we all go."

I watched wide-eyed as Henry slammed his fist into the wall, making the entire room tremble. I started to slide off my stool, but stopped when I winced in pain. Moving wasn't a good idea right now, and it'd only make Henry angrier.

"Fine. But she leaves the instant it is over."

"Agreed."

With fury radiating from him, Henry stormed across the room to where I sat. Brushing his lips against my cheek, he whispered, "Kate, I am so sorry."

"Whatever it is, it's okay," I said, trying to remember a promise he'd made that he might be forced to break. Nothing came to mind.

He straightened up and set his hand on my shoulder. I could feel how tense he was, and it did nothing to help my own nerves. "Brothers and sisters, nieces and nephews, may I present to you Katherine Winters."

I started to chastise him for introducing me by my full name, but my breath caught in my throat when I saw the procession of people walking toward us. I gripped the edge of my seat, too stunned to move.

Walter was first, dressed in a simple white robe. After him came Sofia, her cheeks flushing as she caught my eye.

James was next, and he stared at the ground. I wanted to look away, but my eyes followed him all the way to his throne. His was the one that looked like the arms were made from two snakes. I shivered.

After him, Irene entered, and then Nicholas and Phillip, the gruff stable hand.

Ella, holding Theo's hand.

Dylan from Eden High School, a face so distant in my memory that it took me a moment to place him.

And by the time Xander stepped through the door, looking whole and well, I was too floored to wonder exactly how he'd come back from the Underworld.

Henry's grip on my shoulder increased when the next person stepped inside the circle, and I suddenly realized why he was angry.

Calliope.

But she wasn't the last. My stomach contracted when I caught sight of who brought up the rear.

Ava.

They all stood in front of their respective thrones, giving me a few merciful seconds to stop my mind from reeling. I vaguely noted that two of the thrones were empty—and Walter claimed the massive throne made of glass—but the room spun around me, making it difficult to focus.

"Kate," said Henry. "I present to you the council."

CHAPTER 19

THE COUNCIL

It took every ounce of willpower I had to keep breathing as I stared at the faces of the council. Friends, enemies, but not the strangers I'd been expecting. Dozens of questions darted through my mind, none staying still long enough for me to force it out. All in all, that was probably a good thing, but I didn't understand—*this* was the council?

I looked up at Henry, and he gave me a reassuring smile. It didn't help.

"I will be right here," he said before moving to sit at one of the two empty thrones. I'd never felt so alone in my life.

"I—I don't—" I started, finally finding my voice. "How—who—"

Ava was the one who answered. "I'm sorry for lying to you, Kate—we all are. But this is how it had to be."

"We needed to know that you were able and worthy to fulfill this role," said Ella, all traces of bitterness gone from her voice. "While it may feel like we betrayed you, it's really the opposite. We now know you well enough to decide whether or not you're fit to become one of us."

I focused on Henry, the only one I trusted to be honest

with me. "It was all a setup? Ava in the river, Xander, Theo, Calliope—"

"No." His voice was so firm that I instantly fell silent. "Not all of it. Be patient, Kate. You will find out soon enough."

I was more than willing to shut up and let them get on with it. If I'd been nervous before, now I was petrified. Glancing at James, I noticed he refused to meet my eyes. Slowly resentment filtered through the other emotions churning inside of me, and I balled my hands into fists. No matter what Henry said, it was impossible this was some sort of coincidence. Everyone I knew in Eden was here.

"Before we begin," said Henry, this time addressing the council, "I believe there is a matter that has yet to be decided."

Calliope, who was to my right, stepped forward. She looked furious.

"Sister," he said in a booming voice that echoed through the room. "You have admitted to killing at least eleven mortals in cold blood over the past hundred years. Do you plead guilty?"

She sniffed and narrowed her eyes. "Yes."

Henry looked at me, the gravity of his stare making my heart thud. "As her only surviving victim, Kate, her punishment falls to you."

Bewildered, I looked back and forth between them, trying to figure out if he was joking. He wasn't. "I don't—" I froze. How was I supposed to do this? Taking a deep breath, I said in a small voice, "Um, what are the options?"

"Whatever you wish," said Henry, his eyes as hard as diamonds as he glared at Calliope.

I opened my mouth and shut it again. This was the job, wasn't it? The one I was supposedly signing up for. Deciding people's fates. If I couldn't figure this out when I was the one she'd tried to kill, how was I supposed to decide for people I'd never met before?

As I stared at Calliope's pale face, I realized it wasn't knowing her that made me freeze up. It was knowing why she did it. She loved Henry, and like me, she must've hated seeing him hurt. Putting up with Persephone, knowing she didn't love him, having to watch him go through losing her—and then being faced with girls who were supposed to take Persephone's place when she'd loved him first? No one could've possibly been good enough for him, not when she was standing right there waiting for him to notice her. It was no excuse for murder, but I understood wanting to be the one to make Henry happy.

I chose my words carefully, keeping eye contact with her as I spoke. She stood across from me, looking like she wanted to kill me all over again. "I know you don't like me. I know you think I'm not good enough for Henry, and I know you want him to be with you. I get why, too. I get that you love him and just want him to be happy. I get that you probably thought the girls who came before me were too stupid or petty or selfish to love him like you do, and I know that love can make people do some really dumb and hurtful things sometimes."

I glanced at Henry, but his expression was impossible to read.

"I can't punish you to eternal torture or whatever it is just because you loved someone enough to try to protect him. While you went about it the wrong way, I get what you were trying to do. And that makes this really, really hard."

Again I looked at Henry, although this time he was looking at the ground. "I want you to spend time with every girl you killed," I said, my voice breaking. "I want you to get to know them and appreciate them for who they are. I want you to stay with them, one by one, until you understand their individual worth. I can't make you like them, but I want you to respect them and appreciate them as people. It can't be superficial, either. You have to mean it. And I want you to make amends with them as well."

Calliope glared at me with such intensity that I considered myself lucky to still be in one piece. Angering a goddess wasn't the smartest thing to do if I wanted to stay alive for much longer, but I trusted Henry to make sure she didn't turn me into a pile of ash.

"When all of this happens—and when they forgive you for what you did to them—then you can go on and live your life, or whatever it is that you have. But you're never going to see Henry or me again after today. Not because I want to hurt you, or because I hate you. I don't. Like I said, I understand why you did it, in a way. But neither of us can trust you anymore."

Even though I was sure I was being fair, my decision felt cruel. She loved him. The possibility of never seeing Henry again tore at me, and I'd only known him for six months. How could I possibly be okay with separating her from the person she loved for the rest of her eternal existence?

"And I wanted to let you know that I love him, too," I said quietly. "If—if I pass, I'm never going to hurt him like Persephone did, and I'll do everything I can to make sure he's happy. I promise."

A long moment passed before Calliope reacted. I half expected her to scream and shout and tell me how unfair I was being, but instead she nodded, her eyes brimming with tears. Stepping back to her throne made of cushion and lace, she sat down looking like I'd ripped her heart out of her chest. I felt like the most horrible person on the planet. The only thing that kept me from taking it all back was the ache in my abdomen from where her knife had slid inside of me.

"And so the decision has been made," said Henry in a grimly satisfied voice. "I will uphold Kate's ruling no matter what the council decides."

"As will I," said James weakly. I felt a stab of pity for him, but there was nothing I could say to make it any better, not when I didn't understand it in the first place.

Henry sat back down, and it was several seconds before anyone spoke. I stared down at my lap, too afraid to see the looks on their faces. Was I fair? Or did they, too, think I was being cruel?

"Katherine Winters," said Walter as he stood, and I looked up. "You were tasked with seven tests, to be distributed throughout your time in Eden Manor. If you have failed any of these, you will return home and live out your existence without any memory of the past six months. If you succeed in all seven, you will be married to our brother, and you shall rule his realm with him for as long as you wish. Do you accept?"

There was no backing down now. "Yes."

Irene stood next, her hair flaming in the bright light. "For the test of sloth, Kate passed." She gave me an impish smile. "Your study habits were quite inspiring, you know."

Was that what Henry had meant when he'd said I couldn't possibly fail after nearly killing myself studying for that stupid test? It had to be. But they couldn't all be so simple.

Sofia was next. She looked as warm and motherly as ever, and it was hard to imagine that she could be part of something so terrifying and official. "For the test of greed, Kate passed." She must've seen my confused look, because she smiled and added,

"Your clothing, dear. When you were offered a new wardrobe, you didn't hesitate to allow your friends to help themselves as well."

I breathed a sigh of relief. Apparently not liking dresses was a virtue.

"Gluttony," said Ella, standing. I furrowed my brow—out of all of them, I'd have thought Calliope would've been the one to handle that. "While Kate was made aware it was a test, and while she was unconscious for much of the time afterward, she did willingly make the choice to stop eating." She raised an eyebrow. "Although I would recommend three square meals a day outside these walls."

Ava stood next, twisting side to side with a childish grin on her face. "As for envy, Kate passed with flying colors."

"Envy?" I said, my voice cracking as I tried to think back on what that could possibly be.

"The day Xander died." She shot him an apologetic look, and he winked. "You didn't let jealousy interfere with your decision. I mean, not that you were jealous—that's the point. You were fair, and you were patient with me, even though I didn't deserve it."

So Xander—or whoever he was—really had been killed. Or whatever it was, because I was pretty sure gods couldn't die. I found some relief in knowing that not everything about the past six months had been scripted.

Calliope stood next, pale and shaken, though her voice was surprisingly strong. "Wrath," she said, raising her eyes to meet mine. For a moment, I thought I saw a ghost of a smile on her face, but it was gone as quickly as it came. "With her decision today regarding the punishment for my actions, Kate has passed."

I was sure that what Calliope had done hadn't been scripted either, which meant that not all of the tests had been decided on ahead of time. What would it have been if she hadn't tried to kill me? Either way, five down, two to go.

Walter was the one to stand next. "Lust," he said, and my heart sank. He couldn't fail me for this. They had to know what Calliope had done. "You engaged in lustful relations with our brother, an act that is strictly forbidden before the council makes a decision and a marriage occurs." He pressed his thin lips together, and suddenly it was hard to breathe. Didn't he understand that we'd been set up? There had to be a trick, a loophole, something that would make them forgive that night.

"But—" I started, but Walter's voice cut through mine.

"I am sorry, Katherine, but for the test of lust, you have failed."

Failed.

The word echoed endlessly in my head. The room spun around me, and it was only my iron-tight grip on my stool that kept me from falling. My chest ached, and I felt as if the air itself was pressing in on me, making breathing impossible.

This couldn't be happening.

"Brother," said Henry in a strained voice. "I would like to contest the council's ruling on this."

"Yes?" said Walter. I looked hopefully between them, struggling to keep myself from spiraling downward into despair. There was still a chance.

"As you know, the test in question was compromised. We were both given large doses of an aphrodisiac that affects both the mind and the body, allowing for our inhibitions to be lowered. If anyone is to carry the blame for that evening, it is me."

"No," said a small voice. Calliope. "It's me. I was the one who did it. I thought—I thought that if they failed a test…"

Walter frowned. "Yes, I am aware. But you know as well as I do that our rules are firm. No matter the circumstances, they must be followed."

Henry sighed, and something inside of me broke. He looked as crushed as I felt, wearing his pain clearly, but it was the way he glanced at me that was agony. His eyes were cloudy with anguish, and already I could see him pulling away. He'd dared to hope because of me. He'd tried because I'd made him, and it was my fault he looked like that. It was my fault he was hurting so badly.

"No," I blurted. "Henry doesn't deserve this. Calliope said it was her fault, and she did it on purpose. That shouldn't count. It can't count."

"I'm afraid it isn't up to you." Walter frowned, and against my better judgment, I glared at him.

"He's your brother, and if you do this, he's going to die or—or fade out of existence or whatever it is. I don't care how strict your rules are. If you love him half as much as I do, I don't understand why you don't get that this isn't *fair*."

"It isn't always about fairness." Walter's voice was gentler than I expected, and his expression was strangely compassionate. "Despite evidence to the contrary—" he looked at Ava, and she rolled her eyes "—we do not abide lust."

"But it wasn't lust!" I stupidly tried to stand, and pain exploded in my chest, but I refused to let this be the end. "I'm not guilty of lust, because I love him. You can't accuse me of something I didn't do, not when it means that Henry's going to die for it. Anything else, fine—do whatever you want to me,

I don't care. But don't do this to Henry," I said, tears blurring my vision. "Please. I'll do anything."

"Kate," said Henry. His face was pinched and his shoulders were strained, as if he were struggling to stay put. "It's all right."

"No, it's not. It's not fair."

"Katherine," said Walter. "You say you will do anything, yet you do not do the one thing we ask of you."

"What?" I wiped my cheeks with the sleeve of my dress.

"Do you accept your failure and the consequences of it?"

No, of course not. This was a cruel joke, a mockery of justice. Henry and I finally had a shot at being happy, and now we'd both lost it. I couldn't look at Henry or any one of the other faces surrounding me, unable to stand seeing their disappointment.

"I accept that the council has chosen to fail me, yes," I said in a choked voice. "And I understand what it means." Better than they did, apparently. "But I don't think it's fair that you're doing this to Henry, and if there's anything I can do to change your minds, I'll do it."

Walter eyed me, and there was something so intimidating about it that I wondered if he was going to smite me or whatever it was gods did to people they didn't like. "You have failed, Katherine. There is nothing you can say that will change that fact."

I blinked rapidly, struggling to pull myself together. I didn't want Henry's last memories of me to be this. Turning in my seat as much as I dared in order to face him, I managed to force out a small, "I'm sorry."

He didn't meet my eye, and I couldn't blame him. I'd failed, and now he had to suffer for it.

Caught between anger and despair as the room seemed to press down around me, delivering blow after crushing blow, I wished more than anything that I could turn back the clock to that night in order to stop it from happening. Henry deserved so much more than this, and I wasn't able to give it to him, no matter how badly I wanted to.

The silence seemed to echo in the ballroom as no one said or did anything. Only seconds passed, but it felt like an hour. As bitter disappointment settled in the pit of my stomach, one rational thought came to mind:

What now?

A noise from behind me caught my attention, and I tried to turn around to see what it was, but any movement now made my chest feel as if it were on fire. I heard the thud of a door closing, and the soft click of heels against marble echoed through the ballroom.

"Sister," said Henry, his voice full of rich golden warmth that made my pain ebb away. As I looked into the faces of the other council members, I realized they all seemed happy and relieved. And smug, I noticed, glancing at Ava. Even James seemed happy to see her.

"Hello, Henry."

All the air whooshed out of my lungs as her voice filled my head, chasing away my thoughts until there was nothing left but her. Forgetting the pain, I strained my neck to see her, watching as she greeted all but Calliope with a smile and a kiss on the cheek. Making her way around the circle, when she reached Henry, she stepped into his open arms.

In the back of my mind I realized I was gawking, but I couldn't stop. She separated herself from Henry and took a seat in the throne next to him, the one made of branches and vines that had previously been empty, and something inside of me fell into place.

"Hello, Kate," she said, and I opened and shut my mouth several times, but nothing came out. Finally I forced myself to swallow, and when I managed to speak, it came out more like a croak.

"Hi, Mom."

CHAPTER 20

SPRING

My mother looked exactly as she had in my dreams. Healthy and whole, as if she'd never been sick a day in her life. But there was something about her, some indeterminable quality that made her seem as if she were glowing from the inside, like light straining to be released.

"What are you doing here?" As I asked it, I knew it was obvious. The only thing that kept me from seething was my joy at seeing her again, but even that was rapidly being replaced by confusion.

"I'm sorry," she said with the same sympathetic smile I'd seen on her face a thousand times before. Every time I scraped my knee, every time I dragged home hours of homework and barely had time for dinner, every time a doctor had told us she only had months to live. In so many ways she was a stranger, but with that smile, she was still my mother. "Deception was the only way you could be properly tested. I never meant to hurt you, sweetheart. Everything I've ever done was to protect you and to keep you as happy as I possibly could."

I knew she was telling the truth, but I couldn't help but feel the humiliation of being duped. Even if it had been for my own good, that didn't make me feel like any less of an idiot for not realizing who she was.

My own mother was a goddess. It wasn't something I could simply shrug and accept.

"Diana," said Walter, and she stepped toward me, the white silk robe she wore moving with her as if she were submerged in water. She wasn't close enough for me to touch, but close enough for me to see that her eyes were shining. Whether it was from tears or pride or power, like Henry and his eyes made of moonlight, I couldn't tell.

"For the seventh and final test, pride and humility." My mother paused and smiled. "Kate passes."

I didn't understand. The ruling was over, wasn't it? Hadn't their decision already been made? I couldn't fail any of the tests. Walter himself had said it. I waited for some kind of explanation, but it didn't come.

"Those who agree?" said Walter.

Wildly I turned from face to face, but none of them gave any hint. Ava, Ella, even Henry gave no sign of what was happening. One after the other they murmured their agreement. To my surprise, Calliope, who looked so pale and miserable that I couldn't help but feel a stab of sympathy for her, also nodded.

They were saying yes, I realized. They were voting. Even though I'd slept with Henry, by some miracle I hadn't failed completely. But when the vote reached James, my breath caught in my throat, and I was sure he would shake his head.

Without meeting my eye, he, too, nodded. The others continued to vote, but I stared at him, and when at last he looked up, I mouthed a simple *thank you*.

"So it has been decided," said Walter when the vote reached him. "Katherine Winters will be granted immortality, and she will be wed to our brother, to rule the Underworld with him as long as she so chooses." And then he smiled, his ancient eyes twinkling. "Welcome to the family. This session of the council is adjourned."

The finality in his voice confused me, and dumbfounded, I waited as the council stood and headed toward the door. Some—Ella, Nicholas, Irene, Sofia, even Xander—squeezed my shoulder or gave me a word of encouragement as they passed. Ava grinned widely. Others, particularly Calliope, said nothing as they left. James, too, passed by without a word, his shoulders hunched and his head bowed. Remembering his nod and thinking of what it must have cost him to give it, I wanted to reach out to him, but I was frozen on my stool, unable to move in fear all of this would shatter and reveal itself to be nothing but a dream.

Soon only three of us remained. Me, Henry and my mother. She stood once the others had left, and without a word she enveloped me in her arms, hugging me gently. I rested my chin on her shoulder and buried my nose in her hair. Apples and freesia. It was really her.

I don't know how long she held me, but by the time we let go of one another, my chest ached and I'd slid halfway off the stool. She helped me right myself, but it was Henry standing a few feet away from us who caught my eye.

"Was—" I paused and cleared my throat, hating how small my voice sounded. "Was that a good thing or a bad thing?"

Henry stepped beside me, and both he and my mother gently helped me stand. "You passed," he said. "I hope you are pleased."

Pleased wasn't exactly the word for it. Confused, yes. Reeling, sure. And I wasn't going to be pleased until I understood
what had happened. "He said I failed," I said, wobbling on my
feet. "How could I pass after I failed?"

"It was the seventh test, sweetheart," said my mother. "You
did not fail lust. Even if you hadn't loved him, Henry made sure
we were all aware of what happened. This was the only way
the council had to test you on your pride. In accepting your
failure despite wanting to stay, and in respecting the council's
decision, you showed humility."

"And by showing humility, you passed the final test," said
Henry.

"So—" I stopped, hating that I felt so slow and stupid, but it
felt too good to be true. "What does that mean? What's going
to happen now?"

Henry cleared his throat. "It means, if you agree, we will be
married at sunset."

Married at sunset. What had felt like a far-fetched fantasy
hours ago now pressed against me, an impending reality that
was hurtling toward me faster than I could run away.

Not that I was running. This was what I'd wanted, wasn't
it? Not to be anyone's wife, but to give Henry a chance. To
give him the same hope I'd wanted for myself, and now with
my mother here, even if she wasn't exactly the same, we'd both
won, hadn't we?

No...not all of us. Calliope hadn't won, and neither had
James. In order for Henry to be alive and happy, in order for
me to have my mother back, they had to lose. Calliope had
brought it on herself, but James—what had he given up for me
to have this?

With a start, I realized both Henry and my mother were staring at me. We'd somehow made it across the ballroom, and now we were stopped between the heavy double doors that were opened wide enough for the three of us to exit.

"Yes, of course," I said, my face reddening. "I'm sorry, I wasn't hesitating, I was just—thinking, and—of course I still want to do this."

It wasn't until Henry relaxed that I noticed how tense he'd grown. "I am glad to hear that," he said, his relief plain in his voice. "May I ask what it was you were thinking of?"

I didn't want to tell him that I was worried about James, in case it was still a sore spot for him, so instead I asked the question that had been burning in my mind ever since Ava had walked through those doors. "Was it all a setup?"

There was an awkward silence, and this time I saw Henry and my mother exchanging looks, as if all they needed to communicate was a glance. It wasn't so impossible, really, and I bit the inside of my cheek, irritated they weren't sharing.

"Yes and no," said my mother. We continued slowly down the hallway, each step more painful than the last, but my injuries were the least of my concerns. "After the decades Henry spent searching for a new queen, when it became apparent his search wasn't yielding the results we needed—"

"I was going to give up," said Henry. "Each girl failed before they'd begun, or if they showed any promise at all, they turned up dead. We know what was happening now, but I cannot tell you how heart-wrenching it was to watch those young women die, knowing it was my fault. I could not bring myself to put anyone else in such danger, and I was determined it would end."

"And I was just as determined that he try until we had no

more time left," said my mother. "So we compromised. Per-sephone…" Something in her expression changed, and for the briefest of moments I saw shame. "Persephone was my daughter. Your sister. It's my fault she was never happy, and because of that, Henry was never happy either."

"It wasn't your fault," said Henry with quiet fierceness. "It was no one's fault but my own. I am the one who could not make her happy—"

"And I'm the one who pushed you together to begin with," said my mother. "Don't argue with me, Henry. I mean it."

He fell silent, though I thought I saw the barest hint of a smile.

"As I was saying before I was so rudely interrupted." She ran her fingers through my hair, and I knew she didn't mean any of the sharpness in her voice. "You always had a choice, sweet-heart. If you didn't want to do this, we would have all accepted it and proceeded without you. You have always been in control of your life—all we did was offer you the opportunity."

My throat tightened as I imagined what might have happened if I hadn't. "Why didn't you tell me before?"

"It would have given you an unfair advantage," said my mother. "It needed to be your decision, not one I influenced you to make or one that you automatically rejected because you knew what you were getting into. Besides," she added gently, "even if I'd told you, would you really have believed me?"

Of course not. And when I left for the real world, who would possibly believe me if I told them how I spent my winters? Nobody sane, I was sure of it. "Does Eden even exist? Every-one there, even Ava and Dylan—was that part of giving me a choice?"

"Eden does not exist outside of the few weeks you occupied it," said Henry. "If you decide to go back to where the town stood, you will see nothing but trees and fields. I am sorry for the deception."

So was I. I pursed my lips, trying to come up with something to say that didn't make me sound like I was twelve. "Just—don't do it again, all right?" I looked between him and my mother. "No more lies, and no more holding out on me."

To my surprise, my mother laughed, but it wasn't the laugh I was used to. It was a strange combination of sounds—a gurgling brook, the chirping of crickets and somehow the first day of spring. It was incredible.

"Of course," she said, her voice filled with affection that spilled through me and made it easier to walk the next few feet. "Now, before we get to your wedding, is there anything else you'd like to know?"

My wedding. A lump formed in my throat, and it was all I could do to speak around it. "Yeah," I said hoarsely. "What kind of name is Diana for a goddess, anyway?"

She laughed again, and the knot in my throat loosened. "Ella was rather put out I took her Roman name, but she did not want it, and I've always been quite fond of it. We all choose new ones throughout the years."

"Ones that match where and when we are," said Henry. "We are most famous within Greek mythology, and that is why we are known throughout by our Greek names."

"But we have no real names," said my mother. "We were created before names."

"And we will survive long after names are needed," said Henry.

My mother glanced at him. "Some of us, anyhow."

Her words brought an image of James crashing into my thoughts, and I tried to push it away, but he remained stubbornly in the forefront of my mind. "You're really the Olympians then?"

"All thirteen," said my mother. "Plus Henry, on a good day."

He grunted, and my frown deepened as I struggled to put the pieces together. "Then—who's who? I mean, I know who you two are, Hades and Demeter, but everyone else?"

"You mean to tell me you haven't figured it out already?" said Henry. I gave him a dirty look.

"Not all of us are omniscient, y'know."

"Neither are we," he said, his eyes sparkling with amusement.

I chewed on my lower lip as I thought about it. "I could probably guess if I had to. Not all of you though." I shook my head. "Olympians. That's—" Incredible. Unspeakable. "A warning would've been nice."

I must've sounded bitterer than I'd intended, because my mother hugged me tighter and buried her nose in my hair. "No matter what I'm called or who I am, I'm still your mother, and I love you very, very much."

I nodded, not trusting myself to speak. She was my mother, but my mother didn't have laughter that felt like sunshine. My mother gave up her life for me, and what was left of her was cold and stiff. Not this warm, bubbly being who was so much stronger than I would ever be.

"Come," said Henry, apparently sensing my change in mood. We stopped in front of a pair of richly decorated doors depicting the earth and the world below, and my breath caught in my throat. Persephone's bedroom.

"Henry?" I said, but he shook his head and offered me nothing but a smile in return. I tugged self-consciously on the white lace of my dress, making sure my bandages hadn't leaked.

The doors open, and instead of the shrine it had been only months before, it was empty except for a small white arch decorated with a rainbow of daisies. Standing off to the side were nine of the other council members, all but Calliope and James, and Walter stood underneath the arch, waiting for us.

"I hope it will do," said Henry. "I was not sure if you wanted something more elaborate."

"No," I said breathlessly. "This is perfect."

My mother took my hand, her eyes shining with tears. "That's my girl," she said, and even though I never wanted her to leave again, I knew it was time. This was my life now, and while she would always be part of it, she would no longer be the center. It was a shift I hadn't been expecting, but somehow these past six months had prepared me for it.

I let go of her hand, and she walked away to join the others. Henry led me to the archway, and as Walter spoke, I could feel every eye on us. Henry and I repeated our simple vows, and in a voice with such unshakable authority that the very stones of the manor seemed to quake, Walter proclaimed us husband and wife.

Henry leaned forward to kiss me, and as he did, heat started at my lips and ran through me, leaving coolness in its wake that replaced the pain. By the time he pulled away, my body felt whole again, healed and strong in a way it never had before. But that wasn't what mattered; what mattered was the way he looked at me, as if this moment were the happiest in his long life. And deep inside of me, I knew I would never be alone again.

★ ★ ★

We spent our wedding night in my suite playing card games and making every effort to avoid mentioning what would happen the next day. It was my last night in Eden Manor for six months, and even though I knew I would return, something about it felt final. Half a year was no time at all for Henry, but for me, it stretched out in front of me, the end nowhere in sight.

Married one day and gone the next. Somehow it didn't seem fair. I could return early if I wanted, I knew that, but my mother was adamant that I spend my first summer without Henry.

The next morning we had breakfast in bed, me sitting cross-legged in my pajamas on one side and him on the other. I was allowed to eat now that it was spring again, and even though I wasn't any hungrier than usual, I attacked my pancakes with unusual vigor, making a mess of myself in the process. Henry didn't seem to mind; every now and then he leaned toward me and kissed the syrup off my lips, smirking when he saw me blush.

Packing took no time at all, and much sooner than I'd anticipated, I stood facing the majority of my new family on the winding drive that led to the front gates. Once again Calliope was missing, but it was James's empty spot that made my insides twist unpleasantly.

One by one I hugged them goodbye, even gruff Phillip, who smelled of horses and looked like he wanted to be anywhere but witnessing this tear-filled display of sentimentality. Before I'd even reached her, Ava was crying, and she threw her arms around me so tightly that I thought she might never let go. "Oh, Kate—I'm going to miss you!"

"I'm going to miss you, too." No matter what had passed

between us that winter, I hoped her tears meant all was forgiven and that I would see her when I came back in the fall. "One day you'll have to fill me in on everything that happened when I wasn't looking."

She nodded, too choked up to speak, and with one last hug, we finally let go of each other.

My mother was next. She stood serenely in the sunlight, looking as if she were glowing, and for a moment I was afraid to touch her. She fixed that for me, gathering me up in a hug and giving me a wet kiss on the cheek. "Have fun," she said warmly, but there was a glint in her eyes that made it clear she expected me to uphold our deal. I would stay away for six months, but this was the only summer I'd let her boss me around. "Go experience mortal life before it passes you by."

I wasn't sure I'd ever be able to enjoy mortal life again, knowing what was waiting for me in the autumn, but I nodded. "Love you," I said, suddenly as choked up as Ava. My mother gazed at me, and for a long moment it felt as if we were the only two people in the world. But as quickly as it had come, the feeling vanished, and then it was Henry's turn.

I didn't know what to say, so instead I wrapped my arms around him, and he embraced me. I was crying in earnest now, making a mess of what little makeup Ava had talked me into that morning, but I didn't care.

"Take care of Pogo, yeah?" I said with a sniff, pulling away to wipe my eyes.

"Cerberus and I both promise to do so," he said, his eyes never leaving mine. "Kate…whatever is waiting for you outside that gate, remember that the summer is yours to do with what you please." His voice was strained, but he seemed to make an effort to push past it. "It is none of my business what you decide to do with that time."

"I know," I said. "And I also know that the way I feel about you isn't going to change just because the seasons do. So if you don't mind too much, I'm going to stick to the vows I made." I gave him what I hoped was a reassuring smile. "You can't get rid of me that easily."

He managed to return it. "I cannot tell you how relieved I am to hear that, but that still does not change—"

"Henry," I said firmly. "Enough about that. You're stuck with me whether you like it or not, so you might as well get used to it."

He hesitated, but finally he gave in. "Anytime you need me, I will be by your side. You have my word."

I nodded, and he pressed his lips to my forehead. It was such a chaste kiss that I wondered if he would give me a proper goodbye or not. Probably not, I realized. Not with my mother watching.

"I will be waiting for you when you return," he said. "And I love you."

This time I hadn't imagined or dreamed it; he'd really said it, and not because of some test or bet or obligation. Because he meant it. Something inside of me swelled, and I felt as if I was going to burst. "Love you, too."

With that, he braved the mess that was my face and kissed me deeply. I tried to make it linger, but he pulled away, and I knew it was time to go.

I trudged down the drive, glancing over my shoulder every few seconds as I took my time. While Henry's presence behind me pulled me back, knowing that I would have to leave before

I could see him again pushed me forward. This was my home now, and nothing could keep me away forever.

When I reached the top of the gentle hill that hid any view of the manor from the outside world, I turned and waved, startled to see Henry was the only one still there. He raised his hand in return, and I forced myself to continue forward.

The gate came into view and with it a sight that made me stop in my tracks. Suddenly I understood exactly why Henry had been so adamant about reminding me I could do what I wanted with my summers.

James leaned against the same car he'd used to drive me to Eden Manor, and he wore the same humungous headphones he'd had in September. The only thing that was different was the lack of a smile on his face.

I slipped out from between the gates and hesitated, not sure what to say. Wordlessly he stepped around to open my door for me, and I thanked him, but he said nothing. It wasn't until we were driving down the gravel road that I finally found the courage to talk, and even then my voice came out as a squeak.

"I'm sorry," I said, my hands clasped together so tightly that my knuckles were white. "For everything."

"Don't be." He turned the corner and the hedge disappeared from view. "You did what you had to do, and so did Henry. So did the council. I knew it was a long shot anyway after I met you."

I pressed my lips together, not knowing what to say. I was sure he'd meant it as a compliment, but it didn't help the guilt that gnawed at me incessantly. "You'll exist for a long time, right? I mean, the world isn't going to end tomorrow."

"I don't know," said James, and for a moment I heard a hint of the boy who liked to build things with fries. "With Calliope on the rampage, anything's possible."

Leaning back against my seat, I let myself relax. At least he was still in there somewhere. "Where are we going?"

"Someplace I think you should go before you leave for the summer," he said. When it was clear he wasn't going to give me any more details, I resigned myself to looking out the window and trying to think of something to say that wouldn't hurt so much.

Henry had been telling the truth. What had once been Main Street in Eden was now a dirt road surrounded by trees on either side, and the spot where Eden High School had stood was nothing more than a meadow. Even though I'd only been there for a few weeks, I felt a pang as we drove by. There would be no going back, not to the life I'd known as a mortal, and it was a loss I hadn't been prepared to deal with.

By the time we reached our destination, we'd found civilization once more. It wasn't New York City, but it wasn't all dirt and trees either. Several small buildings clustered together to form a town near the hospital where my mother had stayed. I looked around, trying to find something familiar, but there were only small factories and churches and grocery stores.

James drove past a pair of wrought-iron gates, and my eyes widened as I realized where we were. I could hear the gravel on the road crunch underneath the tires, and he wound the car down the path slowly, coming to a stop a quarter of a mile inside.

"Come on," he said, opening the door. "I want to show you something."

I stepped out and stared at the cemetery that surrounded us, the headstones and statues rising out of the brown grass. Some of them were newer, the names clear and readable, while others we passed were so old and worn that I could hardly make out any kind of engraving at all. James kept his distance, shoving his hands in his pockets as if he were afraid to touch me, and I trailed behind him, busying myself with avoiding the mud and the melting snow.

He stopped in front of a fresh grave, one that was so new that there was no tombstone. Just a temporary marker with a name written in black marker. James stepped aside so I could see it, but there was no need. I knew exactly where we were.

"Diana Winters," I said softly, running my shaking fingers over the letters that formed her name. "But I thought she was—"

"Alive?" said James, and I nodded. "As a deity, yes. But she took a mortal form to raise you, and that mortal form died ten days ago."

I was silent, wondering what he expected me to say to that.

"She's still your mother," he said, "but you need to understand that things won't be the same between you now, and things won't be the same between you and Henry or you and the rest of the council either."

I bristled at that. "Just like things aren't the same between you and me?" I said, but instead of showing any signs of anger or frustration, James shrugged.

"Somewhat different, given you're closer to both of them, but yeah. Something like that."

I crouched down next to the marker, running my fingers

over it as I stared at the mound of dirt that held my mother's human body. I wasn't sure what to feel—sadness was unavoidable, but there was a jumble of other emotions I didn't fully understand. Relief, maybe, that her battle had ended. Fear for this new reality I faced and the truths I'd learned while she'd been wasting away in a hospital bed.

But most of all I felt a hollow ache inside of me, and it took me several seconds to realize I missed the life we'd had before we'd come to Eden. Not the years of sickness and pain, but the trips to Central Park. The Christmas trees. The days when I knew my best friend was only a short walk down the hall. Those were over now, and a new existence stretched out before me, blank except for the faces of Henry, my mother, and the rest of the council.

"I know it's the end," I said, placing a hand on the raised dirt. "I've known that for a long time."

"No, it's not," said James, moving to stand beside me. "It's the beginning."

We stayed there until the cold seeped into my clothes and the fog clung to my hair, leaving me chilled and damp. I accepted his hand as he helped me up, and I touched the marker one last time, proof of my humanity and my brief existence in a world where all things died. At last, with a heavy heart, I tore myself away.

"So what are you going to do during the summer?" said James as we walked to the car. Even though it was an obvious attempt to lighten the mood, it took me several moments to reply, my mind too clouded with thoughts of my mother. I felt anchored to her grave, but with each step I took, the weight became a little easier to bear. It would never go away completely, I knew that, but at least I was sure that one day I would be able to accept it.

"I don't know," I said, and I stared at the muddy ground as I entertained the possibilities laid out before me. I could go back to New York City, but there was nothing for me there. I could stay in Eden with the trees, but I figured that would get boring after the first month or so. "Maybe try some authentic Greek food. I've never been to Greece, y'know."

"Greece," said James, and there was emptiness in his voice that ate at me. "It's nice in the summer."

Tentatively I reached out to slip my arm into his, and he didn't move away. "Do you want to come?"

His eyes widened. "Really?"

"Of course." I grinned with effort, but that didn't make it any less real. "I don't want to go to Greece on my own, and I can't imagine a better tour guide than one of my best friends."

Slowly a smile spread across his face, but there was a hint of distance in his eyes I couldn't completely ignore. "I'd really like that."

The gravel crunched underneath our feet as we reached the car, and he opened the door for me, the silence between us now comfortable instead of tense and ugly. I sat down and re-laxed against the seat as he slid behind the wheel. There was a lingering doubt in the back of my mind as I smiled at him and saw that look in his eyes again, but I pushed it away. Things weren't anywhere near perfect, but no matter what happened, at least I had my friend back.

As we drove away, I twisted around to see my mother's grave, dark against the remaining piles of white snow. James was right; this wasn't an ending. It was the beginning my mother had wanted for me and the beginning I'd wanted for myself all along. I may not have planned on living forever, but now that I was, I was going to make the most of every moment.

★ ★ ★ ★ ★

What happens when summer is over?
Find out in
GODDESS INTERRUPTED

GUIDE OF GODS

ZEUS .... WALTER

HERA .... CALLIOPE

POSEIDON .... PHILLIP

DEMETER .... DIANA

HADES .... HENRY

HESTIA .... SOFIA

ARES .... DYLAN

APHRODITE .... AVA

HERMES .... JAMES

ATHENA .... IRENE

APOLLO .... THEO

ARTEMIS .... ELLA

HEPHAESTUS .... NICHOLAS

DIONYSUS .... XANDER

ACKNOWLEDGMENTS

In one way or another, everyone who has ever been a significant part of my life has helped me down this path, and I'm grateful for everything. I'd like to acknowledge the following people in particular:

Rosemary Stimola, my lovely agent who never gives up. Thank you for taking a chance on me.

Mary-Theresa Hussey, my amazing editor, and Natashya Wilson, Senior Editor at Harlequin Teen. You've both been wonderfully supportive, and I'm so excited to continue this journey with you.

The many teachers I've had over the years, especially Terry Brooks, Jim Burnstein, Kathy Churchill, Larry Francis, Wendy Gortney, Kim Henson, Chris Keane, Bob Mayer, Mike Sack and John Saul. By teaching me how to tell a story, you showed me who I am.

Shannon and John Tullius. Your tireless support gave me hope that maybe I wasn't as terrible as I thought I was.

Sarah Reck and Caitlin Straw, the two best friends and first readers I could ever ask for.

Melissa Anelli, the world's greatest cheerleader.

And Jo, who changed my life just by living hers.

Thank you all so much for everything.

Facebook.com/HarlequinTEEN

Be first to find out about new releases, exciting sweepstakes and special events from Harlequin TEEN.

Get access to exclusive content, excerpts and videos.

Connect with your favorite Harlequin TEEN authors and fellow fans.

All in one place.

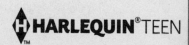

From *New York Times* Bestselling Author
JULIE KAGAWA

Book 1

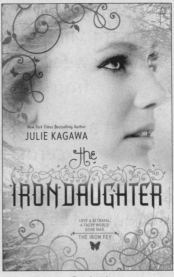

Book 2

www.TheIronFey.com

HTIRONFEY3BKTR1R2

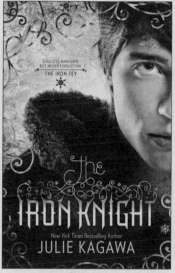
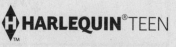

THE GIRL IN THE STEEL CORSET

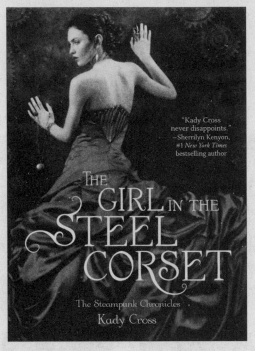

When servant girl Finley Jayne is run down on the streets of London, she is swept into the world of Griffin, the mysterious Duke of Greythorne, and his crew of misfits, all of whom have mysterious powers—just like Jayne. As they search for the Machinist, a shadowy villain using automatons to commit crimes, Jayne struggles to fit in and to fight the darkness that is growing inside her.

Available wherever books are sold!